FORDLANDIA

Thomas Dunne Books

ST. MARTIN'S PRESS ⚘ NEW YORK

FORDLANDIA

Eduardo Sguiglia

TRANSLATED FROM THE SPANISH BY

Patricia J. Duncan

THOMAS DUNNE BOOKS.
An imprint of St. Martin's Press.

Title page photograph courtesy of Photodisc

www.stmartins.com

Book design by Victoria Kuskowski

Library of Congress Cataloging-in-Publication Data

Sguiglia, Eduardo.
　[Fordlandia. English]
　Fordlandia / Eduardo Sguiglia; translated from the Spanish by Patricia J. Duncan.
　　p. cm.
　ISBN 0-312-26592-1
　I. Duncan, Patricia J. II. Title.

PQ7798.29.G85　F6713　2000
863'.64—dc21

　　　　　　　　　　　　　　　　　　　　　　　　　00-031667

First published in Brazil by Iluminuras

First U.S. Edition: September 2000

10　9　8　7　6　5　4　3　2　1

For Jutta and my children:

Nicolás, Fabián, and Sebastián

TRANSLATOR'S ACKNOWLEDGMENTS

I would like to thank my friend and agent, Laura Dail, for bringing this gem of a novel to my attention. Special thanks also to my dear friend Ellen Kresky for donating her valuable time and editing skills. And above all, a world of thanks to my mother, a relentless editor and my ultimate critic.

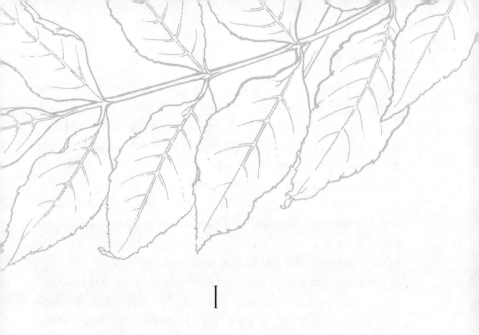

I

The Moacyr moved slowly down the river that June morning. In the summer, the Tapajós was low and full of sandbars. Near the shore there were tide pools, where the water looked as blue as the sky. From the passageway between the decks I could look out at the sleepy river, the rippling clouds, the jungle that breathed, drowsily, and the entire mystery of the landscape.

After breakfast I lit a cigarette and walked toward the bridge. I passed through the second-class cabin, continued along the deck, and climbed up the metal stairway, which led to the captain and his men. The captain, an Englishman with a thin, tanned face, remained steady on the bridge. He was consulting an expert, making notes in a small notebook and giving orders to his assistant, who instantly translated them for the helmsman. The helmsman, a black man who earlier had appeared confident, almost unpleasantly so, now looked sweaty and tense, like someone awaiting an ambush. Five days had passed since we had gone aboard in Belem, almost three since we had left the course of the Amazon at the port of Santarem, and in a few more hours, perhaps by midafternoon, we were due to arrive at our destination.

I watched the captain and the helmsman for a while. Then I returned to my seat, settled in comfortably, put out my cigarette, and stared out at the riverbanks. I had spent hours looking at those banks. I recalled how for years, practically from the time I was a child until I was a young man, I was passionate about travel books and how after the last line of the last page I would wonder (in vain) how much truth and how much fiction those tales contained. To think that what was being told no longer existed or, even worse, had never existed, used to make me suddenly depressed. On this trip, after watching for hours the world that surrounded the boat, I was learning that some things existed as they were supposed to. Where writers had enthusiastically reported the presence of trees and more trees, I saw trees, millions of massive, immense trees, like a wall that went on and on to the point of absurdity. Where the chronicler had recorded rings of white mist condensing over the jungle, I saw rings of mist float, like a bright, transparent fabric above the jungle. It was a world of jungle, water, and silence. A world of an imposing restlessness. There was not a sound. Nothing moved about or shook. Later, I would grow accustomed to that illusory peace, and I would have virtually no time to be afraid. I would also realize, as did Pliny twenty centuries before, that a land covered with thousands of tall, beautiful trees is not always a good thing, except, of course, for the trees.

The *Moacyr* was a simple cargo ship with a lightweight roof held up by stanchions. On deck, besides the bridge, there were two passenger cabins, one for first class and one for second, which were separated by doors and windows, and a kitchen hold. During the day the doors and windows were kept open, and at night they were covered with mosquito netting. In the first-class cabin there were ten comfortable wooden double seats, five on each side, and each passenger, unlike those traveling in second class, had a folding bed made of canvas that could be extended across the space between the rows of seats and the door that led to the second-class cabin. In that same space there was also a seat that could be folded down at mealtime. They served fish, black beans, and turtle eggs; for breakfast, coffee and moist biscuits.

After disembarking in Santarem, there were only three of us left in first class—a very tall, thin American and a German priest whose order I did not know. Jack, the American, had boarded in Belem just as I had. The priest, however, along with his assistant, a tiny native who was traveling in second class, had boarded in Santarem. There, the torrent of the Tapajós River joined up with the Amazon River, forming a vast lake. At the confluence of these two rivers the vegetation was gentler, the trees smaller and in bloom, and patches of grass were visible.

Jack slept through most of the journey. He would only wake up to eat, which he did quickly and quietly, at noon and in the late afternoon and on a few other occasions. When he did wake up, he would be agitated, walk around the cabin a bit and, looking at me as if he had never seen me before, greet me with a slight smile. "Take it easy, there is nothing to fear here," he would say, and then he would be quiet. After that he would sit down, reach his arm beneath the bed, pick up the red leather case where he kept his Spanish guitar, and rest it on his lap. He would open it, look inside, close it, and put it back in its place underneath the bed again, next to his backpack. One afternoon, as the shadows of the jungle stretched out into the mist, he removed the guitar from its case and began to play. But a few moments later, he was silent again, his eyes fixed on the wooden floor, and he put the guitar back into the case. He had blue eyes, rugged hands, and a beard that accentuated his adventurer's looks. Each time he finished checking his guitar and putting it away, and before turning over and going to sleep, he would glance around the cabin and take a big swig of whiskey from a flask, which he kept hidden under his pillow. The beds were narrow but of standard length. When Jack stretched out on his back, an arm and both feet hung over the bed.

While Jack slept, sprawled out on his bed, the priest would talk endlessly with the rest of the passengers and the crew. His conversations were one-on-one, and he spoke quietly, although I sometimes saw him waving his arms, reprimanding the person he was speaking to at the time. In the second-class cabin there were ten people all talking and laughing among themselves. They were all men from the area, and they would only remove their hats when they were speaking with the priest or the captain.

Shortly before noon I got up and walked through the cabin. I had smoked a lot that morning; my mouth was dry, and I wanted to stretch my legs. I called to the waiter, a black man from Bahia, and I ordered a beer. The sun was high in the sky, and for a while now a few parrots with red, green, and blue feathers had been escorting the boat. In this ocean, carved into rivers, the hours, the minutes, do not matter much. Time seems immutable, and you have to adapt little by little to adjust your appetite or sleepiness to the position of the sun. The sun rules with impunity. It, and not the moon, regulates the torrent of the waters, and it dictates, as it sees fit, the customs, the clothing, and the occupations of those who inhabit this part of the world.

I was finishing my beer when the priest entered the cabin. It was clear that, after a lengthy intrusion into the second-class cabin, he now wanted to talk with us, and it was also clear that if Jack did not wake up, his next victim would be me. I felt fine, somewhat anxious to reach my destination, and the idea of a chat with the priest disturbed me. I felt as if I had to justify my actions to him, and I didn't feel like doing so with him or with anybody. Besides, there was something ominous and mysterious about his blond, solid figure. He wore white linen pants and a worn-out, sweaty black cassock. The perspiration on his chest formed an inverted triangle with the base at his chubby neck. He had an inquisitive look. I greeted him with a smile, gulped down the rest of the beer, and went back to my seat to smoke. The priest fixed his attention on Jack. From the way he was looking at him I saw that he knew he was drunk, but he began the task of waking him just the same. First he shook him by the shoulder, and then he slapped him on the cheek with increasing force and frequency. Jack grumbled in response and shifted his body to get comfortable again. His only brief reaction was to feel beneath the bed to see if the guitar case was still there. The priest knelt down beside him and began to talk into his ear. "Wake up. Wake up, Jack, come on, we have to talk," he said, pleadingly. The appeal was in vain. In some way the scene seemed merciless, useless. The night before we had boarded, I had seen Jack get sloshed on whiskey in a cabaret in Belem.

My stay in Belem was too short, just long enough for the interview and the medical exam. The city had traces of a more prosperous past. It was located at the mouth of the Amazon River, and the roar produced by the union of that great river with the ocean used to resound through the narrow streets of the port on nights when the moon was full. That location had allowed Belem to become an important place for commerce years before, during the height of the Brazilian rubber fever. The flow of money, easy and plentiful, had left its mark in the shape of avenues, buildings, and stately mansions from another era. The port was filled with small sailboats, much like those that I would later see sail down the Amazon and the Tapajós. The boats were crammed full with fruits and merchandise, and the crew lived on board. This type of floating market was known as Ver-o-peso. I stayed nearby in a modest hotel.

On my first day in Belem I took a short walk around the port.

The journey on the Italian steamship on which I had sailed out of Buenos Aires had been calm, and we had made various stops at different Brazilian ports. But the monotony of the sea and the sight of a distant coastline had exhausted me. During the journey, voluntarily isolated from the rest of the passengers except for one night when I had a few drinks with a sweet, passionate French woman, I had had time to organize my thoughts. My own decision had brought me there. Until then, Buenos Aires, the district of Palermo, the suburbs, and my friends, had been all there was for me. But I had made three successive, terrible mistakes, and I couldn't bear the prospect of my life becoming a mediocre existence full of compromises. A heavy weight loomed over me, and I had to get out from under it. My mother would have understood. In her day she fought with her own—stubborn Irish—in order to go her own way. She ended up marrying an Argentine. My mother thought the most important thing in life was to act with a clear head, be the captain of one's own ship, and I shared this opinion. But she was no longer here. When I made up my mind to apply for the job and agreed to leave the country, I thought of her and the sparkle in her blue eyes.

The Ford Motor Company had founded a city in the Amazon Valley, with the objective of supplying its own rubber, and it needed reliable personnel. The challenge was attractive, the pay excellent, and the company, if everything went well, had agreed to transfer me, after a time, to Detroit or to a European subsidiary. I would live for the present, without possessions, without yesterday hanging over me. This was my chance.

The offices of the Pickrell House, where I had to appear for my final interview and to sign the contract, were in the business district of Belem on the first floor of a sorry-looking building that resembled a convent. I had no trouble locating it, since no one in the city spoke of anything other than the Ford Motor Company's plans. When I arrived early in the morning there was a line of applicants outside the building. The line went from the first floor, down the staircase to the street. Most of the people were barefoot and looked like peasants, and the murmur of their lively conversation resonated in the stairwell and in the hall. Later I would meet others like them: they were Brazilians from the northeast who were prepared to exchange their free and miserable lives in the desert for a job with a salary in the middle of the jungle.

I did not wait my turn. I went directly to the secretary, a fat woman who barely looked at me over her glasses, and gave my name. The fat woman searched through a list that was on her desk and then smiled as if she knew all about me. A few minutes later she led me, obligingly, to the conference room. In the middle of the room there was a round pine desk, and maps and photographs of historic figures hung on the walls. The din of the peasants could be heard even there. Just as I had settled into one of the wooden chairs the doctor came in. He was a skinny little man with a thick mustache that concealed a harelip. He took my pulse and then told me to take off my shirt and pants. He walked around me, examining me carefully. He asked me if I had played sports professionally. Surprised, I responded that I had not and that I had played a lot of sports but none on a professional level. He paid no attention to my response and sat down to write some notes. Then he told me to get dressed, wished me luck, and left as discreetly as he had entered. I began to feel somewhat uncomfortable. I looked out the window. Rain clouds were beginning to fill the sky. I had not yet finished buttoning my shirt when the door opened and one of the directors came into the room. He was of average height and ordinary build. He introduced himself, shook my hand, and invited me to accompany him into an adjacent office. Another man was standing in the office waiting for us. He was taller and wore, as did the other man, an impeccable brown suit with white pinstripes and a white vest. He spoke with an American accent. They had me sit across from the only desk in the office, and they offered me coffee and water. On the desk I recognized the forms that I had filled out in Buenos Aires and the recommendation that a neighbor, a foreman in the Argentine subsidiary, had written for me. After looking over my papers and the doctor's notes they asked me four vague and puzzling questions. They listened attentively to my answers, without interrupting me. Then they showed me some papers with ink stains, and I had to give my opinion as to what I saw in the shapes of the stains.

Once we finished the test, they completed a form, whispered some things to each other, and gave me the information I would need in order to report the following morning to the port. A steamship was leaving for the Tapajós, and the company was urgently requesting my presence. There, the managing director, a man called Rowwe, would fill me in on the specifics of the job. The contract was written in English. I read it and signed it on the spot. On a separate sheet of paper I had to designate a beneficiary for a one hundred dollar insurance policy to be paid in the event of an accident. I thought of my father, but I finally filled it out with the information of a friend with whom I had some outstanding gambling debts. Before saying good-bye they asked me, ironically, why, according to the doctor's report, I did not have the imprint of Ireland on my body. Supposedly, those of Irish descent have some natural marking on their skin that, no matter how small, looks like the outline of old Eire. I shrugged and answered evasively. They didn't ask anything else.

When we said good-bye in the hallway, under the glare of the fat woman and the peasants still waiting in line, they hugged me, as if instead of going into the center of Brazil I were about to leave for the center of the Earth. Once on the street, I was overcome with a sense of emptiness and loneliness. It was cloudy and a fine rain was falling. I felt like drinking, and at that moment I wanted only to find the nearest bar.

I walked a short distance and found one, a hole-in-the-wall between the business district and the port. I hung out there until late afternoon. The bar was poorly lit, to conceal the presence of prostitutes, and almost every table was empty. I chose one near the door and ordered a drink. They brought me a glass filled to the rim. I raised it and downed it in one gulp. The women were by the bar. I saw two or three of them leave alone, only to come back escorted. At an adjacent table an American and two Brazilians were talking and drinking. When the gringo took one of the women to the private room that was visible at the back of the bar, the Brazilians began talking with me. They asked me where I had come from and where I was going. They were both journalists and one of them, Joao, who wrote for the city newspaper, *Folha do Norte*, seemed very interested in the journey I was about to embark upon. He promised to make a trip to visit me and to write about the experience. The other one, a Spaniard by birth, his face thin and drawn, remarked bitterly about how some thirty years ago he had been president of a remote rubber-producing jungle state that bordered Bolivia. The coming and going of the women, who approached us every couple of minutes, and the jokes of his colleague, perhaps tired of hearing the same story, did not allow him to tell his story coherently, and it was hard for me to follow. Nevertheless, I managed to learn that the old Spaniard had uncovered a plot between the United States and Bolivia to seize that region and that he, with the support of the governor of Manaus and twenty armed men, had capitalized on the weakness of the Bolivian authorities and the indifference of the Brazilian central government in order to incite the rubber producers to rebel and to form an independent republic, the Republic of Poets. He showed me tattered newspaper clippings and some poor, blurred photographs that he kept in a worn-out silk handkerchief, which he carried in the top pocket of his jacket. The state, now part of Brazil, was called Acre. An abundant wooded area, isolated from the world, ruled by free and just poets. I looked at the photographs. In the worn-out photographs you could see a group of men, some serious, some smiling, with weapons and flags, surrounded by vegetation. Their garments, their disheveled hair, and their mustaches lent them a comedic air. I had doubts about the photographs and asked why there was no book on the subject. "It is still too recent," he replied. For a moment I imagined myself embarking on an adventure like that, and my expression must have changed with my thoughts because the two journalists pointed at me, looked at each other, and burst out laughing.

Their faces were a purplish blue as they proposed another toast. A short while later the American returned, said good-bye to the woman, and with his guitar, got up onto the shaky platform in the middle of the bar. He was completely drunk, but when he began to sing we were quiet. His voice was hoarse. The song went

> *Dear God up in the sky*
> *I know that you're listening*
> *I know that it's a little late for my first prayer*
> *I'm not here asking you to have pity on me*
> *I'm not here asking you to forgive me*
> *Or to change the way I am*
> *Time's not on my side anymore*
> *I'll take my chance on the final judgment day*
> *But once I make it to the mysterious river*
> *Help me, help me*
> *Keep the devil down there, way down there in the hole*
> *You've got to help me.*

Now, on board the small steamship, sprawled out on a canvas bed, Jack, the American, tried to keep sleeping while the German priest did everything possible to wake him. After I finished my beer I went back to my seat and was passing the time smoking and watching the jungle closing in on the shore. I have never been particularly sensitive to other people's problems nor do they interest me very much, but when I saw the priest, now tired of insisting, pick up a bucket full of water from the river and prepare to throw it at Jack, I had to stop him. I got up, walked over to him, and asked him to leave Jack alone and to come talk with me. The priest looked at Jack, then at me, dropped the bucket on the floor, and sat down next to me. He rested his left arm, thick as a tree trunk, on the back of my seat. I didn't accept the cigarette he offered me, and he looked at me as one who is used to dealing with people of questionable motives.

"My name is Theo and I am here to give hope to troubled men. But I don't know why, my son, you are coming to this blessed place. To make money, seek refuge, or are you motivated simply by a scientific interest?" he asked.

"To make money, of course, what do you think?" I answered.

His look reflected a certain uneasiness.

"Rubber. Once again rubber," he said, and he was pensive.

The priest crossed his legs, wiped the sweat from his forehead, and leaned back in his seat. Then he leaned forward again.

"In Fordlandia, right?"

"Yes, that's where I'm headed."

"Look at that poor drunk pretending to be asleep," he said pointing his thumb at Jack. "He is here for rubber too, just like you. He is the *jefe*, an important man, yet he only confides in alcohol. He thinks that alcohol makes him less vulnerable. He doesn't want to talk to me, and here in the jungle it is not a sign of strength for white men to be quiet. Quite the contrary."

I did not respond, but he went on.

"I don't know, son, nobody knows why we go mad when we live in the jungle. The silence, the shadows," he looked toward the shore, "have their way of fighting us. I don't know. There is something inhuman in the jungle, something that holds us back at first, then shakes us up, and finally calls to devour us. When that time comes, no reasoning, no knowledge is enough. The devil is right there, cunning, tempting, and nothing can save us. Nothing except faith. I can promise you that."

"Is that so, Father?"

"That's right. For ten thousand kilometers around, from any direction you are returning or any direction you are going, you will only be able to prove two things: one, your ignorance, two, the immense power of the Creator. Faith is the only answer I can offer for a problem so alien to common thought, mediocrity and superstitions. Only faith can save us. And you know what else?"

"No."

"In the Amazon, witch doctors and those who are superstitious cause the same damage as cowards in an army."

"How is that?"

"They are afraid and they cause fear."

I did not know what to say. I had never been particularly interested in religion, mysteries or invocations. In order to change the subject I asked him about the riches of the jungle.

"The white part of the Brazilian nation is too small. And these rich and beautiful lands have been waiting for centuries for men with good intentions. Real men. They don't settle for the natives. They can't settle for idlers, for pagans who resist progress. Not at all, son, not at all," he repeated, almost shouting.

Theo's face had grown red as he was speaking, and beads of sweat ran down his forehead and his neck. The air was warm but not heavy. Beyond the riverbanks one could now make out small hills covered with vegetation. With a bit of difficulty, Theo stuck his hand in his pants' pocket and took out a small piece of bark and offered it to me.

"Here, it's quinine bark," he said, calmer now, "chew a little every day and it will help protect you from malaria. It's simple: if they—the Indians, the blacks, and the mulattoes—lived together, if we had them all together, all of them in a valley, or in a city, so we could civilize them, tame them, maybe our work would be done, we would swim in abundance, and there would be no need for witch doctors or fortune-tellers. No, sir. But here, in this interminable and colossal Garden of Eden, one has to walk a long way to come across just a few men, unfortunately. A few here, some downriver, a few more upriver or on other rivers. That is my problem. Do you see? Do you understand, son?"

"Yes, I understand."

"Yes, *you* understand, but if only my colleagues in Rome, in Rio, in Tibet or wherever the hell they are knew of my difficulties and would send me more resources, more money. Like Henry Ford. You people have money, all right, money and machines!"

He paused again, as if he were thinking; then he added, "Although you people, from what I understand, settle only for the bodies and not the souls of those poor people too. Where are you from, son? Your accent is not American."

"I am Argentine, from Buenos Aires."

"Argentine. Rubber fever again. Be careful, my son, the jungle knows how to defend itself against your scourge. In the jungle you must distrust what you think you understand too easily as well as the things you don't understand. But don't be afraid, I will always be by your side if you need me, always," he said.

Then he got up, patted me on the shoulder, and moved his face close to mine. He asked me for a donation. I had put my wallet with my money and documentation under my shirt, in my underwear, and I had kept only a few coins in my pants pocket.

I gave him the coins. The priest looked at them greedily, then put them in his jacket and left. As he went toward the second-class cabin he looked at Jack with contempt. I could never have imagined that that German would save my life. A short while later, the steamship slowed down and began to approach a white sand beach. The motors sputtered as if a piece had broken. A flock of parakeets crossed the river, from one bank to the other. Through the foliage I saw some huts of mud and straw. A canoe made of tree bark, steered by a mestizo, came looking for the priest. As he went down the stairs with his assistant he turned around and nodded his head to say good-bye to me. The water was green and crystal clear. I waved good-bye and went to the bridge to ask the captain how much longer. "We'll be there before nightfall," he responded solemnly.

11

The gold clock that rested on an elegant mahogany cabinet showed that it was ten minutes before one. Ernest Liebold compared the time with the chronometer in his vest pocket and hurried to finish reading the correspondence that his secretary had given him that morning. The English colonial-style oval table was set for four. A smoky blue crystal vase, filled with fresh roses, sat in the center of the table. Liebold, who was in charge of all company operations, liked to arrive a few minutes early to all meetings, showing that his enthusiasm for his job extended even to the dining room. There were two objects in the room that distracted him: a portrait of the boss in profile, standing with his right hand resting on the back of his favorite armchair, and the quote by Thoreau that the boss had engraved in the cypress wood that covered the walls: "The wood stumps warmed me twice—once while I was splitting them, and again when they were on the fire." When the other two executives entered the room Liebold removed from his pile of correspondence a telegram that had arrived from Brazil. It contained valuable information about the topic that they had chosen to deal with that June afternoon, 1930. Edsel Ford and Charles Sorensen greeted Liebold and sat down facing each other in the Jacobin chairs. The three men were silent. Edsel reviewed the notes that he had brought with him in a folder, Sorensen looked out the large window, and Liebold again compared the time on his chronometer with that on the gold clock and reread the telegram. The large window looked out onto the factory parking lot. Through the glass, one could see hundreds of brand-new automobiles waiting to be loaded onto railway cars.

At one o'clock sharp the door opened and a young-looking man of average height came into the dining room. To some, he was a simple man erroneously thought to be complex; to others, he was a complex man whose genius projected a deceiving aura of simplicity. It was Henry Ford, the richest man in the world and whose business was well known and admired.

Henry Ford sat down next to Edsel, his only son, to whom he had handed over, in writing, the presidency of the corporation, and he looked toward the large window. Then he looked back toward Liebold and Sorensen, who, seated across from him, smiled back.

"What news do we have today, Mr. President?" he asked Edsel.

"We had agreed to discuss the situation in the Amazon."

At that time, the company was consuming a fourth of the world's rubber, and Ford was fed up with the conditions imposed by the British monopoly. His interest in supplying his own rubber for his company went back to the early 1920s, and while he was supporting costly and unsuccessful attempts to produce it in an artificial form, he entrusted his people to find a suitable place to establish an enormous plantation. Experts traveled throughout Panama, Colombia, and parts of Asia and Africa, but Ford decided on the Brazilian Amazon. He bought millions of acres there with the objective of producing as much rubber as the automobile industry would need for tires. It was, as he had so proudly stated to Congress, the most ambitious colonization in the history of the Amazon. Its blind strength and extraordinary fertility had only to be transformed into disciplined energy. The Amazon, under the influence of our will and our work, will become, he said, the first chapter in the history of a new civilization.

"What problems could there be there? We sent enough money, tractors, a good administrator, and we have excellent relations with the government. What more do we need? The only thing that remains is to produce rubber, tons of rubber to achieve two things. One, that the bloody English stop gouging us with their ridiculous prices and their control of the market. Two, that Charlie always has enough raw material to make Ford cars run throughout the whole world. "Huh, Charlie?"

"That's right, Henry. Of course."

Charles Sorensen, who managed the vast complex on the Rouge River, agreed and shot a contemptuous look at Edsel. Sorensen believed that he had reached the top because of his own merit, and he was right. It had really been Sorensen who was responsible for the innovation of the assembly line, which would make his boss famous, a myth almost, among politicians, industrialists, and scientists. At the old plant in Highland Park fifteen years before, he had had the boldness to take concepts that were floating around at that time and put them into practice in the form of a thin band that transported automobile parts so they could be assembled in much less time. One constant, synchronic, and uninterrupted movement connected those who assembled the chassis with those who mounted it and welded the engines and the bodies. At Highland Park, located in a Detroit neighborhood, twelve and a half man-hours were needed at the time to assemble a Ford Model T. After Sorensen installed the assembly lines, the same work took only one hour. Henry Ford took credit for the innovation, stating publicly that the idea had occurred to him while he was visiting a clock factory. Sorensen never revealed the secret nor did he contradict his boss's apocryphal version. "Iron Charlie" professed unwavering loyalty to the man who had hired him early in his career as an industrial designer, making it possible for him to climb to the top of the company ladder. Highland Park had been replaced by a complex of ninety buildings in Dearborn, on the outskirts of Detroit, on the banks of the Rouge River. The Rouge plant, in addition to producing ten thousand automobiles per day, also smelted and molded all the pieces used by Ford products. Sorensen, with his extremely strong and melancholy personality, managed the Rouge Plant, and he saw Edsel as the only obstacle preventing him from achieving complete control of the company.

"There are some difficulties though," Edsel replied.

"What kind of difficulties? Come on, tell us once and for all," urged Ford, who never missed a chance to show his son who was boss.

"It's not easy to get reliable personnel for the plantation, and what's more, the person who was in charge has fallen ill to malaria."

"I had malaria when I was a boy too, and here I am. I can't believe that that is holding us up. Let them look for replacements and do whatever is necessary to produce, soon. Edison and Firestone assured me that it's impossible to make artificial rubber, so there is no alternative, unless you want to surrender to the British. President Herbert Hoover himself even told me that. The British even took the seeds they used for their plantations in Malaya and Ceylon from the Amazon. So, gentlemen, we have no choice. We've got to stop wasting time and get to work."

"I have good news from the office in Brazil," Liebold inter-rupted, showing the telegram. Liebold, unlike Sorensen, pre-ferred not to be the center of attention at meetings. His voice was low and monotonous, and he got angry when asked to repeat something he had just said. Ford was aware of that weakness.

"What did you say?"

Liebold cleared his throat and then responded.

"I said that I have some good news from the office in Belem, in Brazil. They sent us a telegram."

"What's the news?" Edsel asked.

"They say that they already have a replacement for the job. An Argentine."

"Italian or Argentine? There are lots of Italians in Argentina," Ford inquired.

"I said Argentine, an Argentine whose mother was Irish."

The door opened and a waiter came in to serve lunch on an engraved silver tray. He brought a pitcher of fruit juice, three plates with soybean-based dishes, and another with a piece of very rare beef. For some time now, Ford insisted on eating only vegetables, and he credited the soybean with extraordinary properties. "If people would learn to eat what they should there would be no need for hospitals or jails," he asserted. The menu for the day was celery stuffed with soybean cheese, soybean cro-quettes, and for dessert, apple pie topped with soybean ice cream. Only Sorensen, who quickly went for the plate with the meat, dared to defy the strict diet imposed by the boss.

Ford asked the waiter, an Italian who had waited tables in the executive dining room since the days of Highland Park, to come over when he was done serving. When he came over, Ford looked at his hands and then looked him straight in the eye. The man waited silently for the question de rigueur.

"I imagine, dear Umberto, that you have not been smoking or drinking alcohol, right?"

"No, Mr. Ford, not at all."

"What do you think if we hire an Italian like you to teach cooking in the city we are building in Brazil?"

"That's a good idea, sir. I would go myself if it weren't for my family. You know that I would do anything I could for you and the company."

Ford seemed satisfied with his response and dismissed him with a smile. Then he picked up the pitcher and smelled the fruit juice. Before filling his glass he glanced over at the other three men.

"Well, problem resolved with the Argentine. Send one of your men down there anyway, Charlie, to sniff around and find out what's really going on in the jungle. Oh—and while you're at it, ask them to send some birds from the region to my home in Fairlane. There must be good ones down there."

"I'll do it this afternoon," Sorensen answered.

"Now, Mr. President, gentlemen, with your permission, let's eat," Ford said.

Edsel had intended to discuss other matters, but he closed his folder, exchanged glances with Liebold, and began to eat. His brown eyes revealed confusion. He felt like an imposter at Ford. Once again, that afternoon he had tried to show his worth without directly confronting his father.

III

Shortly after rounding the curve where the Tapajós gets wider and comes together with the Cupary River, one of its larger tributaries, the captain appeared in the cabin. He seemed relieved. He informed us that we were nearing Fordlandia and should prepare for arrival.

Jack got up quickly, as if impelled by a spring. He took off his shirt and began to wash himself with the bucket of water that the priest had left next to him. I, on the other hand, went to the bow and stood there, waiting anxiously for that creature to appear. That stretch of the Tapajós was wide and straight with high banks, like railway embankments. The current was stronger, and the *Moacyr* crawled along like a centipede along the floor of a lavish hallway.

A little while later I spotted Fordlandia. Nothing visible to the eye was either monumental or noteworthy; however, seen from the river the village was a pleasant interruption in the unending succession of dense greenery. Set on the left bank, it looked like a vast and seductive refuge. Sailing toward Fordlandia, the first thing visible was the long and sturdy wooden dock built on piles and the large water pump in the river. Two enormous sheds of cement, metal, and glass stuck out on one side of the dock. Beyond that, following the route of the asphalt street that stretched down from the dock through an open space without any bushes or trees, there were other sheds, streets, and a hundred houses with white walls and reddish roofs. Some distance from those buildings, conical in shape and steel gray in color, stood the tank of drinking water, tall and straight, like a watchtower. The terrain was slightly rolling, and behind the last roofs small hills were visible. In the distance, on the outer limits, the jungle unfurled its arrogant trees, which stood guard, and its majestic palms. In the Amazon, all the villages are near the rivers. The river nourishes, transports, and seduces, but it also subjects men to a primitive existence. Fordlandia, however, penetrated inland and sought to create conditions for an autonomous life and a particular way of living. A couple years back, two boats had left Detroit, the *Lake Ormoc* and the *Lake Farge*. They had been the first to bring materials, tools, and men into the region, which at that time was an uncultivated ravine called Boa Vista. Jack, who had come up next to me without my realizing, handed me his bottle of whiskey. He was smiling and had shaved and combed his hair. A few drops of water ran down from his still-wet hair onto his forehead.

"Here, drink, not everybody dares to talk to that pest, Theo," he said, handing me the bottle.

I took it and after a swig gave it back to him. He tipped the bottle all the way up, and once he was sure that there was not a single drop left, he kissed it and threw it into the river.

"In the wonder city," he said pointing to Fordlandia, "we have to live clean; clean and pure."

Three men were waiting on the dock next to some crates. As we went ashore the three came forward and greeted Jack effusively. One of them threw Jack's pack over his shoulder, picked up the case with the guitar, and left with him for the center of the village. I would see Jack again the next day, at my first official meeting with the authorities of Fordlandia. The other two men formed part of a guard that maintained order in the village. It was an armed guard, run by Fordlandia directors. Brazilian officials had no authority there. The guards, who wore blue overalls and had revolvers fastened to their belts, asked me and the second-class passengers to wait on the dock while they checked the passenger list and some notes that the captain had handed them. In one of the crates, which would later be loaded onto the steamship, there were a couple of toucans struggling to stick their orange beaks through the wooden slats. The crate bore a sticker indicating that the cargo was fragile and that it should be delivered express to its final destination, Fairlane Mansion, Dearborn, Michigan, United States. One of the second-class passengers went over to the crate and tried to stroke the beak of one of the toucans with his finger. The frightened birds, in disarray, sought refuge in one of the corners of the cage, just as the guards ordered us to follow them to the nearest shed.

The guards entered the shed and began calling us, one by one. Each interview lasted no more than a few minutes, and those who came out said that they had been given vaccines, made to drink a quinine potion (a medicine to prevent malaria), and, depending on the individual, they had been forced to leave behind their liquor bottle, their knife, or their tobacco. Nevertheless, they seemed agreeable, and as some left directly for the village hospital, where they would have to remain for two days of observation, others remained outside, waiting for their names to be called.

As I stood there waiting along the small road that led to the shed, I noticed that the crew, after loading the crates, were carrying onto the boat a man on a stretcher who was wrapped in blankets and whose face was as white as a ghost. A doctor, who accompanied the stretcher to the foot of the gangplank, talked with the captain until he ordered the departure whistle to be blown. I saw the helmsman head sluggishly from the bow to the bridge. Our eyes met. The mulatto looked at the sick man and then acknowledged me with a gesture loaded with irony. I looked back toward Fordlandia. The last rays of the sun accentuated the dark green of the vegetation. I wondered what I was going to do there.

I had to wait a little longer until one of the guards called me. But instead of having me go into the shed he introduced me to a colleague of his and asked me to follow him to Mr. Rowwe's office. The director himself had made a telephone call to the guard post asking for me, and he wished to meet me right away. We walked toward the main buildings. On the street people were coming and going without any apparent purpose. They moved slowly, like sheep, calmly and impassively. In front of the main building, there was a spacious square planted with grass. This was where festivities were held on special occasions. Apart from those occasions, the square was so empty and quiet that it seemed larger, particularly in summer, when the brilliant sunlight and warm air filled it in such a way that the idea of walking across it was not at all appealing. Between the square and the river, there was a short winding path with banana trees, palm trees, and a few benches for resting. We followed the asphalt road up to the top of the hill. There the road split into three paths. The widest path led to the main administration building, a bright redbrick structure. The adjacent alleys were dirt, and between the houses and the huts there were open spaces covered with patches of grass, some of which were planted with bushes and large trees.

J. F. Rowwe began to speak as soon as he saw me. He did not invite me to sit down. He was tall with red hair and he wore glasses with thick lenses due to premature nearsightedness. He showed me a map of the area that the Ford property covered. Three million acres along the Tapajós River, between the Cupary and the Tapacurá Rivers. One hundred ninety-six kilometers of waterfront. The map included the village and other areas marked in red ink.

"Look at those areas. We have to plant as many rubber trees as possible there. In a few years we must be able to produce three hundred thousand tons. Quite simply, one half of the world's production. At this time we have not moved far enough along. There are problems," he said.

"What's wrong?"

"We have only found a few people to work here, few and inferior."

"And how do you intend to solve that problem?"

"That, starting right now, is your problem. I was informed by the office in Belem that the results of the test you took indicate that you are very capable of finding needed solutions, or no?"

"I think so."

"You think so or you are sure?" he inquired.

"I'm sure," I answered.

I thought for a moment about the answers that I had given in my interviews in Belem. I remembered one, but I could not see how it related to what Rowwe was expecting of me. When one of the interviewers, the one who spoke American English, asked me whom I would rescue first in the event that my house was on fire with my family inside, I replied the one who was most able to help me fight the fire.

"Find men, hands, do it however you want, wherever you want, just find them. In doing so you will be contributing to the progress of Brazil and the company, as well as to your advancement. Read this, think it over, and tomorrow I will see you at eight o'clock for a meeting with the rest of the executives," Rowwe added.

He handed me a folder containing what was called the General Plan of Operations, Tactics, and Strategy and some descriptive notes about the personalities of the people there. On a wooden cabinet next to the desk there were some glass tubes that contained dissected spiders. When Rowwe realized that they had caught my attention, he said smugly, "Don't be afraid of them. The only ones here that can really bother you are these two," he said, opening a drawer on the side of the cabinet.

I went over and looked inside. There was a dead snake and a small bottle. It was a bluish green cobra with a yellow stripe running down each side of its body. Its eyes were pierced by a black line.

"The *surucucu* kills quickly. This pest, on the other hand, does it little by little," Rowwe said, pointing first at the snake and then at the bottle.

I picked up the bottle. Inside was a brown mosquito with black-and-white legs. It was an anopheles, transmitter of malaria.

Rowwe put a hand on my shoulder.

"Welcome aboard, and don't forget to go by the hospital early tomorrow morning. You need some shots to protect you from diseases. That's all."

The same guard who had accompanied me to Rowwe's office led me to what would be my house for the duration of my stay in Fordlandia. When I explained that I was Argentine and not a gringo as he had thought, he was friendly, and began explaining to me what the different buildings were along the road. The lights had been turned on in the village. The wooded area, the streets, and the sky began to transform, invaded by the first nocturnal shadows. The vegetation was enshrouded in darkness, and the trees, their crowns outlining the profile of the hills, reached out toward the sky in shapes never visible in the day. The landscape lost its scattered essence and came together in large, dense masses. Along the way we passed the hospital, the school, the stores, and the factory, and we saw groups of people in circles talking.

The house, located in the area where the Americans lived, was made of wood and had a pointed roof. The walls were whitewashed, and the windows and the door were painted green. It was clean and had only one bedroom with two single beds, a wardrobe, and a desk. In Fordlandia, there were residences for officials that were similar to or larger than mine, more rustic houses for the foremen and a series of spacious huts for the single workers. The few who had brought wives to the village lived in larger huts. Across the street and to the left there was an entertainment hall for officials. From the bedroom window you could hear voices and music from the hall. I put my bag down on one of the beds and glanced around the house. I checked thoroughly inside the furniture and underneath the sheets and the pillows. I found only a line of ants coming and going across the floor from the sink in the bathroom to the small garden at the entrance. Dozens of them were covering what was left of a bar of soap on the sink. I lit a cigarette—I hadn't dared to smoke in front of Rowwe—went over to the bedroom window, and looked outside. There was no moon, and the lights in the streets and on the porches lit up the pitch-dark night. Rowwe had made an impression on me—a bad impression. As the managing director of Fordlandia, people obeyed him. But he did not inspire either affection, fervor, or even respect. He was neither polite nor impolite. I never saw him smile. He was a common administrator. Implacable and common. He was there as the result of the current purges among the company's executives. When he was managing the engineering department in the plant in Detroit, he had let himself be seduced by the plans of a designer who, encouraged by Henry Ford's son, sought to replace the Model T with a more modern automobile. The other executives—at the direction of Ford himself, it was said—had cornered him. He was offered a position abroad and told to take it or leave it. The resentment had pierced his spirit, and that was apparent in everything he did.

I opened my bag and looked for the cologne. I walked across the room and into the bathroom. I watched the ants for a while, at work on the soap. Then I sprinkled the soap with cologne and lit a match to it. The flame rose and then went out quickly.

That night I went to sleep early. In the morning, before going by the hospital and to the meeting, I wanted to read the papers that Rowwe had given me. It was clear that things in Fordlandia were not turning out as they should, but I would not be fully aware of this until much later.

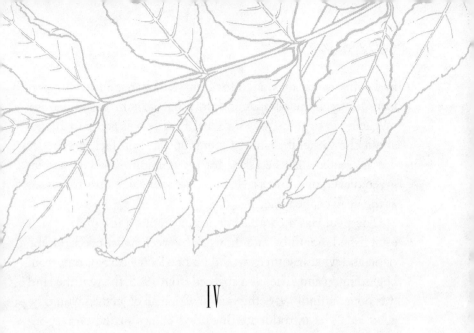

IV

I went to work the next day. The whistle signaling the beginning
of the workday on the plantation and at the sawmill got me out
of bed early. It went off four times a day from Monday to Saturday. At six fifteen in the morning, then at eleven and twelve,
the lunch break, and finally at five-thirty in the afternoon,
announcing the end of the workday. Its sound was abrasive,
and the system used in the village was the same one that had
been used in Europe to announce bombing raids during the
war. I got up, scrubbed my body and legs with a wet cloth, and
after making sure that there were no insects hiding in the folds
of my clothing, got dressed and left.

It had rained during the night. The air was thick and heavy.
When I got to the meeting all of the officials were there except
for Rowwe. There were six U.S. officials in all. Five worked rou-
tinely assisting Rowwe. They had that look and the manners of
those who are used to controlling and managing men. The sixth
was Jack. He greeted me with a smile and asked me if I had gone
by the hospital. I showed him the pricks on my arm left by the
vaccines and I sat down next to him. He looked worried. We

had coffee while we waited for Rowwe. We made trite compar-
isons between the pampas and the jungle. There was something
menacing in the air. I was sure that Rowwe was going to ask me
about the General Plan of Operations and, in fact, no sooner
was he seated than he asked for my opinion. Rowwe came in,
greeted everyone, and sat down in the managing director's spot
at the head of the table.

The plan was a complex series of graphs and numbers that
established month by month, week by week, what needed to be
done and what resources would be needed to carry it out, from
beginning to end. The plan covered from 1926, the year the land
was bought, until 1956, the year in which all objectives would be
achieved. The introduction included copies of the correspondence between the governor of the state of Pará, the Brazilian
ambassador to the United States, and Henry Ford, as well as
copies of the law by which the extensive region was conceded to
the company and which allowed it to establish its own authority
there. There was also a copy of a long report produced by two
scientists, La Rue and McCarrol, addressed to Henry Ford. The
report contained a chronicle of the history of rubber, which
emphasized its importance in the modern world and encouraged, in particular, the installation of a village in the Amazon,
along the banks of the Tapajós River. One of the many explorers
who traveled throughout the Amazon long ago, a Frenchman
named La Condamine who had been commissioned by the
Académie des Sciences to prove Newton's theory on the shape
and size of Earth, had been the first to send samples of rubber to
Europe. The natives, who called it *cahuchu*, used it to make bottles and pots. It was first used in Europe for waterproofing material, shoes, and military boots. But after Charles Goodyear
discovered by accident in 1839 that rubber combined with sul-
fur in the presence of heat would stabilize and vulcanize, its use
became more general, from hoses and tents to condoms. After

Goodyear's discovery, rubber became one of the stars of industrial civilization. The report pointed out that rubber was present in all stages of life, from the nipple on a baby's bottle to the tires on a hearse.

The report even included the opinion of an English politician who was then governor of Ceylon, Sir Henry Blake, who suggested "paving the streets of London with rubber in order to prevent the noise of the traffic from disturbing businessmen at work." The British did not hesitate to get involved. Toward the end of the last century, the Foreign Office had sent an agent to organize the secret gathering of seeds from rubber trees on the banks of the Tapajós River, between the port of Santarem and what is now Santarem and what is now Fordlandia. The baskets of seeds were sent to a nursery in Kew Gardens in London, and from there, once they had grown into seedlings, they were shipped to Ceylon, Malaya, Java, Cambodia, and Cochin China. The agent who took part in this operation received money and honors. Toward the end of his life, he was knighted. Some years before, the very same Foreign Office had organized the shipment of Peruvian chinchona seedlings—quinine—with the aim of combating malaria in His Majesty's remote holdings.

In just a short time the production of rubber in the British colonies in the Orient eclipsed that in Brazil and the rest of the world. The dream in the Amazon had ended. However, these events, La Rue held, did not detract from the potential for a large-scale plantation on the banks of the Tapajós. Quite the contrary.

Organization, capital, and discipline were all that was needed. He pointed out that in the last century the United States had made the most famous sailing exploration in the Amazon, and that the brother-in-law of one of the naval officers, a fellow named Maury, who would eventually become director of the National Observatory, had already proposed colonizing the region with slaves from the south. Tapajós, located in the state of Pará, was an area where rubber trees grew naturally, and what's more, the price of land was ridiculously low, and the rubber produced could easily be transported down the river to the ocean. La Rue's report concluded with a map of the world that traced the route from Fordlandia to the plant in Dearborn, Michigan. Two rivers, an ocean, a canal, and a great lake, all easily navigable, joined one point to the other. The diamond to its skilled cutter. As a footnote, La Rue, aware of Ford's weakness when it came to word meanings, offered his own speculations about the etymology of the word *Amazon*. He disqualified the versions about Orellana and Walter Raleigh. It was said that in their day, both conquerors attributed the failure of their expeditions—the first to rescue Pizarro and the second to extract gold in the Guianas—to savage blond women who confronted them along the riverbanks, just like the legendary Amazons in Herodotus's *Histories*. According to La Rue, it was correct to associate the name of the most magnificent river in the world to the women's resistance and to history, but the reference to Herodotus's writings was mistaken. La Rue assured that the word *Amazon* came from the Greek *Amazona*: "joined by a belt," and that Orellana as well as Raleigh, when they used the word, evoked a remote race of women conquerors in Africa who fought in teams of two, joined not only by prayers but also by their belts. The only thing that La Rue carefully failed to mention in his report was the close friendship that he maintained with the speculator who had sold Henry Ford the thousands of acres near Fordlandia.

That morning, instead of reading the plan of operations, I had amused myself reading La Rue's report and the notes about the people there. When Rowwe looked at me impatiently, waiting for my response, I lied.

"I don't have any doubts about the plan. All we have to do is carry it out."

"Exactly," he said.

Jack turned toward me.

"What do you think about La Rue's optimistic report?"

"Very interesting," I said.

"Very interesting? I believe that rather than a good chief of personnel we have hired a good diplomat," Jack replied, smiling.

"Again with your doubts, Jack? When will it stop? When are you going to understand that success depends on us and on nothing or no one else? Of course for that to happen we have to be convinced . . . and sober," Rowwe replied.

One of the Americans got up and flipped the switch that turned on the ceiling fan. The windows were open, but it smelled humid and stale.

"Everything boils down to one thing," Rowwe continued, addressing me. "The jungle works day and night, and we work only during the day. It is intent on resisting; we, on the other hand, are dispersed. In order to make up for that discrepancy in power we need people, many more people, and that is your challenge. Ideally they would be white or Chinese."

"Chinese?" Jack asked.

"Yes, Chinese, why not? Right now we have to make do with the natives, but if we don't succeed in doing things as they should be done, we are going to have problems."

Rowwe was not the first to mention the Chinese. La Rue stated in his report that "a million Chinese in the rubber-producing areas of Brazil would be a gift from the Gods." Instead of Chinese, Rowwe would be able to import only a few West Indian blacks to Fordlandia, a move that would prove to be a bad one.

Jack looked at Rowwe and smiled.

"When there are problems, changes in executives are inevitable and painful," he said.

Rowwe got up and walked around the table, furious. When he was directly behind Jack he leaned over and whispered into his ear.

"Get out, now."

Jack stood up and turned around to face Rowwe. He was three inches taller. Then he looked over his shoulder at me, threw his pencil on the table and left. The pencil kept rolling until it fell on the floor. Rowwe picked it up and clenched it in his hand.

"Alright, let's continue."

"I would like to see the plantation, if that's possible," I said.

"Yes, of course. I'll call one of my assistants to show you around the facilities, including the dining hall, of course. We'll talk again in a couple of days. You can go now," he said.

I spent that afternoon and the following three days walking around the plantation. It was an enormous clearing in the jungle, separated from Fordlandia by a hill. I had never seen anything like it; I was impressed. On one side were the sawmill, the orchards, and an area for livestock. The rest, as far as the eye could see, was paths and more paths. A network of paths that ran through large trees, through seedlings, through thick grass, through the denseness, over and under rock formations, over and under hills scorched by the sun. The ground was sandy, not very solid, and the tractors and other vehicles used to clear the land could only pass through a short tract of the plantation. An advance crew cleared the vegetation (except for the rubber trees) and left it to dry out; another group was responsible for burning it. After that came those who dug up the roots and leveled the terrain, and then those who laid out the paths, and finally those who would till the land. There were men working on some of the paths. On others there wasn't a soul. The foremen and the tallymen stayed in cabins scattered around the grounds, and a couple of them came out to greet me as I passed by. Rowwe's assistant had suggested that I not go too close to the virgin forest. I walked where there were trees in production. Men were making slanted cuts in the trunks and letting the milk of the tree drip until it had filled the tin container that was fastened near the base of the trunk. They worked with a short knife that they were required to give back to the tallymen at the end of each workday. The men went barefoot and wore lightweight clothing and straw hats. Rowwe's assistant told me that the workers were afraid of cobras, the indigenous savages, and the darkness of the jungle. Each one attended to a long row of trees. Every two hours the latex in the containers was poured into large buckets and carried to the warehouses. There, it would be coagulated and fumigated until it was converted into *pelets* of rubber, blackened by the smoke, and then be put on a boat to Dearborn, Michigan. Each tall oval-crowned tree was separated from the next by a dozen meters. The workers explained to me that in the past it was customary to cut down the rubber trees in order to bleed them dry with blows from sticks and axes.

The workers called themselves *seringueiros*, and they called the tree that produced the rubber *seringal*. Father Manoel de Esperanza, long before the Frenchman La Condamine, had seen the natives use rubber. He was the first one to use the word *seringa*, derived from the Greek and later adapted into Portuguese, in order to name the milky sap of the tree. But, in fact, most of those men were not seringueiros, nor did they have any experience at all in that kind of work. They were northeasterners, like the men I had seen in Belem when I showed up for my interviews at the Pickrell house. They were there, punching their time cards when they came and when they went and obeying the rules in order to work, so they could eat and earn a living, because their land, which was hot and dry, had driven them out.

There were almost three thousand men, and they were all ready to leave as soon as they could save enough money. They seemed peaceful, but in a moment of frustrated desperation could become almost more dangerous than a savage beast.

On the way back I bumped into Jack. He was squatting down and giving orders to the workers, who had formed a circle around him. He got up to say hello to me. We arranged to have lunch together the following day. Jack could be seen around the plantation at all hours of the day, with men armed with shovels, machetes, and hoes, giving orders to clear a path and measuring the terrain with his footsteps. He would order them to clear and plant in one place, then in another, then he would interrupt them and take measurements again. He would stop work at nightfall, and it was likely that the following morning he would decide to resume working in the same place. Sometimes he would not been seen around the village for an entire week. I never found out if the reason for his zeal was because on the plantation he did not have to deal with the authorities or put up with the opinions of Rowwe or anyone else, or if it was because working the land brought back fond memories of the beautiful lands in Michigan, where he spent his childhood, the only truly happy time of his life.

As I went up the road that led to Fordlandia, the whistle blew, and I looked back at the jungle out of the corner of my eye. That afternoon I had the feeling that the jungle was waiting patiently for the invasion to occur. When I got home I stretched out on the bed and reread the report on the people of the Amazon from beginning to end. It was a detailed report about the customs and beliefs of those people. It had been produced by Ford's sociology department, and the only incomplete chapter was about the natives that inhabited the area. The report went off into the description of the different feats that a young Indian named Teró had to accomplish in order to be recognized as the new warlord of the Munduruku tribe. I had the impression that a woman had written it. When I finished reading. I went across the street and into the entertainment hall. Inside I saw one of the Americans whom I had met that morning. He was at one of the tables playing solitaire with a deck of Spanish cards.

The hall was large and well lit, but smoking and drinking were not permitted. There was a pool table, a Ping-Pong table, another for chess, and a Victrola. I ordered a coffee and some chestnuts and then played pool with him. He was a surly type who spoke quickly. His name was Frank, and he had worked for Rowwe at Ford in Detroit as a machine operator. He played well but was lucky too. After a trick shot, he came over and spoke to me quietly.

"Don't pay any attention to Jack, take my advice."

"Why? Do you know him well?" I asked.

He swallowed and I noticed how his Adam's apple went up and down.

"No, but he was in jail. He's a bad seed," he said.

We played two matches and I lost both. Then we went outside to smoke. The air was pleasant and the village was silent. I saw a man prowling around my house. Frank lit his pipe.

"If you get too close to Jack, you're out," he persisted.

I put out my cigarette, said good-bye to Frank, and crossed the street. The man I had seen was now leaning, expressionless, in the doorway. He was rolling a cigarette. When he saw me, he took off his straw hat and came toward me. He walked uncertainly, wobbling. He did not seem drunk but rather tired. He was hunched over, and his arms hung down at his sides as if they were dislocated.

"You're the Argentine?" he asked.

"That's right."

"I am Enéas, your assistant."

I looked at him suspiciously.

"Rowwe sent me, but don't worry; I will work for you," he said.

He held his hat in one hand and his cigarette in the other. As I lit a match and gave him a light, cupping my hands around the cigarette, I noticed that he was missing two fingers on his left hand. Enéas inhaled the smoke. Then he said quietly,

"I lost them in the sawmill. But eight good ones are better than ten regular ones."

"I hope so."

"Me too, *mi blanco*."

Enéas had a dark complexion and dark, frizzy hair. In the Amazon people categorize each other by the kind of hair they have. They distrust skin color and physical features, but not hair. White men were those with fine, straight hair and thick beards. Mulattoes and *caboclos* had thick, black hair, and their beards consisted of only a few hairs on the jawbone. The flat nose indicated Negro ancestry. The almond-shaped eyes implied the presence of indigenous blood. Of course money counts too, a lot, as a criterion for classification. One time, while we were sailing down one of the many small rivers that cut through the Amazon Valley, we came across a commercial boat equipped with a shiny diesel motor. It was being steered by an arrogant-looking black merchant whom Enéas knew from childhood. As the black man's boat moved off, Enéas said, in a tone of admiration that he used on very few occasions, "Well, well, look at that, now Orlando is white." I responded that if Orlando was the one behind the rudder then something was wrong with his eyesight because to me the guy was as black as night. "Orlando was black, but now he isn't anymore," he answered decisively.

People thought that Enéas was a caboclo with indigenous and African ancestors. For him, however, the natives were the real caboclos. The only thing that he asked me, shortly after we met, was that I not call him caboclo. "Calling someone caboclo," he said, "doesn't offend me but it makes me sad." As for me, I got him not to call me "mi blanco" but only at the end, the unfortunate end, of our relationship. At that first meeting I asked him to report to me every morning after breakfast. He smiled at me and left for his hut. I watched as he left quickly and unsteadily. I wondered if that man of few words and fake expression could be useful to me. The doubts lingered with me for a while. Then I went inside the house and fell asleep.

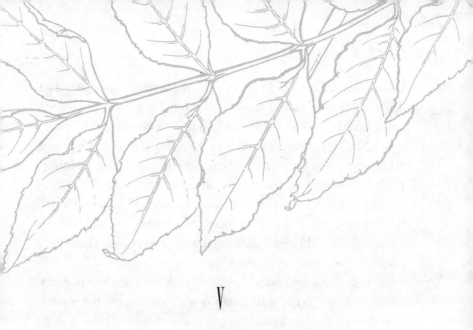

V

In the morning Enéas and I visited the stores, the refrigeration plant, and the administrative offices. Enéas walked two or three steps behind me. He seemed ready to fulfill any request that I had, and if I didn't speak, he remained quiet. I preferred his cigarettes to my American Lucky Strikes. When we stopped, or when I would linger to watch someone working, Enéas would invariably squat down or lean against the closest wall. His movements lacked what I considered normal flexibility. He looked like an old, tired horse and his expression annoyed me. For a while I had wanted to shake him; to hit him. But I contained myself. I merely showed my annoyance by giving him abrupt, terse orders. Later we went down to the dock.

Another boat had arrived. It brought food and mail. There was a Syrian on board who sold cigarettes, liquor, alligator skins, and used books. The Syrian unfolded a small table on the dock and placed the bottles and cigarettes on it. He placed the stack of books on the floor next to him. Nobody dared to buy anything other than books from him. I looked around. As they were unloading the hold, several workers waited off to the side to board. Two armed guards were going through their baggage. They made one of the workers leave behind some mandioca, some rubber, and a machete, which he was carrying in his bag. I watched the worker, who before boarding the steamship took advantage when the guards weren't looking and used his foot to push the mandioca, the rubber, and the knife into the river. I wasted no time. I went over to the salesman and asked for a bottle of liquor and a carton of cigarettes. The Syrian looked at me, confused. Then I looked through the stack of books. There were poetry books, geography books, and books about political subjects, and they were bound in leather with gilt titles and borders. I bought one about the Brazilian desert, and for the three items I paid more than it would have cost me to have dinner and go dancing at the Palais de Glace in the heart of Buenos Aires. The Syrian wanted to sell me more things. "Don't you need a whistle or a mirror?" he asked. "I don't think so," I answered. I handed my purchases to Enéas and asked him to hide the bottle and take it to my house.

I met Jack around noon. He was waiting for me outside the dining room. He was being entertained by two Brazilians from the administrative staff who were talking with a parrot. The parrot, which was tied to the window with a string, replied with squawks. In the dining room, lunch was not ready yet. We sat down at the table that faced the window where the parrot was. The dining room was small and exclusively for directors and their guests. I looked out the window. The Brazilians looked at us and then went away.

"Why are you here?" Jack asked me.

"For a job and money," I answered.

"And what are you running away from?"

"I'm not running away," I lied.

"Why are you punishing yourself then?"

"What kind of question is that?"

Jack looked at me, surprised.

"Ah! Then you are a volunteer. I am happy to meet volunteers among us. It's a pleasure, Mr. Volunteer," Jack said.

I couldn't avoid asking him what had been the driving force behind his coming to Fordlandia.

"To get well and save my soul," he said.

"After being in jail," I added.

Jack was pensive for a moment.

"Ah ha! How quickly news gets around. Something like that, sure, why not? A couple of years here and then I can search for my destiny elsewhere, in sales or something else. Why else would I have traded my beloved Michigan for this shitty, humid place. Tell me, Mr. Job and Money."

"Maybe to get ahead at Ford."

"Get ahead at Ford. Ha! Like Rowwe, perhaps, or maybe like your little friend, Frank. Of course, good idea. Absurd! Those guys are losers. This is a lost cause, old man. From the beginning. Make no mistake about it. And in Detroit you don't get ahead by organizing papers or going through the formalities but by having new and effective ideas, with real inventions. That is Detroit, old man. And those guys are useless here, in Detroit, or wherever the hell they are. Useless strays in a lost war," he said.

He just stared at me. The waiter brought us our lunch. It consisted of a bit of spinach and mandioca, a chopped egg, and a piece of boiled fish. He also brought us a bottle and two glasses. I picked up the bottle and smelled inside. It had a fruity smell, which one moment seemed very sweet and the next sour. The label said: "Fruit juice, made in Fordlandia." I filled the two glasses and we made a toast.

"What is this," I asked.

"Papaya and *guanábana.* It complements our daily requirement of two thousand five hundred calories. Two thousand five hundred for us, two thousand three hundred for the natives, no more, no less. The exact amount needed to replace the strength that the Tropics takes out of you. Didn't you read that in the report?"

I told him that I had still not read up on that matter, and we starting laughing.

"Should I order something else?"

Jack smiled.

"Don't even think about it." He shook his head and looked outside. "Do you know the only thing about rubber that I like?" he asked me.

"No."

"You can pick up women and not get any diseases."

"What are you talking about, condoms?"

"Of course, what else? Old Henry thinks of everything, boy. What is the automobile? It is the promise of freedom and youth. You can't change your body, your ailments, or your wrinkles, but you *can* change your car. With a car it's easier to meet women and seduce them, and with condoms you avoid complications."

"I don't like using them."

"You don't say. A mysterious volunteer with the soul of a priest, a priest with syphilis. Well, well. I'll tell you something: I've read about the history of condoms. It is a noble history, old man. Of princes and courtiers. It began long before Saint Goodyear discovered the vulcanization of rubber and began producing it widely. What a guy Goodyear, huh? Did you know that two hundred years ago the Scottish wrote a song making fun of a certain Quondam, who wanted to prohibit its use so that there would be less sexual activity among the poor? "Then Seringe and Condum / come both in request / while virtuous Quondam / is treated in jest."

We were finishing our lunch when Rowwe came in, alone. I noticed that he looked tired. He came over to us and without even looking at Jack asked me, "When do we get to work?" His voice seemed tired, too.

"Soon. I will see you tomorrow afternoon and tell you what my plans are," I answered.

Rowwe nodded without a word. Then he turned around and sat down on the other side of the table. The waiter brought a plate of chestnuts for dessert and coffee.

"What can I do to recruit people, Jack?" I asked softly.

"Promise them paradise: a job and money," he said.

"Where can I find them?"

"Ask your caboclo, he knows," he said, pointing at Enéas.

I looked out the window. Enéas was waiting for me outside the dining hall as I had asked him. I got up and shook Jack's hand. I asked him quietly, "And the guitar?"

Jack looked at Rowwe out of the corner of his eye. "One night when there is a full moon I'll invite you to one of my concerts," he said.

While we had been eating, the sky had opened up, but the downpour had ended quickly and the sky had cleared again. Enéas's clothing was soaked. The final drops from the rain shower had caught him between the employee dining hall and that of the executives. I had intended to tour the plantation, but the humidity and the insects, which appeared by the thousands, discouraged me. We went to my office and I asked Enéas to tell me in detail how many towns and rubber villages he knew of nearby, what the distance was between them, how many people lived in each one, and what we needed to take with us if we undertook a trip through the area. My proposal made him happy, and he told me what he knew. We talked that afternoon in my office and the following day as we walked along the paths on the property.

The following afternoon I went to see Rowwe to tell him my plans. In the middle of my presentation I felt a certain pride.

"Have any of you or anyone from Belem traveled the area before to spread word about the village and offer jobs?"

"No one has, until now."

"Good, I think in a couple of days I will be prepared to do just that. I will visit huts, towns, and small plantations along the Cupary and Tapacurá Rivers. I will need money, plenty of money, credentials, pamphlets, a good motorboat, and provisions," I said.

Rowwe got up and asked me to trace the route on the map that was hanging on the wall behind him. While not exact, I pointed out the rivers and the areas I intended to visit.

"It's bold, okay, I buy it. You can count on those things as well as some weapons. I also want you to take notes on everything you see out there," he said.

Then he opened a desk drawer and took out some typewritten pages. He gave them to me for a few seconds.

"When you return, successful or not, we'll set this thing in motion," he said.

I only managed to read the title page. On the top left I read: "For C. Sorensen. Dearborn Office. Strictly confidential." The title, in capital letters, said: "PROPOSAL TO EXTEND THE PROPERTY TO SIX MILLION ACRES, SOLVE THE PROBLEM OF MANPOWER, AND MOVE FORWARD INTO THE AMAZON." Signed: J. F. Rowwe.

I said good-bye to Rowwe. I promised to send him my ideas and what I would need in writing. I was left thinking about the contents of those pages. The subject interested me and I was intrigued. But later, preparations for the trip absorbed all of my time. Organizing my first trip on the tributaries of the Tapajós was not easy. I clearly did not know the area or the jungle. And what I had seen during the voyage aboard the *Moacyr* had been truly awe inspiring. This trip into the Amazon would help to understand the real potential of Fordlandia: if it were all just an enormous glass container, a cavity made of precious crystal, into which an eccentric millionaire had poured his eccentric dreams; or if, in fact, it really was a pioneering adventure whose goal was to raise the flag of progress in an unknown territory, as unknown as it was beautiful, never to leave. I went for a walk around the plantation. The workers were still working and they looked at me briefly and, at times, mockingly. On more than one occasion I tried to talk with them, but the attempts failed. They knew that we were different. They communicated with each other in a rustic and obscure Portuguese. As I walked along I was carried away with the excitement of the trip. That was not a good thing. My mother used to say that when you are excited, you are a prisoner of your nerves. I walked around for half an hour. Then I returned to the village on the paths, which were still flooded with sunlight and heat. I looked for Enéas and found him sauntering around one of the side streets. I told him that Rowwe had accepted my proposal, and Enéas then suggested that we round up an assistant and said he would take care of that. It seemed reasonable to have another man to rely on in case problems arose, so I accepted his suggestion. What's more, I was certain that Enéas, reluctant to do any kind of manual labor, as if he were nobility, was thinking that the assistant would be the one actually responsible for the daily work. And that's just how it was. The assistant's name was Roque.

Roque was a mulatto and shorter than Enéas. He looked young—almost like a boy—and was born in an old village on the banks of the Tapajós. He had a little mustache and only a few stained and crooked teeth left. Unlike Enéas, Roque walked quickly and proudly. Enéas had the ability to find his way around the rivers and the jungle, even under difficult circumstances. Roque, on the other hand, proved throughout the trip to be a good cook and an unbeatable conversationalist. He knew all the legends and myths of the Amazon. From the simplest ones—universal ones, I would say, versions of which could be heard in Buenos Aires, for example—to the most improbable. When we wanted to be quiet and Roque would begin one of his long stories, the only way to shut him up was to call him by those four words that wounded his pride: "Shut up, worthless Negro." Roque had a sharp but unstable mind, capable of dazzling us one moment only to die out the next. With only rudimentary morals, he was able to reflect on the most complex questions.

In the late afternoon I met with both of them in my office, which was a cubicle, just like that of the U.S. official's, across from Rowwe's office. I repeated the objectives of the trip several times, and I unfolded a map on the desk. We made a rough itinerary, calculated the time we would spend traveling from one place to the next, and I jotted down everything we were going to need. I asked them if they knew how to handle weapons. Rowwe's assistant had brought me a revolver and a .22-caliber shotgun, several cartridges, and ammunition. Enéas said that he had experience in handling shotguns. We arranged to meet the next morning to finish the preparations. Then I locked my office and headed home, taking the map and the shotgun with me.

When I got home I went into the bedroom, dropped the gun on the bed, and went over to the window. I opened it onto a dusk that was now fading into night. The afternoon was fading into a reddish sky. I went back over to the bed, sat down, and unfolded the map, still nervous. I went over the details again and tried to memorize the different names of the rivers and towns.

When I was small I had a passion for maps. My father used to take me on trips around the islands of the Delta, where he had some friends and relatives. Once, after a ride in a motorboat, one of his friends gave me a map of the Delta made by military cartographers. I spent hours and hours looking at that map, and for months I dreamed I was in the middle of an exploration. I was a lonely hunter. I also remembered a passage from a book by Mark Twain. In *The Turning Point of My Life*, Twain wrote that in his childhood he had really wanted to sail through the Amazon, and that in New Orleans, before setting out on the Mississippi, he had looked unsuccessfully for any boat sailing for Pará.

I folded the map, got up, and put it down on the desk. Then I picked up the shotgun. I uncocked it and looked in the barrel to see if it was clean. I removed the safety catch and aimed at the small lamp hanging from the ceiling. A few insects were flying excitedly around it. I gently pulled the trigger. The spring was taut. Out of the corner of my eye I saw a shadow approaching the window, and then the flicker of a match. I pointed at the flame. The shadow disappeared and I heard the sound of someone falling down. For a moment it was absolutely still.

Then I saw the drawn and tired face of Frank slowly appear at the window.

I lowered the gun.

"What are you doing? Are you crazy?" he shouted.

"I wasn't going to shoot you."

He raised a pipe to his mouth. He lit another match, and as he puffed away at the pipe, he looked at me resentfully.

"Seeing as you're leaving the day after tomorrow, I came to see if you wanted to play some pool," he said.

I like pool. In fact, I could spend the rest of my life with a cue in one hand and a stiff drink in the other. I accepted and put the gun down on the desk. When I was ready to leave Frank stopped me.

"Wait, wait. Aren't you going to offer me a drink?"

I looked at him, surprised. I hesitated for a moment, but then I went to the wardrobe and took out the bottle and filled a glass. I lifted up the mosquito netting and passed the glass through the window. Frank downed it in one gulp.

"That Syrian sells pure shit," he said.

That night Frank told me some of the details of his life. I learned that he had been raised in a working-class neighborhood of Detroit, that he had run away from home as a boy, that it had been hard for him to find a job, that he had been about to join the U.S. Navy, that if not for Ford and Rowwe, especially Rowwe, he would be on the streets, maybe stealing or committing violent crimes, or lost in some remote place.

"And this isn't a remote place?" I asked him.

"In some ways, yes. But we created it and we control it," he said.

The other Americans, except for Jack and Rowwe, were in the canteen. While we played pool, the other four organized a poker game. They were playing for money and drinking a lot of coffee. Every now and then they took a break and went outside to smoke.

Playing poker without smoking or drinking seemed ridiculous to me, and I almost told them so. They, however, seemed to be having fun. Two of them were accountants and the other two were engineers. Frank was Rowwe's right-hand man. The gringos always acted through assistants and Brazilian foremen, and they were rarely seen outside of their offices, where twice a day at the same time they would receive reports and give orders to the foremen. Jack was the only one who walked around the plantation and had direct contact with the workers. For that reason they tolerated him, even though they did not hide their contempt for him. They constantly alluded to him in their jokes and comments. In one such comment I learned that Jack thought he was hiding something from them, an invention, which they actually already knew about. I stayed at the canteen until after midnight. Before going to bed I decided to take a walk through the village. At that hour, the village showed hints of modernity illuminated in the darkness of the night by the scattered lights.

VI

It was a mild, bright day, and the morning was filled with that incredible brightness typical of summer. Even the mist over the jungle rose at dawn like a curtain. The Tapajós glittered calmly, and the scores of trees were perfectly still. Their aroma floated from bank to bank throughout the drifting summer's air. We had just set off when I looked back and saw Jack walking along the dock next to Caroline. I stared at them a while. I would remember that image until I returned.

Jack had been at the dock early that morning to help us inspect the boat and store our bags. He also brought me a flask of whiskey hidden in a cardboard box. He seemed nervous until Caroline's canoe appeared on the lower course of the river. Caroline was returning from a trip to a community of Mundurukus, and she was accompanied by a caboclo and a native woman. The canoe was small and filled with fruit and handicrafts. Jack helped her ashore, and as he took her by the arm he introduced her to me. Caroline was smiling.

"This is Caroline, the one responsible for much of what you have read about this paradise."

Caroline was tall and blond. Her eyes were gray and slightly almond shaped. She wore what to me seemed like the typical explorer's outfit, which fit her loosely.

"This is the Argentine, a new director, who is about to set off in his boat and conquer the kingdom that only few people, you being one of them, dare travel to," Jack said, pointing at me.

She looked at me.

"Is that right?"

"Completely false. It is just a trip to get to know the people and offer them work," I said.

She laughed. I noticed her expression. According to Rowwe, Jack talked for some time about the way I had looked at Caroline that morning. Caroline was Canadian and had been hired by Ford's Sociology Department. The department had a team of investigators and social workers who visited the houses of the Ford employees to insure that they were saving money and weren't living in sin. When the social workers showed up at their homes, they had to show their savings books and their marriage certificates. The workers would distribute a pamphlet entitled "Standards of Living," which urged employees to use soap in their daily hygiene, not to spit on the ground, to avoid buying things on credit, and if they were foreigners, to attend the Ford schools where English was taught. The wives of the employees were advised not to have guests to eliminate the risk of infidelity while their husbands were at the factory. Rowwe had the pamphlet translated into Portuguese and Tupi, the native language, so it could be distributed to the people at Fordlandia. As for me, despite his insistence, I never carried or distributed those leaflets at any of my meetings or visits around the area. The Sociology Department, according to Ford, had to improve men in the same way that the assembly line installed in his plants had allowed him to improve cars. The Department also hired ex-convicts and vagrants in order to give them an opportunity with the company. An ex-convict who had become a successful sales director was one who had arranged for Jack, his former cellmate, to join the company. But Caroline was not a sociologist or a social worker. She was an anthropologist, and her work in the Amazon was to study the character and customs of the natives. She traveled and wrote a lot. Her reports, in some way, hinted at the possibility that Henry Ford's ideas would fail there.

When the dock in Fordlandia disappeared from sight, I looked up. There was not a single cloud in the sky, but in the distance, behind the hills, the intense darkness turned golden and fiery as lightning pierced it. Enéas cleared his throat and then asked me if he could take off his shoes. I said yes. Roque smiled and asked Enéas if he too could take off his shoes. Enéas looked over to me and I gave him my consent. Roque was at the bow, holding the rudder. Enéas was at the stern, across from me. As soon as he took his shoes off, he put on his straw hat and sat quietly, smoking and staring out at the river. Every so often he addressed Roque and told him the course. The plan was to reach a commercial post located at the mouth of the Cupary River around noon. The post provided goods in exchange for rubber to some sixty families in the area, and according to Enéas, those people would love to be hired at Fordlandia. The motorboat had a powerful diesel motor and plowed quickly through the current. After navigating for a while, Roque touched my shoulder. I turned around and looked at him. He swallowed and then said, "You aren't the first Argentine to come around here, mi blanco. There was one a long time ago, and he was a famous foreman."

"Very famous?"

"Extremely famous, and feared. Right Enéas?"

Enéas did not like the allusion.

"I don't remember, and how could you remember if you were only a boy?" he said.

"Well, I didn't meet him, but everyone knows about the fame of El Argentino," Roque replied. "Especially around the area of Manaus."

"And what did the famous Argentino do?" I asked.

"The same thing as you, only different. He hired men but for himself, not for others. He had land. He was rich."

"And how do you know he was Argentine?"

"That's what they called him El Argentino."

"I see. And why was he so famous?"

"For how he lived. He made the people work like slaves and gave them nothing in return. Nothing. Just a little bit of mandioca and liquor. Whoever protested was tied to a tree for the insects or cobras to finish off. Very, very cruel, El Argentino."

"And what happened to him?"

"One night the Anhangá killed him. He cut up his entire body, piece by piece, and threw it into the river, to the piranhas. His own people celebrated the Anhangá."

"I see. And who was this Anhangá?"

"Ay, mi blanco! Anhangá is a spirit that floats in the jungle. Sometimes he appears as a bird, sometimes as an animal. As a person he appears incomplete. He is missing an eye or a leg, or his feet are facing backward. He hides in order to eat the souls of those who get lost in the jungle. He is very dangerous, mi blanco. It's best not to run into him."

"Shut up, worthless negro," Enéas said.

Roque's eyes filled with rage and he was quiet. We moved forward in silence. The noise of the motor scared the birds that were flying over the boat, and they took refuge in the trees. I unfolded one of the maps and estimated we would be at the post in four hours. Then I opened my pack, took out the flask that

Jack had given me, and took a drink. The whiskey burned in my stomach. It was ordinary whiskey. Enéas looked at me. He got up and took from his knapsack a small bottle wrapped in paper. He offered it to me.

"Do you want to try this? We make it at home, it's good," he said.

I took a couple of swigs and gave it back to him. It was a very sweet liquor with a pleasant taste. Enéas seemed satisfied. Before putting the bottle away he too took a drink. A little while later, Roque tapped me on the shoulder. When I turned around he handed me a brown glass bottle.

"Try this, mi blanco, this is the really good stuff," he said, taking a drink and reaching his arm out again to hand me the bottle.

I took a big swig. It was a strong, dry liquor known as *cachaça*, and its heat spread throughout my body.

"It's good, Roque, really good," I said.

Roque looked at Enéas and smiled.

We approached the post just after noon. The shadows of the high, thick clouds were slipping across the river. The post was on the right bank, surrounded by thickets. Behind the weeds, the trees came together in crowded rows. There were several canoes docked at the narrow, rundown pier, and in one of them a man and a boy were fishing with a line and tackle. The canoe overflowed with fish, and some red and black birds fluttered around it. The birds flew here and there. The post consisted of the pier and three wooden buildings painted red. There were two small houses located on either side of what looked like a grocery store. When we drew closer, the man and the boy in the canoe stopped fishing and left their canoe. Other men and children came out of the store and from one of the houses too.

We docked and hopped out onto the pier. The children and the fisherman came to meet us, and they stood staring at the motor and the final turns of the propeller. The other men remained at the door of the store. We walked over to them and I recognized Theo, the German priest, among the men. When he saw me he came forward and shook my hand. Then he introduced me to each one of the customers, and we all went inside the store. Theo was accompanied by a Norwegian scientist who was in the Amazon to study the birds of the region. He was a likable guy with an easy smile, and he was staying at Theo's mission. He carried a camera. We exchanged a few words in English, and he asked me if he could take a photo of us next to the motorboat. I agreed to grant him his request before we resumed our journey. Theo was at the post because the owner, Francisco, had called on him to officiate at a forced marriage. A farmer had deflowered a young girl, and the father had appealed to Francisco asking him to help catch the young seducer and force him to marry. Francisco was also the justice of the peace, but the young girl's parents had demanded the presence of a priest. The ceremony would take place in the afternoon at the bride's house, a few kilometers from the post, on the same river, and the Norwegian had loved the idea of going with Theo on that special day.

The store was small and crammed with goods. One could see bags of rice, beans, boxes of matches, rolls of fabric, and large carafes of kerosene, beer, and liquor. There were also some small bottles of Atabrinea, a drug used to combat malaria. Once a month in the summer, the rubber producers would fill the store, bringing the rubber they had produced. In return Francisco would give them the goods they needed. The *caucheros* usually took more than the amount that Francisco gave them for the rubber. The people called Francisco's game "credit."

Francisco, in turn, had credit with the boats that carried the pelets of rubber from his store and brought him goods from

Belem. The boats visited the post every month in the summer, and they belonged to merchants from Belem. The land that the caucheros worked on belonged to Francisco, even though his title was vague if not nonexistent, and they were prohibited from selling the rubber independently to other posts or buyers. A list with the names of the families that resided on his lands was posted on the door of the store. Francisco kept a close eye on the caucheros by posting guards armed with .44 caliber rifles at the mouth of the rivers and tributaries that surrounded his lands. Every month, Francisco would welcome the caucheros to his store and offered them, in addition to music, food and drink at no charge. There were a few small metal tables and a few chairs. The floor was packed dirt, and the locals preferred to remain standing while they drank and talked. I sat down at a table with Theo; the Norwegian was leaning up against the bar. I invited everyone to a beer. Theo looked dirty and sweaty, just as he had when I had met him on the boat. I reached into my shirt pocket and took out the piece of quinine bark that was left.

"I still have your gift," I said to him in English.

"I, however, already spent your money," he said.

I leaned back and looked over at the group next to the bar. Enéas and Roque had joined the group and were talking excitedly. No one paid any attention to our table.

"The village needs people, Theo, a lot of people, and I thought you could help us find them."

"Me? Why would I do such a thing?" he asked.

I was pensive. I had always disliked the words: *state, development, nation*. I had heard them standing alongside my parents at certain meetings in the suburbs of Buenos Aires, and I had read them in proclamations that turned up at my house. But they had always sounded hollow, worn-out, and I refused to say them. They would be even less useful outside the limits of the civilized world. Theo, however, was intelligent and educated, and I did not want to offer him, right off, something material in exchange for his collaboration.

"Well, in doing so you would be contributing to the development of the region, and we would be very grateful to you," I said.

"Who are we?"

"Ford, the company, the state, Brazil," I said.

"All that is a long way from here and has its own religion, my son. What's more, I do more for the people in this region than all of you."

I was hungry, and when they brought our beers I ordered something to eat. Theo picked up the mug and took a drink. A small brown spider appeared on the table. I pushed it onto the floor with the back of my hand and squashed it with my foot. Theo shook his head.

"Your manners will destroy the jungle," he said.

I stared at him. "Why don't you think of some way to help us?"

"I'll think about it, but don't say anything to Francisco," he said, looking toward the pier.

Another canoe was docking at the pier. All of the children, a woman who came out of one of the houses, and one of the men who was in the store went out to meet Francisco, who had stopped for a moment in front of our motorboat. Then he came toward the store along with the man who had gone out to meet him. He wore a suit of coarse linen. He was short with thick lips and a quick step. When he entered the store, the villagers stopped what they were doing and greeted him respectfully. He said hello with a nod of his head and looked at Theo and then at me. His eyes were riveted on me.

"Cheers, amigos," he said, coming over to us.

I picked up my beer and drank half of it. I wiped my mouth with my hand.

"Cheers," I said.

Francisco sat down and slapped Theo on the shoulder. He looked even shorter at the table.

"Everything's set Theo, so in a little while we'll leave for the wedding," he said.

Theo put his hand on my shoulder.

"Allow me to introduce this young man who has come from Argentina to work for Mr. Ford. He is a very generous man."

"I hope you know the rules of rubber production," Francisco said.

The rules of rubber production were an agreement between merchants and vendors, who in the past imposed eviction, fines, and prison terms on all caucheros who harmed the trees, bought goods at a store other than that which had given them credit, or ran off leaving their credit unpaid. The agreement prohibited the vendors from giving refuge to fugitives, and the caucheros used to rebel against those conditions. On one occasion, on the lands of a fellow named Pereira Silva, they overcame the guards and seized a boat in which they sailed to Belem. But in Belem they were captured by the state police, who as the legend goes, sent them back upriver and forced them to work the rest of their lives in the most remote seringals of the very same Pereira Silva. Caroline's report stated that the rules had, in fact, been abolished twenty years ago, when the peak of the Brazilian rubber industry passed into the hands of the British colonies in Asia. Caroline described the rules based on the work of two local writers, Ferreira de Castro and Euclídes da Cunha.

I leaned back and looked at Francisco for a few seconds. Theo wiped the sweat from his forehead with a piece of paper. I had the feeling that everyone was now looking at our table.

"Those rules are a thing of the past, they don't exist anymore," I said.

"You are mistaken, señor, maybe that is so in Santarem or in

Manoas. But here the rules still exist and are observed," Francisco responded, seriously.

The same man who brought us the beer now brought our food. There were two plates of fried fish and farina. The fish smelled like cod, and its meat was white and thick. I took out my pocketknife, opened it, cleaned the blade on a piece of paper and cut off a piece. It was delicious. I asked the waiter what kind of fish it was.

"*Pirarucu*, the best. Shall I serve you, *patrón*?" the waiter asked.

"No, I'm leaving now."

"Eat something with us, hombre," Theo said.

"No thank you. But as soon as you finish, come by my house and we'll leave. It was a pleasure, señor," Francisco said, and then, addressing the waiter as he left, added, "Don't charge the señor or his friends, they are guests, as are Theo and his foreign friend."

My thinking was that Francisco would collaborate with us in exchange for money. Apparently I was mistaken. We ate in silence. Theo quickly finished his fish and asked me for a match so he could clean his teeth. He leaned forward with both hands on the table and let the match hang from his mouth.

"Would Henry Ford agree to send a letter to the head of my order praising my work and help me to erect another church in the area?" he asked.

"Of course. I don't see why he would have any objections."

"Good, I will help you then, I will send you people. But you must know that I don't believe in rubber or in those who produce it. They are difficult, unstable nomads. Rubber is a thing of the past, anyway. Why don't you look for gold?"

I shrugged. Theo stood up and looked at me. I reached into my pants pocket, took out a few bills, and handed them to him. He seemed satisfied. He counted them and then pulled open the neck of his cassock and put the bills away in a small pouch that he wore hanging from his neck. Then he offered me a piece of quinine bark.

"Here, my son, I bless you and will always be by your side if you need me. Good-bye," he said.

We bought some provisions and left. We had arranged to visit the caucheros who worked for Francisco after we left the post, and we had a short trip ahead of us. When we raised anchor and started the motor, the children on the pier got excited. The Norwegian accompanied us to the boat and took three photographs of us with his Kodak. Francisco and Theo appeared at the door of the house and watched as we reentered the canal.

The day had become heavy, and the air was hot and humid. I put on my straw hat and lit a cigarette. As I watched the post grow more distant I thought about Caroline and Jack.

"Tell me, are Caroline and Jack a couple?" I asked Enéas.

"I don't think so."

"But they looked very tight," I said.

Enéas was smoking too. The smoke from his cigarette crossed in a spiral in front of his black, quiet expression before disappearing in the breeze.

"I don't think a woman like señora Caroline would fall in love with a crude man like Jack, mi blanco," he responded.

We went up the Cupary, which was low. On the banks there was a border of reddish purple earth that was covered with rubble from the jungle, and different-colored butterflies fluttered over it. The vegetation was lush, overgrown, tangled up in jumbles of climbing plants, lianas, shrubs, and branches. I passed the time by picking out a tree farther ahead by which I could measure our progress toward the caucheros' dwelling, but I invariably lost it before we passed it. An hour later we spotted the first house. It was a hut set in a small clearing. Tree trunks and burned branches were piled up on the ground surrounding the house. The caucheros burned the jungle in order to make a clearing on the land and remove the acidity from the ground. With fire and machetes they cleared the riverbank and the excess foliage, and then they planted some mandioca, squash, and peppers there. It was hard work. The better the burning and cleaning, the better the harvest. A cauchero who stopped his work to welcome us told us all the details about the burning and the planting. He was barefoot, scarcely dressed in some old, torn pants, and only Enéas and Roque could understand his Portuguese. The guy was eating his words. His skin was sallow, and his hands and ears were swollen from insect bites. He had heard about Fordlandia and did not seem suspicious. When Enéas told him our intentions and added that we intended to pay for his help, he agreed to go and look for the other heads of families and to organize a meeting at his house.

The homes of the other families were located only a short distance from his, but they were not easy to find. Some were on the Cupary River and others toward the interior of the jungle, on the banks of narrow tributaries. The man's name was Juca, and he left with Roque, who was not pleased with the task. The sun was beginning to go down, and the possibility that night would catch him mid-trip scared him. Juca, on the other hand, was excited at the opportunity to drive a motorboat. Enéas and I stayed behind with his wife and his five children. The feet of the oldest and youngest children were cut and infected. The woman barely looked up when Juca introduced us, and after offering us coffee in some small containers made of squash rind, she started repairing some nets that were spread out in the house. The house had practically no furniture. In the kitchen there was a table, two crates, and a wooden bench, and the bedroom contained two trunks made of palm leaves, which were painted red. Some nets were rolled up and piled on the floor along one wall.

On the floor up against another wall was a statue of a saint, the same one that I had seen off to one side of the bar at Francisco's post, St. Benedict, surrounded by four lit candles. In the Lower Amazon, St. Benedict, a black saint not formally recognized by the church, was adored. In my opinion, St. Benedict was a vulgar saint who had performed no miracles and had no unique history. Nevertheless, the caucheros dedicated the first day of their harvest to him, and during the days in December immediately before and after the celebration they organized meals and dances in every neighborhood. During the feast days of St. Benedict, there was not a soul left in Fordlandia. Next to the statue of the saint there was a small mattress rolled up and tied with a string. Juca and his wife had a net for everyone, and the children shared the remaining two nets. Juca told us that he and his wife used the mattress only "when they wanted to touch each other." Behind the house was a clay stove, which was covered by a roof made of palm leaves, where the latex from the rubber coagulated.

I walked for a while with Enéas and Juca's oldest son along the paths that began near the house and penetrated deep into the jungle, forming a kind of circle that ended more or less at the point where they began. The paths were forested with rubber trees, one every eighty or one hundred steps, and according to Enéas, they were several kilometers long. In the summer months, Juca and his oldest son went along those paths collecting the latex from the trees. They would leave before dawn and spend each morning on a different path. In that way, with the cool air and alternating paths so that the trees were not overworked, they extracted, so they said, the greatest amount of milk possible. Every morning they went down the same path twice. The first time they made cuts in the trunks, and the second time, midmorning, they collected the latex from the containers tied to the trees. Juca's family helped him clean the weeds and vegetation from the paths and also to open small clearings that connected one path to another. The work was suspended in the winter, from December to the end of May, because the daily rain flooded the paths and the containers into which the latex flowed. It became impossible to keep working, and so the cauchero would swing in his hammock or gather *timbó* or cut cedar wood. In the winter, the water in the rivers rose to astonishing levels, overflowing the banks. The water was low in the summer. August was an idle month, for the rubber trees were in bloom, and the flowers would fall into the containers and ruin the milk. In Fordlandia they had told me that the caucheros feared the cobras that hid in the leaves of the trees and the hostile natives who used to come through the area. Juca and his son, however, complained about the length of the paths and they feared only malaria. The paths went through solid ground as well as swampy terrain. Narrow tree trunks served as bridges to cross the marshes or the waters that had not yet receded during the summer. Juca and his oldest son would take a small machete and a shotgun with them, in case along the way they had the opportunity to hunt a *cutia*, a paca, or on a lucky day, a wild pig. The paca was the tastiest, but it was also the fastest and most difficult to catch. When pursued, it seeks refuge in the small rivers and flees by swimming underwater, against the current. Without a dog to corner it on solid ground, the only way to catch it is with an accurate shot when it comes up for air. In the last few weeks, Juca did not attempt to hunt because he had caught *panema*. A few days later, when I missed an easy shot at a pheasant with brown feathers that was lying in some thickets, he told me that Juca had given me his panema. I paid no attention to him. It was obvious to me that I had missed the pheasant because I had used the revolver instead of the shotgun. The barrel of the Italian .32 revolver was very short, and when fired, the return was so abrupt that there was no chance of hitting the target. I had practiced, looking over the front sight and trying to avoid the jerk of the small barrel, but I ended up shooting a meter away from where the pheasant was. That revolver was only useful at a short distance.

Juca, just like Francisco's other caucheros, did not make deep incisions in the trees so as not to damage them too much, and his cuts drew a kind of spine on the trunks—a vertical cut and others at an angle starting from that cut. In this way much more milk ran out than with the method I had seen in Fordlandia. Jack would tell me that that spine extracts more milk, but it also means a certain slow death for the tree.

We walked along one of the paths for a while. The ground was a bed of dead leaves, which came up to our ankles with each step. The jungle was frighteningly dense, and the shadows closed in on the premature night. The female anopheles arrived at twilight and foretold the proximity of all fauna. Enéas and Juca's son had gone ahead. I caught up to them and suggested that we go back. Just as night fell, we arrived home. My first night in the jungle, far away from Fordlandia. We made a fire on one side of the house to drive away the insects and we sat talking until the motorboat returned with Juca, Roque, and eight other heads of families. We went into the kitchen. Juca lit two kerosene lamps, and we gathered around him. The lamps gave off a thick black smoke and had little effect in the darkness.

I looked at the faces of those huddled around Juca: unshaven faces, dirty and pale, like after a drinking binge. Their bodies smelled of bitter sweat. While we were having our meeting, Juca's wife, who had changed into an old-fashioned floral party dress, cooked the three cutias that one of the caucheros had brought in a clay pot. The cutia is a large rodent whose shape and flavor resemble a rabbit's. The cauchero who had brought them told of how he had caught them. What you have to do with them, the man said, is wait patiently and quietly, until they come out of their lairs, which are normally holes in fallen trees, and subdue them quickly with a blow of the machete. "They come out to eat and we eat them instead," the man said, smiling. His hands were filthy and his teeth moved unevenly in his mouth. As we were talking and Juca's wife was cooking, the children were having fun playing with the black, shiny skins of the cutias. The aroma of the cutias cooking awoke my appetite. Enéas spoke for us. We had agreed that he would consult with me on every question they had and that I would tell him how to respond. He began just as I indicated, telling them about the advantages of living in a village like Fordlandia, and he spoke in detail about the houses, the dining room, the schools, and the hospital. Then he talked about the work schedule and told them that Sundays were free for them to do whatever they liked, particularly with their weekly pay, which surpassed, quadrupled in fact, what they could earn collecting rubber for Francisco. While Enéas was talking, Roque nodded his head in agreement, and at times he would repeat the end of a sentence. I tried to prevent Roque from putting his two cents in, since I knew that much of what mulattoes say is not believed. But it was no use. Juca was paying attention to Enéas but he was also glancing over at his wife and children.

"Why don't you look for people in Santarem or in Belem?" Juca asked.

"We are looking there too. Many of those already in the village are from Belem," Enéas responded, just as I had told him to.

"Who is the patrón?" one of the caucheros asked.

"Henry Ford, an American who makes automobiles."

"Where does he live?"

"Very far away, in another country."

"So then he's not there?"

"No, he has foremen who are there working for him."

"The señor is a brother of the American?" asked another one, pointing at me.

"No, he is a foreman, a boss."

"Where does he come from?"

"Argentine, from Argentina," I said.

The men looked at each other. I remembered the story that Roque had told that morning and smiled.

I couldn't think of anything else to do but to offer them a cigarette. I shook the pack until three cigarettes popped up a couple of centimeters, and I held them out to them. Instead of taking a cigarette, one of the men asked me for the pack, looked at it, and gave it back to me. None of them accepted my offer.

"What are automobiles?" Juca asked.

"Carts with a motor," Enéas said.

"Yes, carriages that use a machine, a motor, instead of horses," Roque added.

In one of the pamphlets about the village there was a photo with a Model T. I got up, looked for my knapsack, took out a pamphlet, and brought it over to the light. I showed them the photograph, which they passed among them. None of them could read. The last one to see the photo called the children and showed it to them. The children laughed when they saw it.

"Do they pay with money or with goods?"

"With money; you can buy whatever you want with money," Enéas responded.

"Whatever you want, anything you want," Roque reiterated.

I went over to Roque and whispered to him to be quiet or else wait outside until the meeting was over. Roque looked down and was silent. Juca's wife informed us that dinner was ready, and she asked her husband to help her serve. All the caucheros looked at Juca, who replied sternly that that was her job and not to bother him, and he told her to hurry up and serve them. By the light of the lamps she looked young, but her face had a sullen expression. She glanced over at Juca as she put the pot on the table and went to the bedroom. Everyone served themselves on plates made from palm leaves. There were glasses for the liquor. As we were eating I could hear very clearly the murmurs of the night. There were whistles that rose from the foliage and died away, things walking on the straw roof, and other things that howled like children. Not far off you could hear the incessant croaking of frogs. We ate quickly, crowded together in the kitchen, and when we finished I told Enéas to ask the caucheros how and when we would see them. The caucheros were silent when they heard the question. Juca was sucking on a bone. In the midst of the silence, he dropped the bone on the plate, and as he finished the remainder of his food with a piece of stale bread he proposed that each one spread the word about the village and the conditions to the other families, and that it would not be bad if some of them wanted to try it out to see how the work was. "After the feasts of Sâo Joâo and Sâo Pedro," he said, "we'll see each other there." I decided to give a little money to each one, an advance for what will come, I said, and I told Roque and Enéas to take the men back, at least to where the Cupary met up with its nearest tributary, since the motorboat had a powerful searchlight. Roque and Enéas reluctantly agreed.

Juca accompanied them to the riverbank and lent them some small lanterns that were used to light the paths when work began before dawn. The woman cleared the table and took the plates outside where the stove was. Then she returned, served her own dinner on a plate, and went back into the bedroom. With Juca's help I hung a net in the kitchen. When they returned, Enéas and Roque hung up theirs. The smell of food, grime, and tobacco lingered in the kitchen. It took me a while to fall asleep and I awoke several times during the night. In the pampas, the silence of the night is a blessing for city dwellers.

For someone coming from the city, that first night by the window or lying in bed, the silence is overpowering, like a spell, as if you were closer to what was real and good. Nocturnal silence does not exist in the jungle. The night is filled with obscure sounds, rustling, howls, dives, flights, cries, things falling, things climbing or crawling. At one point, when I heard a cry, a real wail of unending torment, and after the cry a plunge, I jumped down from the net and went to where Juca and his family were. Everyone was sleeping. I was about to wake up Enéas and Roque in the kitchen, but a sense of ridiculousness overcame me, and instead of waking them up, I left my knapsack open by the side of the net with the butt of the revolver within reach, and I went back to sleep.

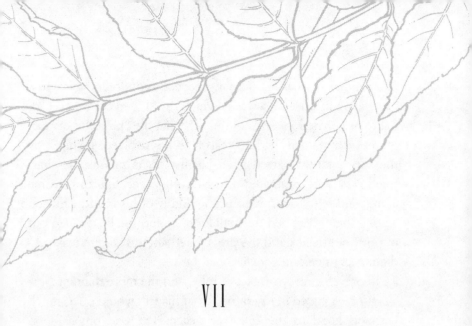

VII

Ford heard the melody of an old Irish song and he sat up on his elbows. There was still a bit of light in the cabin, and he could make out the rug with hues of chestnut brown, the worktable, and the lithographs of naval battles. In one corner, fixed to the floor, was an armchair made from noble Swedish wood. Then he heard someone coming up the stairs, walking down the hall-way, and approaching his door. He had rested for three hours without being disturbed. Everything reminded him of his jour-ney aboard the *Oskar II*, when he had proposed to go to Europe during World War I to mediate and demand peace among the nations. "Men seated at a table, and not men dying in trenches, will resolve the differences once and for all," he had stammered nervously in front of the crowd that had come to the port in New York to see him off that Sunday in Decem-ber 1915.

At that time his actions were receiving great publicity and he was showered with praise, especially after he raised the salaries of his workers high above the industry standard. He believed that he had to render his opinion about every event and, of course, that is what he did with respect to the bloody war that was raging in Europe, a war in which the United States, according to its convictions and contrary to what the "parasites of Wall Street" maintained, had no reason to be involved. Inspired by the support he received from pacifist organizations, he chartered a steamship, invited a few distinguished figures to come along, and left, bound for Europe. Many of his friends, Edison among them, declined the invitation, and as the boat sailed out of port, politicians and the press joked about his initiative, predicting an uncertain conclusion at best.

Roosevelt called it an act of folly, and the more tolerant *New York Times* stated in its editorial that his trip would do as much harm as good to the cause of peace. The bad omens soon became reality. In the middle of the Atlantic, Ford learned that the United States government had broken off relations with Germany in order to enter the war. The pacifists who were with him split into several factions, and Ford spent most of his time locked in his cabin, dejected and recovering from a flu he had caught early one morning when the crest of a wave hit him as he was going down to inspect the machine room. No sooner had the "Peace Boat" docked in Norway than Ford abandoned the project and hurried back to his country. A short while later, he agreed to build submarines in his factories, but as a result of that adventure, his fame had grown in Europe. Troubled by the criticism of some intellectuals and journalists, he set his idealism aside and appealed to practical reason: "If I had tried to burst into the European market out of nowhere it would have cost me millions of dollars. The 'Peace Boat,' on the other hand, made Ford a recognizable name on that continent for very little money."

He heard footsteps approaching his cabin and then saw the door opening and a tall man walk in. The man was wearing a hat tipped down over one side of his face and reeked of tobacco, and Ford felt the same anguish he had felt on those solitary, melancholy afternoons he had spent aboard the *Oskar II*. Ford remained lying down, completely motionless. Then his eyes met those of the intruder.

"Now that we are on the same boat, the course of which is unknown, and you are running our lives, tell me, Henry, what are you exactly? An inventor or a philosopher?"

"I am not an inventor. I merely brought together the discoveries of other men that represent centuries of work. If I had tried my ideas fifty, ten, or even five years before, I would have failed. That's how it goes. Progress occurs when all the necessary factors exist at the right time, when it is inevitable, and I am not so stupid as to maintain that only a few men are responsible for the greatest advances. Nothing is gained by pretending otherwise. I want to give jobs and cars to everyone and, along the way, make money," Ford responded.

"Well, whatever you are, I have to tell you the truth: you are alone, and nobody expects or wants anything from you now."

"Where did I go wrong?"

"You didn't go wrong. It was the men who failed."

"Am I dead?"

"You are alone, not dead."

"I don't see the difference," Ford said, and he leaned forward, trying to determine the identity of that man with a high-pitched voice and rural accent. It was absurd. The image quickly became blurred, like a photograph under water, and then it disappeared in a blink of the eye. He woke up suddenly. He looked at his wife, Clara, who was sleeping next to him, and then he jumped out of bed and crossed the room to the mirror.

He had more gray hairs than he had had in his dream. He looked at his watch and walked over to the dressing room. His heart was racing. He looked at his clothes and at the hundred pairs of shoes he owned for a moment and then went back over to the bed and lay down. He was still, pensive. Who was that man tormenting his dreams? His father, William, perhaps, always skeptical of his ambitions? Or maybe Couzens, his loyal administrator for years, whom he had let go for having criticized his ideas at the expense of the company? Impossible, neither one smoked, he told himself. Then he remembered the Dodge brothers, removed as shareholders because of an underhanded move. The image of the Dodge brothers, who had been the final obstacle between him and complete ownership of the company that bore his name, filled his thoughts for a few minutes. Then he felt like taking a ride on his bicycle, and he got up again. The air was blowing in through the open windows, and day was slowly breaking in the immense garden. He went to the dressing room, put on some pants and a shirt, and just as he finished putting on his leather boots he heard Clara's voice.

"Why are you putting boots on, dear? It's summer."

"Boots? Ah, yes, because I'm going to the Amazon."

"Where are you going? Where did you say, dear?"

"It was a joke. Don't worry, Clara, please."

VIII

Very early the next morning, when it was barely light out, Juca woke me up, and after having a little watered-down coffee that had been prepared the night before, I went with him and his oldest son to make the rounds. Enéas and Roque stayed behind to drain the bilge on the motorboat. We returned after three hours, and Juca was happy. He had tapped about one hundred trees and, according to him, those incisions would bring him two or three kilos of latex, which he would collect on the second round and harden around noon. Before we left we ate some dried fish and mandioca. Juca and his children came down to the boat to say good-bye. Juca wanted to give us a small ball of rubber as a gift, but I did not accept it, and we agreed to see each other soon, with other caucheros, in Ford-landia. We headed upriver to visit another commercial post.

We had a day and a half's journey ahead of us. During the trip I felt I was the master of my destiny and I could do with it whatever I wanted. The weather was nice, and we set up camp to eat and sleep on one of the many beaches along the shore. From sunrise to sunset we were escorted by rose-colored magpies, and I saw toucans, hummingbirds, and parrots flying over the foliage. The river was calm and the jungle watched our passage silently. Some of the trees were in bloom. In the jungle the silence is broken twice a day—at twilight and at dawn. That is when every living thing there sings, coos, and cries out in fear of the night that is approaching or in happiness for the day that is breaking. Not a sound is heard the rest of the day. One has the impression of something artificial, something in a trancelike state. Dawn in the jungle is less colorful than twilight. The light is indecisive, unhurried, and one must wait a long while before being certain that the day will be clear. The ground gives off torrents of humidity, and the vegetation is enveloped in mist. At dawn, everything is a shadowy, dark green. When I walked along the path with Juca, it was only on our return that I saw rays of direct light over the woods. The struggle to survive leads to a fight among the animals, as they climb over each other to reach the treetops and peek out onto a clear sky, under the light of the sun. There is an uncontrollable impulse toward the light. The branches gravitate more to the sunlight than to the century-old trunks. That morning on the path, Juca told me that in northeastern Brazil, the land of his parents, the phenomenon was the exact opposite. Instead of fleeing the suffocation of the shadows, the animals try to avoid and stave off the sun, their brutal enemy. But in the jungle, every sunrise is jubilant. Its manifold sounds are different from those at twilight, and more important, they announce the end of fear and the retreat of terror to the human spirit.

By the time we reached the next commercial post, Enéas and Roque had become enemies. The previous afternoon, while we were resting on a beach, they had had a heated argument, and it had been hard for me to calm them down. We had gone ashore on a large beach on the right bank. We threw our nets on the sand and sat down to talk. It all began when Roque brought up the subject of differences.

"You, mi blanco, are quite different from us, right?" he asked me.

I sat up on my elbows and asked him what had led him to think that.

"The difference is that when I want a coconut, I have to climb a tree and bring it down myself. Whereas if you want a coconut, you pay someone to do the work for you," he said.

"But it doesn't always have to be that way," I replied.

"I think it does, unless I find a treasure. Treasures come to us in dreams, and there are many, many hidden ones."

"Where? In the jungle?"

"Not just in the jungle. One night a cousin of mine, Lobato, dreamed about the exact spot and depth where a chest full of money was buried in front of his house. That night Lobato heard 'the money is there waiting for you' and he got up, crossed the street, and dug up the chest. But his luck didn't end there. No, señor."

"What else happened to your cousin?"

"Ah, many more things. The money enabled him to marry the daughter of a rich merchant and inherit the business. How did Mr. Ford become rich?"

"From what I understand, with work, ideas, and a bit of luck, naturally."

"Oh, mi blanco, here people change only if they find a treasure, receive an inheritance, or if . . ."

Enéas was sitting down, baiting a fishhook. Fish are plentiful in the summer, and Enéas had tried his luck that afternoon. He had caught a good-size *pacú* almost effortlessly. He interrupted the conversation without looking up.

"Or if they steal, right? Isn't that what you were going to say,

Negro? Ford made money through work, hard work, not expecting to receive an inheritance or to find gold underneath the rocks
in the river and not thinking about stealing."

"Look who's talking, a *tapuía* whose wife fishes," Roque muttered.

It bothered Enéas just as much to be called a tapuía as it did
to be called a caboclo. In the Amazon, descendents of the
natives, unlike the Negroes, were bothered by allusions to their
past. Enéas had indigenous ancestors. What's more, Roque had
questioned his ability to support his family by mentioning,
whether it was true or not, that his wife fished.

Enéas exploded. All of a sudden his tired appearance vanished. He stood up forcefully and with extraordinary agility and
threw himself on Roque. It was hard for me to contain him.
Only at gunpoint was I able to get him to let go of Roque's neck
and move off toward the shore. Then night came and the light
became so dim that everyone retreated into himself.

We arrived at the post in the afternoon. I was tired, but
according to the itinerary this was the last post we were going to
visit and I wanted to see Andrade, the owner, before nightfall.
On the pier we saw a few big dogs. They came out of the jungle,
barked at us, and disappeared again into the shrubs. I am not
afraid of dogs; in my house in Buenos Aires there was always a
dog around, and I know how to treat them. Roque asked if he
could stay on the boat, and I went ashore with Enéas. Roque
moored the boat between two big canoes, and we headed
toward the house across from the store. The house was similar to
the other post owner's, Francisco, only it was bigger and had a
straw roof. The dogs did not come out as we walked by. The
door opened and Andrade came out. He introduced himself and
held out his pale, damp, cold hand. He was black, not very tall,
and his hair and mustache were parted down the middle.
According to Enéas, some thirty cauchero families worked on

his lands. We went over to the store with him, where he offered me an awful-tasting drink that he had prepared, showed me his radio (on some nights he could hear stations from Rio de Janeiro), and invited me to sit down. The store was big, and there were a good many bags of rice and beans. When he found out that I was working at Fordlandia and, later, that I did not intend to buy much from his store, he gradually became less friendly. I appealed to him.

"I came to propose that you work for us, that you send us your men, get us hands in exchange for money," I said.

Andrade opened his eyes wide. His dark eyes revealed a calm cruelty. It occurred to me that he would have liked to see me throw up his drink. Before he could respond I explained, "You will earn more with us and, what's more, without any problems for you. We can agree on a fair price for each cauchero you get for us."

Andrade downed his own drink and seemed to liven up again.

"Why do you think I will earn more money?"

"It's simple. We need the most experienced men, and we will pay you for them. The rest of their families will stay here with you. Furthermore, those who come to Fordlandia will also be able to buy their provisions at your store."

"And if they all go? What will I do for a living? Raise fish?"

'I don't think they will all come. We can make a pact," I proposed.

"Wait a minute," Andrade said abruptly, and he went to the back of the store.

Enéas and I looked at each other. Enéas was leaning on the bar. I got up and walked over to him. On the bar next to some pieces of dried meat were a few bottles of American whiskey wrapped in newspaper. I thought of Jack. I opened one, smelled it, and took a drink. I told Enéas to take it to the boat. I unwrapped the others and started to read the pages of the paper. They were from the *Folha do Norte*, the newspaper of Belem, but from a year ago. On one of the pages I saw an article that talked about Fordlandia. The article included a caricature of Ford, in which Ford appeared wearing a royal crown and standing on a map of the Amazon. The headline was "The Great Yankee: Civilization and Work." I read it and then folded the page as meticulously as I could and put it in my knapsack. I kept it for a long time, until I had the chance to deliver it personally to Henry Ford.

I was reading when Andrade returned with another man, a mestizo. The man wore a faded gray uniform with an insignia on the shoulder. He wore no cartridge belt, but he had a pistol stuck between his stomach and his belt. He looked like he had just woken up. Andrade introduced him as a police officer. He said he belonged to the Santarem force and that he was there with three other men on a routine visit. Andrade noticed the unwrapped bottles and the newspaper scattered on the bar.

"One's missing," he said.

"Yes, how much do I owe you?"

"They were a gift from the officer and I don't sell them. So you can give it back to me," he said.

I motioned to Enéas to go get the bottle and bring it back. We remained standing at the bar. Andrade also offered his drink to the officer. The officer smelled the concoction but didn't taste it. Instead he asked for liquor, and Andrade served him obligingly.

"So you are recruiting people to work at the Ford plantation?" he asked me.

"That's right."

"How much do you pay?"

"Quite a bit more than in other parts, and we also offer housing, food, and schooling," I said.

"And Andrade was telling me that you are not satisfied with those from Belem and that you want more men with more experience."

"That's right, in order to carry out our plans we need many, many more men."

"Don't you have problems with them once they are there?"

"So far, no."

Enéas had returned and he handed me the bottle. It was obvious that he and Roque had taken a drink. Andrade looked at it in disgust.

"From what I can tell, officer, they take what they want, with or without permission. They've just arrived and they feel like they own everything. What do you think?"

The officer downed his drink in one gulp. Then he stood up straight, came over to me, and looked at Andrade.

"I think that we have to charge these guys for everything. If they want men, we'll get them men, but they'll pay in advance."

"You are planning to spend the night here, right?" Andrade asked.

"That's what we were thinking."

The officer put his hand over his pistol and looked at me.

"Figure out the bill, Andrade, for each cauchero, for tonight, for the whiskey, and for navigating in Brazilian waters under a foreign flag," the officer said.

Andrade opened a drawer and took out a pencil. He made some calculations on the newspaper. After a few minutes he showed the figures to the officer. What he was asking me to pay for the night, the whiskey, and sailing in Brazilian waters was more than half of the money I had left. What they were demanding for each cauchero was absurd. I told them that I wanted to think it over, and I left the store. Night had fallen. Roque was still on the boat. Near the house I could make out three figures that I assumed were the policemen who had come with the officer. I walked over to the boat, spoke with Roque, and returned. I kept my emotions in check. When I entered the store, the officer and Andrade were talking quietly. Andrade had lit a lamp and put it on the bar. The odor of kerosene filled the air. I took my gun out of the knapsack and aimed it at the two of them. Enéas left his spot at the bar and came over by my side. Andrade looked surprised, and his body shrunk. The officer looked nervous and raised his hands. I told Enéas to get a can of gasoline and take it to the boat. I went over to the bar and left some money on it. Then I took the pistol off the officer and removed the bullets. There were only three bullets in the chamber. When I picked up the bottle of whiskey, Andrade looked like he was about to say something. I smiled and walked backward to the door. I told them not to move until our boat had left. I opened the door and looked toward the house. The figures had disappeared. I barred the door from outside and slowly walked over to the boat. One of the dogs came out to meet me. He followed me closely, barking. The boat was unmoored, with the motor running, and Roque was holding it to the pier with his hands. Before I jumped, the dog bit me on the ankle. No sooner was I on board than we weighed anchor and left. The river was impenetrably dark. We moved along slowly for a couple of hours before anchoring to rest.

Early in the morning the noise of fish jumping in the water startled me, as if I had heard gunshots. I tried to go to sleep lying on the deck. I was half asleep, my head resting on my arm, when I heard Enéas and Roque talking. "This guy is completely mad.

After what he did at the post we are going to have problems. That's for sure," Roque said. "I don't think so. I think he did it to prove he has guts. All foreigners need to prove that here. Although I think he really is brave," Enéas answered.

"No. He's afraid, very afraid, and he's mad, and fear mixed with madness leads to death. I am good, Enéas, but I don't like to obey the orders of a madman. You?" They both agreed that they did not like my attitude and then they made some remarks about the weather, the food, and the caucheros. I thought about moving so that they would be quiet.

I waited for the mist to clear before resuming our course toward Jocotá, the village where both Enéas and Roque were born. The trip was calm. At sunset we would anchor at the nicest beaches and we would resume the journey at daybreak. We cut through the water for hours without speaking. We arrived two days later.

Seen from the river, Jocotá had the same charm as Fordlandia. It stood out clearly and colorfully amid the vegetation. The church, white and radiant, with its clay-colored roof, was the first building I noticed. Then I saw the town hall, a two-story building, and a row of low houses painted in bright colors on the river. There were two piers. One was longer and belonged to the town. It was dark red and set on posts. A neglected sailboat was moored at the other pier upriver, which was smaller. A few enormous mango trees jutted out near the town pier. The boats that came to Jocotá docked at the town pier by the covered shed that was on one side. As soon as I got off the boat and walked along the pier, the romantic setting began to fade. The pier was missing some planks, others were rotted and moved with every step. The streets in Jocotá were dirt, and most of the houses looked like they were about to crumble. Further beyond, far from the river and close to the jungle, there were numerous mud huts covered with palm leaves. In the center of town there was a square surrounded by the four main buildings: the town hall, the church, the first-aid station, and the school. The first-aid station had big windows and a garden in front, and the school was an adobe shed with a tile roof that also served as home to the teacher and his family. Between the church and the school there was a soccer field. Jocotá showed its best side to the river. Close up it looked like an old, broken-down piece of furniture. Nevertheless, I was happy. In fact, any break in the endless woods made me happy, giving me the feeling, incomparable in the jungle, of having arrived somewhere.

Before we spotted Jocotá, we ran into several canoes of fishermen who were traveling up and down the river, casting lines and small, round nets. This was a typical summertime activity. In the winter, fishing is practically impossible. Enéas said that during those months, January to May in particular, the fish swim toward the thickets and don't move from there. In the summer, on the other hand, when they come out to spawn and overrun the rivers all the way to the sources of the Amazon, it is easy to catch them. In the streams some people used a poisonous root known as timbó, which before the discovery of DDT, was also used as an insecticide to ward off the anopheles. They would lower the timbó into the shallow waters, and the poison would paralyze the fish, making them float to the surface.

When we were near Jocotá I took over at the helm, and Enéas and Roque sat with their legs underneath them at the stern. They were happy to visit their people, and when the fishermen recognized them they greeted them cheerfully, proudly and cheerfully. I recalled how in Fordlandia only the officials and those in charge of the kitchen and the restaurant were allowed to fish. Across from the village, some thirty meters out from the riverbank, there was a circular weir with an opening, made of poles from the trunks of palm trees. The weir was used to contain fish being carried away by the current. When they wanted to remove the fish, the circle would be closed. The weir belonged to a privileged merchant in the town, Doña Dora, at whose home I stayed.

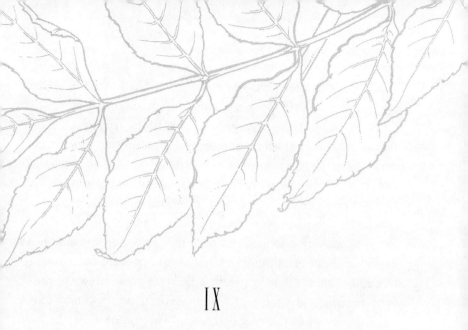

IX

Doña Dora's house was located on First Street. The three main streets in Jocotá followed the river and were intersected by other irregular streets. All were named after saints, but for the people there was only First, Second, and Third Street. First Street was the only one on which there was a row of properly maintained houses. In addition, because of the upcoming feast of St. Apolonius, every day the prefect had some of his men clear the street of the debris from the trees and bushes. The houses, larger than they appeared, were made of wood and adobe with cement and tile roofs, and each had an enclosed garden. The prefect, the mailman, a teacher, and the few merchants in town lived on First Street. Dora was a dark-skinned mulatta, the widow of a black man, and along with her brother-in-law she managed a store called Bola de Oro, the fish weir, and some good land on the opposite bank, which was used for farming. The people referred to the opposite bank as the "poor neighborhood." That was where Roque's family lived. Those lands assured Doña Dora a place and a good reputation in the town's upper class. Doña Dora had a wart on her cheek and she wore gold-rimmed glasses. She looked peaceful and carefree. Doña Dora was the godmother of Enéas's children, and although there was an unwritten law prohibiting sexual relations between a man and the godmother of his children, I am almost sure that they shared an old secret love. Doña Dora's house had two bedrooms, a dining room, and a sitting room to receiving visitors. Both bedrooms had windows and beds with mattresses. Doña Dora put me in the room that had a window that looked out onto the patio, and she took me in with the understanding that she would provide only breakfast and dinner. Many houses in town had no windows to prevent the night air from entering, since it was thought that malaria spread in the night's breeze. The dining room had a door that led to a hallway that connected to a patio. The sitting room was used only on special occasions, and Doña Dora had proudly placed her sewing machine in this room, where she received her friends, among them the tiresome and very religious spinster known as Doña Branquinha. On the patio there was a great variety of fruit trees as well as a henhouse. Late one night, I went outside to walk around the patio and smoke a cigarette. From there I could hear the excited laughter of Doña Dora and the equally excited breathing of my assistant, Enéas.

We remained in Jocotá just over one week. I rested the entire first day. It had been a while since I had stretched out on a mattress, and what's more my ankle hurt. The dog bite had become infected and the nurse, as well as the witch doctor whom Doña Dora brought, prescribed rest and told me to apply a mixture of vegetable resins to the wound. The mixture contained drugs from the Amazon, storax, and *fumo da mata*, and it had a pleasant aroma. While I was resting I did not feel like seeing either Enéas or Roque when they came to see me. But in the following days I would hold meetings with some of the locals and later I would enjoy the celebrations of St. Apolonius.

My stay had created quite a stir, and judging by attendance, my meetings were a total success. I had asked Enéas and Roque to round up all those who might be interested in working at Fordlandia and to distribute the pamphlets we had brought. The first meeting was held at the school, and the second, which was attended by the prefect, was held at the town hall, which had little ventilation, was unbearably hot inside, and was only half built; Doña Dora told me that the other half had actually been torn down in order to make money from the materials. But since, in addition to the prefect, the crème de la crème of the town was present, it seemed like a social gathering. The town had around three hundred inhabitants and a hundred more lived in the surrounding area. Between the two meetings and the feast of St. Apolonius I felt I knew them all. At the meeting held at the school there were practically no questions, and I tried hard to make my speech sound believable and enticing. I appealed to the greatest reason, and I tried not to sound pompous. Entire families came, and except for the children who were running to and fro, they were all completely silent, listening to me respectfully, as if I were a preacher. I gave my speech while standing, and I relied on Enéas to translate some metaphors. At the end of my presentation the teacher, a small, educated man who had introduced himself to me using great words of praise for Fordlandia, encouraged the people to participate. He stood by my side and said that progress calls only once and that he wanted to know if any among those present, especially those who did not have steady jobs, were willing to answer that call. An old man who had been following my harangue attentively raised his hand. The teacher gave him the floor. The man got up from his seat and said, calmly, that he had heard that in Fordlandia the sound of a siren indicated when to eat and when not to, and that "nobody except his body told him when to eat and that if it was like that and he had to obey the siren, he feared he would dry up like paper." The teacher looked at me, forcing me to respond. Roque was the only one who could have said such a thing to these people. It took me a while to answer. I finally said that it was true about the siren, but that it was the only way of organizing work time and rest time when dealing with so many people in the same place. The teacher applauded at the end of the meeting, and some of the others joined in. As we were leaving, I invited the teacher—his name was Flavio—to have a drink. We walked down First Street to the Bola de Oro. The air was humid but bearable. In the store window there were advertisements for Swiss condensed milk and guava jelly, recently arrived from Belem, even though the *Unión* had been the last steamship to dock at Jocotá, and that was a month and a half ago. The store had two sections. In the front, customers were waited on and there were some small tables at which to sit down and have a drink. The grocery store was in the back. Many cauchero and farming families in the area were clients of the Bola de Oro, and they would exchange rubber, oil, sarsaparilla, and vanilla for other food or fabrics. The sarsaparilla and the vanilla were highly valued by the merchants in Belem. We picked a table near the door. Through the glass on the door one could see the pier and the river. Raimundo, Doña Dora's brother-in-law, stopped talking with two customers and came over to wait on us. We ordered beer and liquor. The store had a wooden floor and smelled as if it had recently been waxed. On our way there I had thought about the people who had attended my talk. They had seemed too timid and in some way pessimistic. The teacher had come to these lands at the beginning of the century, at the peak of rubber production. Back then, he told me, he gave private classes in Portuguese, French, Latin, Arithmetic, Algebra, History and Geography. Then he had gotten married. And when the dream of limitless property ended, he had not wanted to leave, and he took over responsibility for the school, the only school within one hundred kilometers. He looked bitter and melancholy. I asked his opinion of the people.

"We are victims of our own greatness," he said.

"I see."

"Even though, to tell you the truth, I always wondered if we men are to blame or God, who offered us riches but also brought us difficulties."

"What difficulties do you mean?" I asked.

"What else? The climate, the environment, the jungle."

"I believe in men," I said.

"Why?"

"Because we are capable of doing new things that last."

"Like what?"

"Well, inventions, machines, projects; in short, ideas."

"Therefore, according to you, men have power over nature?"

"That's right," I said.

"So you don't think, then, that to tamper with Eden is to destroy it?"

"No, I don't think that, nor do I think of nature as a mirror of the divine, if that's what you mean."

"I see. As far as I'm concerned, I can assure you that observing the jungle helped me to understand the mysteries of the soul."

"What mysteries are those?"

"I know what they are, but if I want to explain them to someone who asks, I can't," he answered smiling.

"That virtue is not exclusive to nature. It is also found in good literature or in the cinema," I said.

"I know little about the cinema. I've only been a couple of times in Santarem. But I agree that whoever wants to achieve anything in life will always need to read. What happens, amigo, is that the Amazon is the last page of Genesis, and that page has yet to be written."

"There you have it. Writing is the work of men. Everything that leads to what is beautiful and true is also made by men, teacher."

"By men, not by savage beasts. Your friends from the United States see us as good savages, right?"

"I can only answer for myself, teacher."

"Don't let my questions bother you. Bear in mind that if it's hard to find men around here who read, it's even harder to find men who think. The number of those who think is very small. What's more, neither you nor I is capable of disturbing the jungle with our reasoning. In fact, thinkers will never disturb the jungle. They lack enthusiasm and write for the elite."

The teacher was pensive. He sipped his beer, then lit a cigarette. The customers who were talking with Raimundo said good-bye as they left. He was slow in responding.

"I don't know, I don't believe in man anymore. I don't stand behind any opinion, nor am I responsible for anything else, but I admit that I would like to see Fordlandia," he said.

The teacher had published a weekly paper in the town. When we finished our drinks, he invited me to see where he had worked. We went along a twisting, overgrown road. That road also led to the hut where Enéas's wife and children lived. The place he took me to, which at one time had been a beautiful residence, was in ruins. Inside there was a harp, which still had some of its strings, and a grand piano destroyed by termites that were climbing up a plank of wood that had fallen from the ceiling. When the teacher opened the top they fled quickly into the tunnel they had dug underground. The teacher looked at the piano and stroked the keys. Then he showed me where the printing press had been and where the editors used to sit. He searched in vain for some evidence of the paper between the pieces of wood and scattered debris. In the neighboring lot, the remains of a hearse were also being destroyed by termites. The teacher explained that the car was used in the past when the street that led to the cemetery was clear of brush and that for a long time now the dead could only be carried on a net tied to two poles. The teacher looked at me carefully for a second. "In Fordlandia there is electric light, right?" he asked me. "That's right," I responded. "Then, you will be able to cope with the jungle and you won't end up like us, like an old dirty rag?" he insisted. I hesitated for a few seconds. "I hope so," I answered. I saw the teacher again during the celebrations of St. Apolonius. He was drunk, and unlike that afternoon, he seemed happy.

The common people in Jocotá celebrated St. Apolonius with a parade through the streets in the afternoon, dances in the evening, and on the last day they organized a procession of canoes down the river, led by one that carried a mast with the image of the saint. The prefect and the merchants, in turn, organized their own celebration at Don Raimundo's. Even though the merchants and farm owners participated in their own way, they were not completely in favor of the celebrations, which took place at a rate of one every two weeks during the rainy season. In the Amazon, holidays, including, of course, the day before for the preparations and the day after for the hangover, made it impossible to convince anybody to keep planting or harvesting.

The first day of the fiesta, a group came by Doña Dora's house soliciting donations. The group had a drum, and depending on the generosity of the contribution, played different songs related to the saint. When they knocked on the door, Doña Dora stopped sewing, went out to the patio, and came back with two hens in a bag. While she was off looking for the hens, Doña Branquinha, who had been there since noon, had knocked twice on the door to my room to inform me that the group was there and asked me to come out and join them. The two women had not yet prepared for that night's celebration. I, however, had taken a bath in the river early that morning—it was impossible in the house—and I had gone to a modest barbershop on Second Street. In the barbershop I had looked in the mirror and noticed that I had lost weight and that my white skin had also disappeared along with the fat.

I responded to Doña Branquinha's call, came out of my room, and went down the side passageway to the street. I greeted the group, gave a nice donation to the mulatto who was acting as master of ceremonies, and listened to them until they left. The mulatto began with some short verses that were repeated by the whole group, and they continued with simple, theme-related melodic ballads. Doña Branquinha handed the two hens to them instead of Doña Dora, who stayed next to me on the sidewalk. The sun was slowly setting. Several canoes passed down the river, and others were docked at the pier or along the riverbank. The people tied up the canoes, and after going ashore they hid their oars in the thickets. They knew that after a night of celebrating, ownership of oars was not respected by those who had had a few too many or by anyone in a hurry to get home. After hiding the oars, the men and women, carrying the metal trunks that contained their clothing for the celebration and nets, food, and liquor, entered the village shouting and setting off firecrackers. Some women stopped to smooth their skirts, brush each other's hair, or put adornments on each other. Doña Branquinha stepped in front of me. "Those caboclos organize pure orgies just so they can squeeze up against the young girls, but I think a man as smart as you should have some fun with us, another way, at Raimundo's house," she said. I thanked her for the invitation, even though Doña Dora and the prefect had already extended the same invitation. I said goodbye and went for a walk along the river.

I walked along the shore until I reached the small pier. Narrow and much older than the town pier, it was a virtual cemetery of damaged and abandoned canoes and pieces of oars. Then I headed for town. I went up Second Street, then walked along First Street and around the square. The church was lit up, but the doors were closed. I had heard that Theo, the German priest, officiated at the church when he was visiting the town and that he, with the help of some of the other faithful, had been responsible for painting it white both inside and out. I was expecting to run into him that afternoon, and his absence surprised me. In the middle of the square a tall, wooden pole had been set up and was decorated with the image of the saint, foliage, and whole pineapples. On one side of the pole people were drinking and singing. A little farther beyond, near a corner, a few people were practicing samba rhythms and steps. When I crossed the square two women dressed in old, tight-fitting sundresses who were talking and laughing caught my attention. Some people were saying hello to them, and others looked at them and whispered under their breath. I was particularly drawn to the one with dark almond-shaped eyes and straight hair. *A mulatinha boa.* I looked at her and smiled. Later I found out that those women were prostitutes and they went from place to place, parties to processions, alleviating and dispelling the bad moods of caucheros, merchants, and farmers. The mulatta returned a generous smile. I stayed in the square for a while and then went to the Bola de Oro to have a drink. The teacher, Raimundo, and another merchant were sitting around a table talking. In the center of the table were two bottles of liquor. They made room for me and I sat down. The teacher filled a glass for me and offered a toast. I asked him where Theo was and if they expected him later. The teacher looked at me and burst out laughing. Raimundo blushed and looked down. The other man said he didn't think that Theo would arrive in time. I asked if it was because Theo's religion did not recognize the holiday. "He's a bore, not only does he disapprove of dancing and drinking, but the bastard makes the most of our good mood and stays in his confessional for hours and hours with our women," the teacher said, and he leaned back and then forward. He had the hiccups. He raised his index finger and, with some difficulty, explained to me that that was why they had sent a canoe with a big leak to pick him up, something that could make even a mystical and stubborn German like him not want to make the trip. "Imagine Theo's face," the teacher said. "And Doña Branquinha's when she finds out," the merchant added, and the three erupted in loud laughter.

What Theo must have felt, upon finding himself in an old sinking canoe that couldn't take him anywhere, no matter how hard he tried, was perhaps similar to what I felt when, the night of Raimundo's party, I saw Doña Branquinha get up from her chair and head straight for me, showing me her teeth. The party had begun long before, and around midnight, to the rhythm of marches and sambas played by a trio with a rattle, a scraper, and a drum, it was time to dance. The hall was large and the servants plentiful. The servants were natives of the Munduruku tribe, the same tribe that Caroline had visited. There was pork, chicken, tapioca hors d'oeuvres, and guava cakes. To drink, there was beer, rum, and a bad sweet wine. At the teacher's suggestion, I tried some dark, bitter-tasting hors d'oeuvres, prepared, he said, with *guaraná* seeds, farina, and pirarucu tongue. "Try it," he said, raising his hand, "and let me know what you think."

The men were standing on one side of the room, and the women were seated on the opposite side. They were all wearing party dresses and shiny shoes. The youngest were allowed to dance only with their fathers. They were neither well dressed nor poorly dressed. This was not their era, not their time. The men would cross the room to invite the women to dance. Doña Branquinha was sitting next to Doña Dora, and she had been staring at me since the first note had been played. I noticed that the two women had put on their finest attire for the party. I did all I could to ignore Doña Branquinha, but it was no use. She came over to me, took me by the hand, and we went to dance. The trio started off with a samba. At Raimundo's house the samba was danced without touching bodies. The steps were short, quick, and sweeping, and the body was straight with a simple rocking of the arms so as not to lose one's balance. At the town celebration though, many couples were dancing attached at the waist. I had never been a very good dancer, but that night with Doña Branquinha as my partner, I moved as fluidly as a hanger on a clothes rack. After a few sambas we stopped dancing, and she led me by the hand to the side of the room to introduce me to her friends.

It had been a while since I slept with a woman. The last time had been with one of the women in that bar in Belem, where I met Jack. I thought of Caroline. I would have liked to have had a woman like Caroline there at that moment. I would ask her to dance, have a drink, and then walk down to the river. Maybe we would spend the night together. We would make love to each other all night long in that hot jungle. I poured myself a rum and looked Branquinha up and down while she talked to her friends. I excused myself, saying I needed a little fresh air, and left the hall. Outside, the tune of a lively popular dance captivated me. I headed toward the music.

The town dance was held in a shed on Second Street, which had been decorated for the occasion. The men had to pay to go in. On the street there were several stands set up to sell liquor and mandioca, and the men and women would come out of the shed to eat and drink. The dance was very entertaining, and a small band, made up of a cello, a flute, a *cavaquinho*, a scraper, and two drums played samba after samba. I watched how the exhausted drummers were substituted after playing a while. The couples danced barefoot on the dirt floor. The shed smelled of cheap perfume. Every so often there was an explosion from fire-works being set off in the street. I danced for a little while with a girl from the town who suddenly left me, with no explanation, for someone else. Several couples were hugging and kissing in the middle of the dance floor. I ran into Enéas there. He was with his wife but was spending a lot of time dancing with another woman. Like most of the men, he was decked out in white, and he moved calmly among the women. I confronted him and, whispering in his ear, asked him about the prostitutes. Enéas smiled and told me to follow him. He left his partner with his wife and we left the shed. It was almost morning. We walked down Second Street, moving cautiously in the darkness. Enéas was in front of me, and his step was more unsteady than usual. As we were walking I asked him if he was familiar with the hors d'oeuvres that I had tried at Raimundo's house. "Those are for the white people. We had a little bit of catuaba rind and that was all," he said. After walking a short distance, a large guard dog, angry but restrained, came out onto the road. When he recognized Enéas he went over to him, happy and affectionate. Enéas wrapped his arm around his neck, led him to the side of the road, and, squatting down, talked to him and petted him for a long while. Then we resumed our walk. About a hundred meters farther, he pointed out a street lamp that was next to a bakery, and then he said good-bye. I lit a cigarette and went to check it out. I was hoping to find the straight-haired mulatta there. There was a group of men talking and drinking outside the cabin. When I approached them I saw one of them grab a woman by the waist and push her inside. Then I bumped into Roque, who appeared from the shadows and greeted me enthu-siastically. He told me not to worry, that he knew all the men who were there waiting and that he would talk to them so that I did not have to wait in line and could go in as soon as the girls were free. I hesitated, but Roque insisted, and without waiting for my answer he went over to the group and, with a bit of resistance, achieved his goal. The other men let me go first. A moment later the door opened. I put out my cigarette and went in. There were two rooms, and I was unlucky. The straight-haired mulatta was still occupied and the other one tended to me. When I left I thanked the men who had let me go ahead of them and I returned to the dance. Roque stayed behind, waiting his turn.

On the way back I bought a bottle of liquor. I went back into the dance, crossed the dance floor, and sat down with Enéas and his women. We shared the bottle. When it was almost dawn, the dance ended and more fireworks were set off. I went with Enéas and some others to walk around the pole a few times. It was then that I realized how drunk I was, and I left for home. Enéas shook my hand good-bye. He stayed with his people, not a care in the world. His black face was smiling. Two days later we set off for Fordlandia. But on the way I decided to alter our course a bit so that we could visit the Mundurukus.

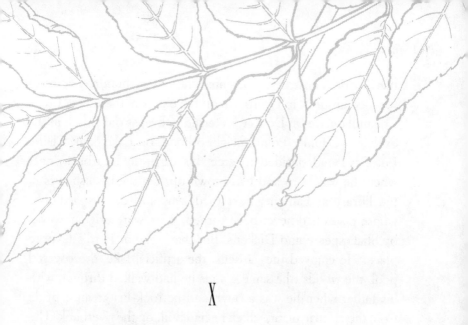

X

The Fairlane mansion was aglitter that October night. The orchestra from the Music Institute of Detroit livened up the dance hall with *paso dobles*, waltzes, and galops. Some of the guests were dancing and standing around the dance floor talking. Others, fewer in number, had formed a circle around Edsel Ford in one of the gardens near the hall. The party had begun at dusk and the music just shortly after that. Henry Ford and Clara began the dance by whirling to an old waltz. Clara looked lovely in a chestnut-colored evening gown, Henry's favorite color. Then the dance teachers whom Ford had hired to give classes at the company joined in. After that, most of the executives and politicians present invited their wives to dance. While the automobile aristocracy, as they were known in Detroit and the rest of the country, was enjoying the dance, a group of artists and friends of Edsel opted for looking through the enormous library and then joining the host's son in the garden.

The Fairlane mansion, named by Ford in honor of the Irish town where his grandfather was born, was designed like a Norman castle, constructed of limestone on six hundred acres of wooded grounds in Dearborn, on the banks of the Rouge River. The millionaires in Detroit preferred to live, as did Edsel, in the exclusive Gaukler Pointe neighborhood, on Lake Saint Claire. But Ford had decided to erect his castle in Dearborn, near where he was born and had grown up. On the bookshelves in the library at Fairlane, next to dozens and dozens of books whose pages had never been turned, there were original works by Shakespeare and Dickens. But that was not Ford's favorite place. He enjoyed the gardens, the artificial lake, the covered pool, the woods (the same woods he had walked through with his father when he was a boy), and he took his greatest pride from the electric plant, which he had built on the riverbank. The plant, with its two gigantic generators and the long underground tunnel that connected it to the house, was the first thing he would show his guests. That October night, after dancing for almost an hour, he invited his two favorite guests, Thomas Edison, in whose honor he was throwing the party, and Harvey Firestone, his sole supplier of tires, to take a walk down to the plant. Henry Ford looked especially happy. He was in an excellent mood and he had been annoyed only once that evening, when a couple of Mexican painters, invited by his son, had proposed to the orchestra conductor that they play a tango. The cautious musician had sent a note to Ford by way of the headwaiter requesting his permission. Ford stopped dancing, refused the request, and after leaving his wife on the side of the dance floor, crossed the dance hall and headed over to the Mexicans. "A gentleman must be able to guide his partner without embracing her as if she were his lover, and in my opinion, the tango does not preclude that possibility," he said to Diego Rivera. The company had its own painter, but Edsel had hired Rivera to paint frescoes on the walls of the museum in Detroit and to do a mural on the universe of the automobile. Rivera was unperturbed by Ford's words, and without taking his eyes off him he shrugged. However, his wife, Frida Kahlo, asked him if it would not be a good idea for the guests, men and women, to take their lovers out on the dance floor to dance the tango. Ford turned slightly red at that peculiar woman's remark, but he said nothing.

The minor incident was in the past and now, on the way to the plant with his two friends, he was enjoying the cool breeze that was blowing from the Rouge River. He was happy and satisfied. In fact, the last few years had not been easy. He had had to discontinue his precious Model T, the boldest and most creative dream in his life, after producing fifteen million of them, and he had had to put up with the fact that General Motors and Walter Chrysler were casting a shadow on his reign. But the new Ford Model A had once again made him a top celebrity, a spot shared only with the feats of Charles Lindbergh, and the production of tractors, planes, and boats that bore his logo complemented that prestige. What's more, a couple of days before, two of his other goals had been fulfilled: inaugurating the Thomas Edison Institute and opening the Henry Ford Museum in a small nearby city, Greenfield Village, which he had helped build. The president himself, Hoover, had been at the inauguration of the Institute, which was a celebration of man's control over energy and the fiftieth anniversary of the invention of the electric lamp.

Henry Ford admired Thomas Edison. In fact, he had worked for him in his early years in Detroit and had always admitted that contact with the dynamos and generators as well as the permission he obtained to use Edison's workshop after hours had been of great benefit to him and his passion for mechanics. He still remembered a short meeting he had had at that time with the inventor as the most important endorsement he had ever been given in his life. In August 1896, a few weeks after the historic race in which for the first time an automobile designed and assembled by him broke the world record for speed, Henry Ford traveled to New York for the Edison Illuminating Company's annual convention. Ford met Edison during a break when Edison, surrounded by colleagues and admirers, was talking about batteries for electric cars. A supervisor from Edison Illuminating recognized Ford, pointed him out, and remarked loudly, in order to penetrate the inventor's deafness, about the advances that Ford had made to make an engine run with gasoline. Edison asked for more information on the subject, and Ford quickly sat down, and explained it to him, drawing an outline of his plans on a piece of paper. Edison gave him a pat on the back and said, "Young man, you're on your way, carry on. This car has an advantage over the electric car in that it supplies its own energy." Ford never forgot that comment. The afternoon of the inauguration of the Institute, the old inventor had refused to join the celebration. He sat outside the hall where the banquet was being held and would not budge. He feared the crowd as well as the microphones that would carry his voice around the country. After a long while, he agreed to go in only when Ford held out his arm.

That pleasant October night as he walked with his two friends toward the plant, Henry Ford recalled those anecdotes and thought that the worst, if he could define the recent past as such, was now behind him. As they skirted the lake and entered the final path, he glanced at his colleagues. Edison looked old, worn-out; there was no trace of the eccentric, genius figure. He walked slowly, looking at the ground, and his shoulders were stooped. Firestone, on the other hand, showed his age only in his bulging, drooping stomach. The music sounded far away, but the notes could be heard clearly. The orchestra was playing a mazurka. Ford whistled along with the music and danced a few steps with his long, thin legs. Firestone watched him and smiled.

"You're happy, Henry. Aren't you?" he said.

"That's right, Harvey. I am. The Institute is a good thing, and furthermore, this week we opened more plants outside the big cities. The real United States, as our dear Thomas always says, is outside the big cities."

"Maybe even outside the United States," Firestone joked.

They both looked at Edison, who did not catch the reference.

"What joke did you tell President Hoover? Tell us," Firestone asked.

Henry Ford looked pleased.

"One day, as I was driving along, I passed a cemetery and I noticed a grave digger digging a huge hole. I asked him why he was digging such a hole and if he was going to bury an entire family in it. The man responded no, that the fellow who was going to be buried was very strange, and that in his will he had requested to be buried inside a Ford, because until now it had gotten him out of every hole and he was sure that it would get him out of the final one too," he said, bursting out in laughter.

Firestone laughed happily and slapped him on the back. Edison kept walking, indifferent. A few steps farther, however, he stopped as if he had run into an invisible obstacle. Without removing his hands from his dinner jacket he looked up and fixed his eyes on Ford.

"And Brazil?" he asked.

The question surprised Ford. He gently took his old friend's arm, and as he was urging him to keep walking he leaned over toward his left ear and said loudly, "Very well. We are selling a lot of cars and trucks. It is becoming the most dynamic subsidiary in South America."

"That's not what I'm talking about. I am talking about your dream: the city in the jungle."

Firestone changed sides, moving over next to Ford.

"Why are you asking?" Ford inquired.

"Because of the birds. I heard that you have new birds here," Edison said, pointing to one of the many cages between the trees along the path.

"Oh, yes, I have received some wonderful, rare ones. I was sent some rose-colored magpies and some other ones whose beaks look like they're not properly attached to their heads."

"And the city, how is it?" Firestone asked.

"As for the village in the jungle, we have had some difficulties, but now it's going well, very well, and soon, Harvey, we will be able to offer you tons of rubber for your tires. That too is going to be a great thing. Or do you think, Thomas dear, that one day it will be possible to make synthetic rubber? Do you think so?"

Ford had financed the inventor for a few years in a vain attempt to produce artificial rubber. Edison shook his head no.

"I heard the city is named after you, is that so Henry?" Firestone asked.

"Yes, that's right, but it wasn't my idea."

"Why? In case things don't work out?"

"No, the village will be a success. It's because of history. I don't want to go down in history," Ford joked.

"You're already part of history," Firestone said.

"You know I don't believe in history and that I wouldn't give a dollar for all the history in the world. The only history I believe in is that which we make every day."

"History's but a walking shadow: 'a tale told by an idiot, full of sound and fury, signifying nothing.' "

"Exactly. Who said that?"

"Shakespeare. You have it in your library," Firestone responded.

Ford smiled.

"I am surrounded by scholars," he said.

When they reached the dock on the Rouge River they stopped.

The night was clear. The family's boats were moored at the end. In the distance you could see the lights and the reddish smoke rising from the Ford industrial complex and, beyond that, the glow of Detroit. The waves in the river were pounding against the dock and gently rocking the boats. Ford looked at the time: it was almost eleven. He peeked over at the house next door. The house, visible only from that spot, was formally occupied by Ray Dahlinger, his former chauffeur and current director of Ford Farms, and his wife, Evangeline. The whole thing was actually a farce, however, set up so that Ford would have no problems meeting the beautiful and energetic Evangeline, with whom he had fallen in love many years ago when she was his assistant at the company.

"Tango," Ford mumbled as he looked toward the house.

"Did you say something?" Firestone asked.

Ford turned around. Edison was shivering and he had the feeling that the cold was making his friend wet his pants. He took him by the arm. "We'd better go. It's chilly."

On the way back, Edison again stopped suddenly.

"Henry, I think you should visit that city in the jungle as soon as possible. Your future lies in the jungle, far from here. Don't let it fail," he said.

"No way, Thomas dear, no way."

The party was at its liveliest. Candles were burning in the silver candelabras and waiters were coming and going, serving foie gras, lobster, caviar, and a few soy-based dishes. To drink there was fruit juice, although near midnight a few bottles of French champagne were uncorked. Things had never gone better. Just a few days later, however, the country's finances would collapse on Black Tuesday, and the world of Henry Ford and his two friends would be changed for a long time.

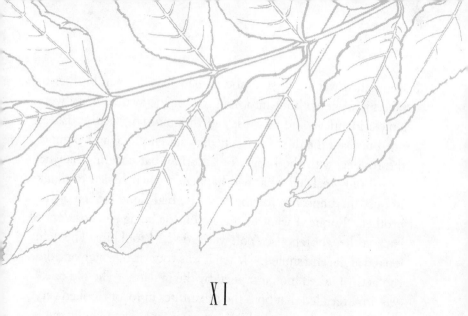

XI

After traveling for a day and a half we reached one of the villages of the Munduruku tribe. The rivers and streams were deserted, and as we moved along I felt as if we were returning to the origins of the world. But we were returning as precursors of change, of progress. We were an excerpt in an epic poem, the epic of the conquest of the kingdom of the trees. The idea fascinated me, and it lingered in my mind for a while.

Near the village the water glistened peacefully, the vegetation gave off a gentle, penetrating aroma, and the evocative, warm, heavy air moved intermittently. The sunlight, however, was not bright. The previous afternoon we had seen how a strange swarm of multicolored butterflies temporarily blocked out the light. The yellow, black, white, and blue butterflies appeared and disappeared suddenly. Roque said that the appearance of butterflies was nothing new in that area and that it was a bad omen. I did not take him seriously. After the days we had spent in Jocotá, Enéas and I were calm and in good spirits. Roque, however, was not. Shortly after leaving Jocotá I had had a heated argument with him, and he still had not gotten over it.

Roque had wanted to stay, and he had sent his twin brother to take his place without informing me of the switch. They were almost identical, and as we set off that morning, neither Enéas nor I noticed the difference. The boy said nothing and clung to the rudder, with the brown of his straw hat covering half his face. I only realized what had happened when I tried to thank Roque, the imposter, for the favor he had done for me at the brothel. "Roque, I want to thank you for being so considerate back at the whorehouse. You were good," I told him. The twin looked at me and smiled. "When it was your turn, which one did you get?" I asked him, intrigued by the mulatta. "The old one," he said. I recalled that both the prostitutes in Jocotá looked very young, and I asked him which one he meant. The twin let out a laugh, revealing a set of teeth that Roque must surely have envied. I lashed out at him and ordered him to return to Jocotá and look for his brother at once. By the time we finally found Roque we had lost almost the entire morning. At first he argued that his brother needed the work and that it seemed fair to share his life with him. After aiming my shotgun at him and telling him that the next time he lied to me or tried to run off I would kill him on the spot, he apologized and got on board. Roque liked to be at the helm. As punishment I made him sit with his back to the bow, facing the sun, the entire way to the Munduruku region, and I handed over the helm to Enéas.

Close to the village the jungle became lower and the river-banks, which were less dense, revealed openings and footsteps. As we were probing the waters' depth in preparation to go ashore, I was certain that someone was watching us from the dense vegetation. The proof was quick in coming. The boat had just begun to approach the bank when an Indian whose body was daubed with red paint appeared on the shore. He was look-ing at us, motionless. He looked serious and savage. Then he turned around slowly, walked along the shore and disappeared into the thickets to our left. A moment later, a dozen children came out to meet us, and, diving into the water, they started swimming around the boat. The bravest ones came right up to the hull. First they gently knocked on the wood and went back to swimming. Then they took hold of the rails on either side and escorted the boat until we anchored, just a few meters away from a small sand beach where there were several canoes without keels made from tree bark. Inside the canoes were oars and fishing nets. The Munduruku were a river tribe, and therefore they were susceptible to all the disasters that ravaged the waters in the region. Long ago, as did all Indians, they felt the pressure of the conquerors, the Jesuits, the Franciscans, and of rival tribes. The conquerors wanted their bodies. They needed hands for rowing, hunting, fishing, sowing and serving. The Jesuits and the Franciscans wanted their souls. The other tribes who escaped the conqueror's siege in the east and the north wanted their lands. The Mundurukus, like the other old cultures that populated the Amazon, were destined to lose all three things. In the last century, when their relations with the white man grew more peaceful and they were bound to the merchants, they became victims of every known epidemic, smallpox in particular. According to Caroline's data, in one hundred years their population was reduced to one-fourth of what it had been— twenty thousand to just five thousand, scattered among several villages. The Mundurukus had a unique history. Their fame came not only from war but from peace as well. They had been powerful warriors who were feared by their neighbors. They were known as headhunters, and they used to carry their trophies in hand when they were hunting or fighting. From among the defeated they were known to take prisoners and then rape their women and children. They were able to resist the Portuguese in several battles and they marched eastward, crossing the basins of large rivers, in order to unleash their fury on encampments of settlers near Belem. The Portuguese and the settlers opted for a truce instead of trying to overcome them by force. The Mundurukus were as good in combat as they were in work. It was said that Karu-Sakaibe, their mythological hero, after creating heaven, since the earth already existed, and before plunging into a hole in the jungle, had devoted himself to transforming prejudiced men into birds and animals, to saving fire in times of flood, and above all, he had passed on to them an interest in farming. At first, the white man would trade metal axes and machetes to them for mandioca flour. Later they would trade goods for rubber. Their loyalty to the truce was unquestionable. As the years passed there were only a few violent incidents of merchants using methods that were too rough, like holding hostages to insure the sole right to the rubber collected, or abusing their women. At any rate, it seemed strange to me that the old and proud masters of the Tapajós had become its modern-day slaves. Perhaps this was the reason behind the curiosity that fueled Caroline's visits and research. My objective in visiting the Mundurukus was to convince them to work at Fordlandia.

The Indian who appeared on the riverbank led us to the center of the village, where there stood a circular building—the house of men. Enéas had explained to him in Tupí the reason for our visit and had asked his permission to go into the village. The short walk that connected the river to the center of town was tortuous, and we had to push back brambles and bushes in order to get through. We had left our weapons on the boat and were carrying only our knapsacks and three young ducks as a gift for the Indian chiefs, thinking they could use them for breeding. Enéas had suggested the ducks, and I had bought them from Doña Dora in Jocotá. Caroline, Enéas said, brought them hens whenever she visited. The Indian, the children, and the women who came out of their huts to join us on our walk were half naked, and their bodies were daubed with red paint.

Two clans resided in the village. One clan used red and the other, yellow and blue. The Indian chiefs told me that they painted themselves in order to better endure the overwhelming monotony of the green jungle. The red clan painted itself with *urucum*, the beautiful fruit of a beautiful tree that had large, soft beans. The merchants in Jocotá and Belem were always interested in that natural coloring. The women and children looked at us and smiled. The Indian women had only a small white cloth attached to their waist by a string that passed between their buttocks to cover their private parts. Some were carrying newborns, and their breasts were swollen with milk. The young women were attractive and smiled sweetly. As I was walking, a couple of them came up to me and timidly touched my hair. When we reached the house of men, the women and children dispersed. The Indians called the house of men *ekcá*. It served as both quarters and temple. Inside they kept the *kaduké*, the sacred flutes, and women were prohibited from entering. Surrounding the house there was a large ceremonial patio adorned with vegetable and animal totems. The rest of the huts were laid out in such a way that they surrounded the patio, like a wheel. Most were made of mud and palm leaves, although I also saw a few adobe ones. Hammocks for sleeping hung inside the huts. According to Caroline, about three hundred natives lived in the village. When we arrived there were almost no men because they were in the jungle collecting rubber, hunting, sowing, or fishing downriver or upriver. They returned at dusk. Apart from the Indian chiefs and a few young boys who were laying out arrows and repairing the adornments, the only men who were in the village were new fathers, and they remained in their hammocks resting and eating light foods. The husband, and not the wife, was the one who had to rest. The Mundurukus, seemed to be one-woman men. Karu-Sakaibe had imposed monogamy on them. On one side of the house of men there was a radio and a camera, both made in Germany. The equipment was in pieces. Two Indian chiefs came out as I was inspecting the pieces and the transmitter. I went over to meet them and stuck out my hand. They greeted me with only a slight nod of the head. I told Roque to give them the ducks, and the chiefs, after lifting them up onto their heads, handed them to the Indian who had accompanied us. I got the feeling that they had been weighing the birds. The Indian took them inside the house. The chiefs were tattooed in red; the tattoo was a symbol of nobility. They did not invite us to enter the temple, and so we sat down in a circle on the floor of the patio to talk. The conversation was unhurried and had the rhythm and musicality of the Tupí language. Enéas translated with some difficulty while Roque, still angry, paid no attention, his eyes following the girls. The chiefs were expressionless during the talk, and they spoke without looking at me. They held their heads upright, and the few gestures they made were noble. Their age was hard to determine. They knew about Fordlandia and they spoke of Caroline respectfully. I proposed that they send people to the plantation in exchange for money, tools, medicine, or whatever they wanted. I assured them that they would be treated well, like the rest of the workers, and that we would be satisfied even if they only worked for us during the summer. And I told them that if we were to begin such a relationship, any member of the tribe would be able to use our medical facilities. The afternoon was fading into night, and the murmur of the jungle was beginning as the chiefs listened to me, emotionless. There was a long silence. Then one of them asked me why I, and not Caroline, had come to them with the proposal. I responded that in Fordlandia she had one role and I had another. The chief asked if the plantation sent the women first to win their friendship and then the men to speak the truth. I smiled. The other one said that they would think about it and then he got up. He went inside the house of men, and a moment later he returned with a third man, a brazier, and some clay cups. The man who had remained with us called to an Indian, and they began to prepare the ritual. I concluded that the conversation was over. I got up and went with Enéas and Roque over to the side of the patio. From there we could see the men returning. They arrived in groups, smiling and festive, and they were carrying bows and arrows, harpoons, spears, and tools for sowing. They brought fish strung by the gills, feathers, and pieces of dead animals. Suddenly, three young, strong Indians arrived, running and shouting. They were carrying an enormous dead snake. One held it by the neck, another by the body, and the third by the tail. They stopped in front of the chiefs. The others formed a large circle around them. Then the women and children joined the group. It was a water boa, the great *sucuriju*, greenish gray in color with a yellow belly and dark ringlike spots. The hunters were proud and felt the admiration for their feat. I approached the circle and forced my way through until I was in front of them and the boa. One of the hunters noticed me. He was almost as tall as I was, his body was tattooed, and his right arm was wrapped in vegetable fibers in order to enhance his muscles. Later I learned that he was destined to be the war leader of the village. Caroline had written about him. The Indian turned around, took the snake's head in his two hands, and shoved it aggressively in my face. I saw the sucuruji's crooked teeth and tongue that was split in three. I pushed it away with my hands. The Indian let out a burst of laughter, and Roque, who was next to me, got his revenge with a short, mocking laugh. I heard only mumbling from the others. That Indian was the famous Teró, and our paths would cross again.

I moved away from the circle and walked around the patio until everyone dispersed to watch the last glimmers of the sun and the chiefs called us to eat and drink. Outside the ekcá, near where we had been that afternoon, they had spread out a cotton cloth on the ground. Burning torches illuminated the area. They held a small ceremony to ensure that a favorable outlook be forever preserved among us and our descendants. They played the sacred flutes and then served a strong drink, a mixture of fermented mandioca flour and fruits from the jungle. We ate *moqueca* (fish prepared in coconut oil), elk meat, and the small ducks we had given them as a gift. When the ceremony was over, the chief showed us to the huts where we would be spending the night. He left us with a torch and a cup of the same concoction we had drunk during the ceremony. Small groups of men here and there were talking and laughing loudly. Their wives and children were in their huts, stretched out in their nets. Inside the huts, the man's net was on the bottom, the woman's in the middle, and the children's on top. For warmth, a few small half-spent logs were burning on the ground. The nets in our hut were all the same height, and they were tied to sturdy poles on the wall and covered with mosquito netting. I was tired. I raised the cup and took a long drink. I lit a cigarette and shone the light of the torch into the corners, leaving it on the ground to burn out. I got into the net to rest and smoke my cigarette. Enéas and Roque were still outside. A short while later I heard footsteps, and I saw Enéas come in with two Indian women. They had followed us. One of them, who was pretty and had her hair pulled back, lifted up the mosquito netting and smiled at me. The other one went back outside with Enéas. I took her hand and invited her to curl up next to me. She caressed me gently, moving her hands through the hairs under my arm, on my chest, on my sex, on my legs, and along the soles of my feet. We made love without urgency, without awkwardness, again and again. The flesh, fortunately, dominates the spirit. I had been told that in native tribes there were women who could not marry because they were chosen for the initiation ceremony of the young. These women belonged to everyone and to no one.

Because of their condition and despite being the prettiest, they do not provoke jealousy. They know everything about love. I thought that the one next to me that night was one of them. What happened in the morning, however, confused me. Teró burst violently into the hut and shone the torchlight on us. He looked angry and savage. There was something ominous in his movements, and he looked as if he was devising some plan against me. I had not gotten completely up when he turned his back on us and left. I tried to ask the woman if she had a problem with him, but she only smiled at my questions and my movements. Teró's visit left me dumbfounded. She stayed only a moment longer, then smoothed her hair with her hands and left.

I wanted to leave early the next morning, but that did not happen. When I woke up, neither Enéas nor Roque was in the hut. Enéas was with a *pajé*, trying to get rid of his panema, and it took me a while to locate Roque. Roque had gotten drunk, and I found him on the beach, facedown in the sun. He had drunk so much that he could not move, and it took me almost an hour to wake him up. Enéas, as far as he was concerned, was convinced that the Indian women had given us panema. When I found him, he was stretched out in a net and a pajé was blowing smoke over his body and rubbing his ribs. Panema, the caboclos said, was an evil, supernatural force that if not removed from your body would hinder you in hunting, fishing, and making love. Enéas's eyes were closed and his mouth was open as the Munduruku pajé blew an aromatic mixture of tobacco, dried pepper, resin from the *cunauru* toad, and deer horn powder on him. The pajé saw me enter the hut and he motioned for me to be quiet. In the hut there were totems, remains of skins, and clay pots that were giving off pleasant odors. The Mundurukus did not accept sacrifices, and they punished witch doctors with death. They did not believe that nature was inhabited by evil spirits. The pajés filled a secondary role in the tribe, and they could only cure ailments such as panema. When the cure was over, Enéas got up, satisfied, and suggested to the pajé that he continue with me. The pajé came over to me and stared. His eyes were painted black and white. He looked like a wild bird. His voice was resonant and deep. Enéas was translating almost in unison. He said that he refused to treat me because I did not believe in him, and he thought I was ignorant. He was right.

When we left, the children plunged into the water again. One of the chiefs said good-bye to us from the shore with a friendly gesture, and his shadow projected onto the river's edge. A moment earlier he had told me that he would send some of his men to Fordlandia. He had also given me a clay pot as a gift for Caroline. It took a while to get the boat going. As Roque kept trying to start its motor, I noticed how Enéas was looking out into the thickness of the jungle, and I followed the direction of his eyes. That's when I realized that Teró, hidden in the curtain of trees, was watching our every move.

XII

Two entire days separated the Munduruku village from Fordlandia. The first day was monotonous, almost unbearably so. The boat struggled against the current, and we advanced slowly. The straight stretches, the bends, and the trees all looked exactly the same. The trip had lasted much longer than I had imagined, I was tired of traveling, and I no longer thought it necessary to map out courses. Nor did I feel like reading or writing down my observations. I took off my shirt, covered my head with a straw hat, and sat back, my legs spread out, to have a smoke and a drink under the sun's rays. In the bow, Roque was quiet as he steered the boat, forcing himself to keep looking where he was going. His eyes were small and red, and he kept yawning. Enéas, who was sitting starboard, had his back to me and was entertaining himself by calling to the fish. He would let out a long, despondent whistle as he gently knocked on the hull. Several fish with bright scales and silvery streaks came over to the boat. They swam on the water's surface and soon were jumping, colliding in the air, and falling back down into the water to the sound of applause. Enéas was enjoying his success. Every so often I would sit up to see how he was doing. He was smiling excitedly, and he raised his index finger to his mouth to ask me to be quiet. I also saw a lot of *botos* approach the boat and then gracefully slip away. They were gray, but both Roque and Enéas insisted on calling them pink. *Botos* are a kind of freshwater dolphin with a round head and a strong, pointed snout. They are harmless, but the locals told numerous tales about them, most having to do with their supposed sexual sensitivity, which was almost human. In Jacotá, I had heard Doña Dora and her friend Branquinha advising women who were menstruating not to bathe or sail in the river during their period, since the boto could not resist the temptation to seduce them. Roque insisted that a boto had cast a spell on one of his cousins, a virgin, and on a friend's wife. Roque wore a bracelet made of boto teeth as an amulet. Enéas, on the other hand, held that the real protagonists of all those stories were the politicians in the region and not the botos. Enéas believed only in the magical properties of the left eye and the genitalia of those cetaceans. A potion of dissected eye and genitalia, grated and mixed with *carajuru* leaves, produced, he said, erections that drove lovers mad. There were multiple uses for the body of the boto, their brain, eyes, teeth, skin, meat, genitals, and fat were all of use. On the beach days before, I had had the opportunity to see a boto close up, out of the water. It was dying, and the waves had washed it up on the shore. Its smell and appearance were repulsive.

Midafternoon a storm broke. The wind whipped up the waves and lightning followed. The storm jostled our boat and the green lit up all around us. It began to rain furiously, and the rain was cool. A short while later the rain carried its final bolts of lightning and storm clouds off to the horizon and disappeared. There was a long, profound silence. I asked Enéas why he had left his town to come live in Fordlandia. Enéas sighed and asked me for a cigarette. He looked at me, a match lit in one hand and the unlit cigarette in the other. "Maybe it was fate," he said. I did not ask Roque. I felt there was nothing inside him at that moment. Only when the afternoon was receding and a wide border of shade had spread out over the water did I drop anchor, and we headed to the beach to set up camp. I told Roque to light a fire quickly so we could roast the *surubim* that Enéas had caught. While the fish was roasting we dug up some tasty turtle eggs and ate them.

When the sun came up there was a white, sticky fog, which was slow in lifting. The only thing I could see was the blurred outline of our boat and a small, hazy strip of water just past the shore. Nothing else. Everything else seemed to have discretely faded away. We stayed on the beach until it had cleared. We were about to set off again, but since it would take only a short time to reenter the Tapajós, no more than four hours, I proposed that we go hunting. I had always enjoyed hunting. Getting the weapons ready, walking, choosing the target, crouching down, aiming, trying not to breathe, and shooting were real pleasures for me. When I was a teenager, despite my fear of snakes, I could walk for hours through the nearby fields of the big, rambling house where I spent my vacations, looking for a good catch. One spring I even went with some friends to Patagonia because I didn't want to miss the chance to organize a hunt in the wide-open plains of the south. Hunting came naturally to me, and it made sense. There was an element of death, of surprise, and of amazement that made me feel happy. I had always dreamed about hunting in the jungle, somewhere in the Amazon. Until now I hadn't had the chance, and that morning seemed like the right time. The idea was well received, and Enéas suggested that we travel up to the next entry in the river until we found a lagoon. At nine o'clock we left in search of an estuary. A couple of kilometers upriver on the port side we spotted an entry. The canal was narrow and curved. Thickets covered the left and right banks. Rising above the shrubs, trees with long, thick trunks crowded together. Further on we came upon a lagoon surrounded by gray sandbanks. It was a world of birds. We spotted herons with dark blue feathers, pink *colhereiros*, chestnut-colored *piacocas*, and, on the shore, some white storks with black beaks, known as *jaburu*. When the bow of the boat entered the lagoon it set off a great commotion. The frightened birds took off in a stampede, and the clatter of their wings ricocheted in the jungle, like an echo. In the confusion, a flock of *guarás* with black feathers and blue-and-green streaks almost crashed into the roof of our boat. In just a few minutes the lagoon and the sandbanks were deserted, and the birds had found their refuge in the nearby trees. Then it was calm again, from shore to shore. There wasn't a sound. The crowns of the trees were splashed with colors, and a few herons were bending some of the branches with their weight. The landscape was beautiful.

We anchored across from a large beach. It was very hot, and I felt like cooling off. I directed Enéas and Roque to unload the weapons and some supplies and I jumped into the water. I swam a few meters toward the middle of the lagoon and then went back. Roque was standing on the shore waiting for me. He looked tense. No sooner did I get out of the water than he asked me, babbling, if there weren't Suyá Indians roaming the area. He said that while I was swimming he had heard a distressing cry, like a dry burst of laughter that broke the silence and rose up into the air. That morning I had wondered if there might be Suyás in the area. The Suyá tribe feared the white man, the black man, and the Mundurukus. They were not usually found near the rivers, as they lived in the jungle in the east, far from the Tapajós. They were hunters of men and weapons, and there were terrifying stories about them. In the morning, shortly after setting off, we had noticed a black spot in the vastness, underneath the sun and on top of the mirror of the waters. The canoe, or what appeared to be a canoe, was moving along swiftly, pushed by the current, and a kilometer ahead of us it dropped out of sight behind some bushes. Several times during the course of our trip we had run into boats crewed by caboclos, natives and caucheros. There was nothing odd about it, except on those occasions the boats did not try to avoid us. "My God, could they be Suyás?" Roque had asked, as he observed the maneuverings of the canoe, his mouth open wide. At that moment my hair bristled underneath my hat, but the only thing I could think of was to ask him to calm down, move quickly down the middle of the river, and be alert as we covered that stretch. When Roque asked me again about the Suyás, I recalled the incident from that morning and I called to Enéas, who was sitting in the sand off to the side and oiling the barrel of the shotgun. He closed the barrel, got up, and came over to me, shotgun in hand. When I asked him if he, too, had heard a cry as I was swimming in the lagoon, he looked over at Roque with a jeering smile and then pointed at the trees with the barrel of the gun. "Yes, sure, it was the *acauas*," he said. The acaua was a whitish sparrow hawk that feeds off cobras. When the caucheros went deep into the woods, they would imitate the song of the acauca with the intention of scaring the cobras away. Roque looked toward the trees and then turned around toward me.

"What I heard was not the song of the acauas, but if Enéas is right, we shouldn't hunt. The acauas herald an imminent misfortune, mi blanco."

"I already said a prayer. Why don't you?" Enéas retorted.

"I'll do it right now, but I won't hunt with you," Roque said. Roque put his hands together and dropped to his knees.

"What do you think, Enéas?" I asked.

Enéas, worried, responded, "I think, mi blanco, that instead of going deep into the woods, I can light a fire and you will see that all the animals will come to us."

I looked at Roque. He was still praying with his eyes closed. I was angry.

"All right, but you are a couple of cowards," I said.

I shouldn't have said it. Enéas looked at me, offended, and it bothered me. He immediately handed me the shotgun and went over to the bushes to look for dry branches to make a torch. A while later he motioned to me from a distance to come over toward the jungle. Roque was sitting on the sand, motionless, watching us. He was pale. Covering my head with the straw hat, as the sunlight was bright, I picked up the shotgun and walked over to Enéas. I took a few steps toward the jungle. Enéas lit the torch and waited for the wind to blow. When the torch was finally lit, he raised his hand for me to stop walking, and he went running into the jungle. I stopped about fifty meters from the vegetation. Soon the bushes began to burn, and then a pillar of fire and smoke rose from the interior of the woods. Some frightened birds took off for the highest treetops. A moment later, Enéas came running out, dropping the torch on the way, and he hurried over to my side. I handed him the gun, put one knee on the ground, and prepared to shoot whatever came my way. Pacas, coatis, *tatouays* and snakes appeared. A good-size tamandua also came bounding out of the fire and the cloud of smoke. Several weeks later, Enéas would insist that he had seen a giant ounce, terrified, run off toward the lagoon. I aimed carefully, shot by shot, choosing my target. First I hit the tamandua in the snout, and then I finished it off with a bullet to the body. The din of the weapons resounded around the lagoon. Then I emptied one chamber on coatis and tatouays. Enéas, perhaps thinking about food, concentrated on the pacas. It bothered me to hunt this way, lying in ambush, without any risk or effort. The

fire had barely begun to die out when I stopped shooting and
got up. Enéas also stopped shooting and stood next to me. I
looked at him. He was sweaty and looked serious, circumspect. I
swapped my shotgun for his revolver. An irresistible force was
suddenly pushing me to enter the jungle, and I thought the
revolver would be more effective there. I went back to where
we'd left our supplies. I loaded the cylinder, put a handful of
bullets in my pockets, and took a swig of liquor. I looked over at
Roque. He was still sitting down, indifferent. I walked toward
the jungle, passing close to Enéas but not looking at him.

I must not have been well. Some time later, I blamed that irrepressible and enveloping desire to challenge destiny on the tropical heat, even when it was inevitable that I would become
marked prey. Destiny. My destiny! I think I knew that I had
always been considered brutally inhuman and unbalanced,
because of fits like the one I had that afternoon. But I think they
were part of my conviction, very firm at the time, that only in
extreme situations is the greatest mystery of life discovered.
What's more, I was accustomed to going my own way and on my
own feet, wherever I decided to go. On the path entering the
brush, I shot a small snake that was still trying to escape the fire.
Before fighting my way through the branches, bushes, and
plants, I turned around and shouted to Enéas to gather up the
best pieces for lunch. Enéas nodded. I removed the safety catch,
cocked the revolver, picked out a large branch, and entered with
determination. I carried the revolver in my left hand and the
branch in my right, to help me make my way through the dense
growth. At first my intention was to find a good catch and nothing else. But I was also fed up with superstitions, witch doctors,
Roque's stories, the myths, and with the fact that every impulse
toward that jungle was thwarted by fear: fear of making a mis-

take, fear of the *anangbá*, fear of what might happen. If we could not overpower those inferior species, I was certain that they would overpower us. And what was there, inside the jungle, but inferior species and thousands of motionless trees, condemned to wait for the hand of man, sooner or later, to hurt them or knock them down. I wondered the same thing about the animals. In the time that I'd been traveling I had known of the wild animals only by their howling, their cries and protests. The ounce was the only truly ferocious animal. But everyone knows that the ounce only attacks when he feels threatened. I was a threat. Yes. But I had faith, perhaps too much, in my own rights, and I was prepared for my unexpected visit to be frightening. I liked to hunt, I had good aim, and I quickly loaded the revolver with seven shots. Seven ready and eighteen more in my pockets.

I had not walked five minutes, however, when I became afraid. I looked around, but everything looked peaceful. Nothing was moving, nothing was following me. I heard only the howling of the *guariba* monkeys high above. But the vegetation, frightfully dense, robust, and thriving, rose like an impenetrable wall, and the few rays of sun that pierced the foliage were not enough to be able to distinguish what was a reflection and what was a tree, what was apparent and what was real. I began to suffer from the warm vapors in the shade and the humidity that clung to my clothes, my skin, and my hair. Then the insects appeared. I hated insects. I hated them in Buenos Aires, I hated them in Fordlandia and I hated them every day we had been traveling. But there, in the middle of the woods, thousands of insects appeared suddenly, buzzing around and sticking to my neck, hands, and arms. Mosquitoes and wasps. I was scared, and I felt like a prisoner, closed in on all sides, and I suddenly took off running with the intention of retracing my steps as quickly as possible.

In the jungle the feelings of confusion, of being lost, of anxiousness, are not long in forming, and one ends up believing in imaginary tracks and nonexistent exits and corridors. The hallucinations begin to stalk you. Nerves become tense, like a rope, and senses betray. Everything seems like something else. Everything is something else. Everything seems like a trap. Everything is a trap. I ran and ran until my lungs were about to burst. I could not find my way out. I stopped dead and breathed deeply. I noticed that the bullets had fallen out of my pockets. I tried to calm down but I couldn't. I took off running again, now going toward my left. I began to gasp for breath, and I ran until my own gasping began to make me dizzy. The ground was soft and spongy. Even so, as I was running I had begun to feel a sharp pain in my right foot. When I stopped again, I took off my boot and my sock. Something had pierced the boot, and my sock was stained with blood. The wound was deep, round, and painful. My shirt was darkened by sweat, I was dirty and sticky, and I had gobs of sap and resin on my face. I put my sock and boot back on and broke off a tree branch to lean on as I ran. I tried but it was no use. I walked. I walked for half an hour but could not find the way out. I was disoriented, lost. I was afraid, and the fear paralyzed me. I aimed the revolver upward and shot two times. The shots sounded harsh and the echo of the bangs was multiplied several times until it vanished in the distance. After the shots I heard only the flapping of wings and the howling of the monkeys. I cried out to Enéas. The monkeys responded by howling and jumping everywhere. I started walking again, this time to the right. The mosquitoes continued to pursue me. They surrounded me in an ominous and plaintive halo but I no longer did anything to stop them from sucking my blood. I was dizzy and began to lose my sense of balance. I saw a small clearing around a fallen tree and dragged myself over to it. At the base of the trunk a tamandua was licking up ants. The tamandua looked at me, surprised, and then scurried into the bushes to hide. I dropped to the ground next to the tree. I leaned my back against the trunk and did not move. I was exhausted, feverish, and the pain in my foot was becoming unbearable. After a while I looked up and saw, over my head in the lower branches, dozens of spiderwebs. It looked as if the small purple spiders were about to fling themselves on me. I moved my body, picked up the revolver, and shot two times. The spiderwebs broke open with the impact, and a few threads came loose and fell to the ground. Three or four spiders fell and disappeared into the dry leaves. I looked through the hole in the spiderwebs. High up and out of reach, you could see the splendor of some orchids. Lower down, on a thick branch, what looked like a liana did not stop moving. It was like an elastic tube that contracted and inflated. The jungle is a world of lies, of appearances. I followed its movements and its shapes, from one extremity to the other, and soon I was able to distinguish the large, rhomboid-shaped head, without eyes, of an actual coral snake. The coral snake's cylindrical tube coiled and uncoiled itself, coming in search of me. I leaned to the left, took a deep breath, and cocked the revolver. There were only two shots left. I took the revolver in both hands and decided not to shoot until it was close. I couldn't miss. The coral snake fell like a lightning bolt a couple of meters away from me. I was carried away by impulse, and I shot at it twice. But my horror grew, and I didn't dare look to see if it was dead. I leaned back against the tree trunk again and stayed there—without a single shot left. Then I closed my eyes and fell asleep. I dreamed. My emotions and fatigue must have created those horrible fantasies. I dreamed I was a cadaver, and I wanted to be buried next to my mother and not there, in the jungle. I had a photograph with a blurred image in my hand. I dreamed that all my friends had also died. The bites from the mosquitoes and the ants that had climbed up on my body woke me from those dreams. I got up, with my weight on just one foot, and I shook the ants off. I took off my shirt, pants, boots, and socks. I had been lost for several hours, and night was beginning to fill the jungle. The darkness began to quiver with frightening noises. I looked over to where the snake had fallen. It wasn't there. A toad carrying its young underneath its skin came over and looked at me curiously, then took three jumps and disappeared beneath the plants. I heard it croak at regular intervals. It sounded like a cow. I had not a single shot left, and I didn't know what I would do when night closed in. I was dazed, lost, resigned. I thought I heard my father's voice, just as it had sounded in his gray days as a widower, when he was fond of reading the Bible. My head weighed me down like a tower, and I put my head between my hands and began to tremble. I lost consciousness.

That is how Enéas and Roque found me. They were carrying torches and had cleared a path that enabled them to retrace the four hundred meters back to the beach. They told me that I did not recognize them and that they had to struggle to take my weapon from me and carry me on their shoulders.

XIII

I was in the hospital in Fordlandia for more than a month. There was a period I vaguely recall—with a strange fascination—when I felt like I was falling hopelessly, without fear, without glory or protests, without desire, into a tunnel of intense brightness. When I came to, I was lying on a bed and a nurse was washing the wound on my foot. I looked at him and shivered slightly. He noticed and told me not to be afraid. I was thirsty and asked him for water. He handed me a bottle and a glass. I rested the bottle on my stomach, and the glass felt cold. Then I drank three glasses of water, in small sips. I asked him where I was. The nurse laughed. "In the Fordlandia hospital," he said. "Fordlandia?" I asked. "Yes, Fordlandia, paradise on earth."

I spent the first two weeks in the hospital in bed, with my right foot bandaged and my body covered with strange, small scars and marks left by bites that did not hurt but which caused a bothersome tickle that would begin suddenly at night, just before I fell asleep. My temperature, which was rarely normal during those days, had the doctors worried. My fever rose and dropped, but my body showed no other symptom to help them figure out a way to restore my strength. I was also experiencing frightful chills and sweats from the malaria. It was not just my body that needed caring for but my mind as well. In the middle of the jungle I had lived through an extreme situation and I had looked over the edge. I had been on the verge of giving up, and while my senses were now more intact and accurate, a morbid memory of what I had experienced made it difficult to direct my emotions, and I felt uneasy. That memorable day in the jungle had left me puzzled. I had never seen or experienced anything like it. My mental images were linked to that experience, and in those days I was no more than a tenacious memory of those events. At night when I couldn't sleep, I thought about the fact that luck, or circumstance, had allowed me to take my feet out of the abyss, and a wave of relief rose in my heart.

Enéas came to visit me. He stayed an entire afternoon, and we talked until my fever would no longer allow me to pay attention to him. He sat at the foot of the bed and told me how surprised he had been to find me in the jungle, and he gave me some news about Roque and Fordlandia. Roque had requested permission to go back to Jocotá. Fordlandia, in the meantime, was overrun by the presence of two hundred new workers from Barbados. A dance hall had also been opened. Before he left, I asked him to help me shave. Enéas went to the doctor's station for a razor and then soaped me up and shaved me. When he finished, I looked straight at him for a second. I felt very grateful to him and I shook his hand and thanked him for rescuing me from the jungle. Enéas smiled sweetly and offered to change my bandages and wash the wound on my foot. I declined but asked instead for two things: that he deliver the report on the trip to Rowwe and that he leave me a few cigarettes. Enéas exited the room and I was left lying there alone. Outside, the day was drawing to a close and the heat was less intense, but I was tired. Shortly after, I fell asleep. I slept soundly, but I still woke up once, startled and bathed in sweat. I looked around me. The darkness was coming in through the windows. The door to the doctor's station was open, and the lamp that was there filled the room not with light but with shadows. I fell back asleep, struggling to escape from my dreams.

The hospital room was long and had large windows on the left side. There were two doors, one leading to the emergency room and to the examination rooms and the other, in the back, which led to the room of the doctor on duty, which is where visitors entered. My bed was in the row of beds situated across from the windows. The room was cool, and in the afternoons, when the heat became worse, the windows were opened and the ceiling fans turned on. It did not smell like a hospital. The afternoons were always peaceful. In the mornings, the ward supervisor and the doctor on duty saw to the sick. When there was an official from Fordlandia in the hospital, they blocked off his bed from the others with a screen, to avoid contact with the other patients. Those from the United States were able—and preferred—to receive medical attention and rest in their homes. But in my case, because of the condition in which I had returned from the trip and the amount of care that I needed, the doctors advised that I remain in the hospital. When I regained consciousness and my temperature had dropped, the first thing I asked was that they take the screen away. I directed the nurses to put it back up after a few days, however, when the condition of my neighbor to the right, an indigenous worker from Santarem, worsened. One morning he became limp and wet, like an aquatic plant, and a line of white foam spread across his purple lips. I notified the doctor's station at once, and the doctors worked in silence for ten minutes, rubbing him with their hands and trying to get him breathing again. Finally, the worker's body trembled, and the doctors broke out in a triumphant cry.

The screen was not my only privilege in the hospital. The ward supervisor had a bell, a dresser, and two chairs put next to my bed, and the bed that was directly across from mine was kept unoccupied. From my bed I could look out the window and ponder the beautiful early evenings in the jungle.

The ward supervisor was kind to me. Once he had finished morning rounds and organized and administered the different medications, he went to the doctor's station, made coffee, and returned with two cups, one for him and the other for me, and a big hunk of fresh bread. The wonderful aroma of the coffee brewing reached my bed. He pulled up a chair, offered me a cigarette, and sat down to talk while I had coffee and ate a piece of bread. He was born in Rio de Janeiro and spoke as if all the geography, fauna, flora, history, and legends in the world existed there. His face had a fixed expression of intelligence, but when the conversation went off into something other than medicine, Rio de Janeiro, or technological advances, he showed little imagination.

Antonio, the chief of staff, loved science and machines, and he was willing to join any attempt to perfect them. He was one of the people familiar with the details of the prototype of the six-cylinder engine that Jack, with the exactness of a goldsmith and the patience of an artisan, was assembling with used parts from tractors and other automobiles in an adjoining room that he had had built onto his house and converted into a workshop. Jack, who ignored or pretended to ignore the derogatory comments that his mechanical work provoked among the U.S. officials in Fordlandia, spent a large part of his energy on that engine and on the innovations that he had thought up—and which according to him would make him a millionaire—such as the starter and the automatic gearshift, the spark plugs located above the engine, and the cooler, which used a water pump. Jack dreamed of showing the prototype to Henry Ford, and Antonio, along with his assistant who was highly trusted by Jack, contributed to that dream by collaborating with him in their free time.

But Antonio, when I met him, was fascinated by the virtues of the electrocardiogram device that Ford had sent to the hospital in the village. At that time, it was already known that muscles generate weak electrical currents and that the heart, when beating rhythmically, gives rise to signals that usually reach the body's surface. Antonio and the other doctors delighted in the possibility of capturing and evaluating the rhythm of the heart, even though in practice they lacked the candidates to test its effectiveness. The monstrosity sent by Ford worked by means of a series of electrodes that were connected by cables to a complex monitor and placed on the neck, the chest, and the legs, and none of his patients, not one, wanted to subject themselves to something like that. As far as I was concerned, considering the attention I was receiving in the ward, I did not object, and I helped Antonio with the testing. I let him examine my heartbeats, and I also got up the courage to handle the instruments myself to evaluate his. The testing took place in the mornings and then during the afternoons of my final two weeks in the hospital, when I started to feel better and they allowed me to abandon, little by little, the strict routine they had imposed from the beginning. During that time I took a liking to my bed, and I must confess that those games with my heart were the only thing, in addition to visitors, for which I would readily give up reading or resting. I had decided to turn my back on the world, and until I had completely recovered, I would not set foot outside the hospital.

One afternoon I was outside the doctor's station leaning against a stretcher in my underwear, electrodes scattered all over my chest and waiting for Antonio to convene his colleagues to begin the electrocardiogram, when Rowwe showed up with another U.S. official. Harry, who had just arrived from Detroit, was short and had a formal air. He wore gold-rimmed glasses, a silk shirt, a belt with a western buckle, and he gave himself more importance than he actually had. He was carrying a wide-brimmed felt hat in one hand and a briefcase in the other. Rowwe introduced him politely but with such an expression of dislike on his face that I guessed them to be rivals. Harry did not like me, nor I him. They stayed only a minute. They did not wait for me to remove the electrodes, and after saying hello to me, as they made themselves comfortable in some chairs that Antonio brought over for them, Rowwe asked me several questions about the results of my trip. As I noticed that he was nervous, I offered to elaborate on the report that I had written on the trip and which I had asked Enéas to deliver to him, and I asked him what was wrong.

"Just routine," he responded.

Rowwe looked at his watch. He was in a hurry to leave. Then he pointed at the electrodes and, sounding somewhat guilty, asked about my heart.

"Is there something wrong with your heart?"

"Everything's fine, just routine," I answered.

Rowwe placed the package he was carrying on the stretcher. He told me that it was a present for me, American cookies. Harry, who was leaning forward with his elbows on his knees, his hat in his hands, listening, interrupted our conversation with his hoarse voice and vulgar accent and asked me to expand the report, since what he had read, he said, could be considered too brief and general, bearing in mind that the company had the right to know even the most insignificant information about its employees and their jobs. Then, with the same air of contempt, he asked me about the number of workers I had contacted, directly or indirectly, and when, in my opinion, they would be coming to Fordlandia. His questions annoyed me, and I shrugged my shoulders to indicate that it wasn't important. Harry smiled and got up from his chair. He looked at the electrocardiogram machine and then over at Antonio, who was standing there calmly, following our conversation with his arms crossed and his head slightly bowed.

"We did not send these machines for doctors to use in their spare time, and if that were the case, it would seem more suitable to send one to examine the brains of the people here," he complained.

Before leaving he looked at me strangely, as if he found me repugnant. I did not see him again until he returned with Henry Ford. Rowwe was confused by his expression and he left in a hurry, following Harry.

"Come see me as soon as you get out," Rowwe shouted on the run.

I watched them leave, amused. Then I picked up the package, ate some cookies, and told Antonio that we should begin the test. Antonio was not offended by Harry's suggestion. On the contrary, some time later in Jack's workshop, he would try to convince us to support him in a business venture that he wanted to present to Ford: he wanted to invent a machine that would study the brain, and he needed funding for his plans.

Rowwe and Harry had come at noon, but visitors were permitted only between five and seven in the evening. In the afternoons, the patients slept, and those who didn't talked across the ward. Very few of them received friends or relatives. During my last few days in the hospital, Jack came to visit me as did, of course, Caroline.

Caroline's visit caught me by surprise. I was in bed reading an old history book that the doctors had lent me, with some of my clothing on the bed and the rest on the floor and my bell close at hand in case I needed something, when I recognized her laughter coming from the doctor's station. Caroline was talking and laughing with Antonio and the doctor on duty. I put the book down on the dresser and quickly put on my shirt, hiding the rest of my clothes under the bed, and I covered myself with the sheets up to my waist. Caroline entered the room with Antonio. I sat up on my elbows and looked at her. She was very pretty and looked younger than when I had first seen her. Antonio returned to the doctor's station, and I noticed how he looked back at Caroline twice. Later, he even popped his head into the room for a second to look at her again.

"Hi, how are you?" she said.

"Hi," I answered.

"Can I sit down?"

"Of course."

She looked around the ward. The men who were awake were staring at us. She sat down on the edge of the bed and smiled.

"The doctors said your heart is fine," she said.

I smiled at her. I couldn't believe she was really there.

"Did you by chance have any doubts?" I asked her.

Caroline blushed.

"No."

"Then I can relax."

"You don't have a fever anymore? Are you better now?"

"Yes, much better."

"Do you intend to visit the Mundurukus again?"

"No, that's your job."

"From what I heard, I thought you wanted to replace me."

"Not at all," I said.

"Why did you visit the tribe?"

I thought before answering.

"I read all your reports, which were very well written, on the one hand, but I realized that the one on the natives was incomplete. I just wanted to know more about them. That's all," I said.

"I'm afraid you've made a mistake."

"I don't think so, but if you want, one day I can tell you about my experience."

"Alright."

"About the entire trip, if you like."

Caroline looked away.

"Do you like to read?" she asked.

"Yes, very much."

Somewhere out in the jungle a bird was chirping. Caroline turned toward the window.

"It's a beautiful afternoon," she said.

I looked out the window. A gentle breeze was moving the treetops.

"Why did you come here," I asked her.

"For my career."

"Is that the only reason?"

"Well, it's not unimportant. I also wanted to prove certain theories, some intuitions, in short."

"On what?"

"My primary interest is in the human condition."

"I see, and in some way you are here in search of the truth?"

"In some way yes, that's right."

"Why not in Montreal, in Canada?"

"At a certain point I felt like all avenues were exhausted."

"I know what you mean."

"You do?"

"Yes. And now can you tell me your conclusions?"

Caroline smiled.

"Not yet. They aren't ready. I still don't have definite answers. And you? What are you searching for, so far from the world?"

"I still don't have an answer either. So you see, we agree."

"I hope I don't regret that agreement."

"Why? I can assure you that I would be unable to do something you would later regret."

We were silent. I observed her face. Her mouth, her full lips, were slightly pursed at the corners. I felt like kissing her. Caroline turned toward the door of the doctor's station and then looked down, in my direction.

"I don't understand what's taking Jack so long," she said.

"Jack came with you?"

"No, but we had arranged to meet here."

"Maybe he changed his mind or forgot," I said.

Her allusion to Jack bothered me, but I tried to conceal it.

"I hope he comes. I'd like to see him," I added.

I heard the door to the doctor's station open. I looked and there was Jack. He came toward us, smiling, looking like he had just bathed.

"Here he is," Caroline said, getting up.

"Where is the famous and courageous Argentine?" Jack asked.

He came over to the bed, leaned over, and gave me a hug. His breath, which reeked of alcohol, hit me in the face.

"You look good, you bastard," he said to me, "much better than I imagined. Why don't you change and get up, so we can better celebrate our reunion? What do you think?"

"I'd love to," I said.

Jack turned to Caroline, "Let's go outside for a few minutes, dear, and leave the gentleman to get ready to welcome a friend and a lady as is fit," he said.

Jack and Caroline stepped out of the room and I got up, got

dressed, and went in to the bathroom. I looked for a mirror, wet my hair, and combed it. I walked across the ward to the doctor's station, where Jack and Caroline were waiting. The three of us then went back inside and sat down in some chairs next to my bed. Jack was carrying a package. When we sat down, he opened it, held up a bottle of whiskey and a box of candy for me to see, and then put them on the ground, next to the bed.

"We brought you some presents," he said.

"Thank you."

"Caroline didn't want to come, but I convinced her."

"It must be hard to convince her," I said.

"Don't be fooled. She is very curious."

Caroline tapped him gently on the shoulder and made a face that only women know how to make when they realize they are the center of attention.

"Enough already," she said.

Jack smiled and took a pack of cigarettes out of his shirt pocket. He lit one for himself and another for Caroline. He drew a puff of smoke from each one. Then he offered one to me, which I declined. That afternoon it was hard to feel like he was my friend.

"How have you been?" he asked me.

"I had two tough weeks, but now I feel fine."

"How did it go with the caucheros?"

"I think some of them will come."

"For sure. In fact, several have already joined on, and all of them have asked for you. You're famous, muchacho," he said.

"Really?"

"The honest truth. And in the jungle? Tell us about it. What happened to you?"

"I don't know, exactly. Maybe it was the heat or the fatigue that pushed me to do such a crazy thing. I don't really know."

"The heat, the fatigue, and not your own will were what drove you into the jungle?"

"Maybe."

"What a disappointment. And I had brought a bottle to celebrate an extraordinary man," Jack said.

"To be carried away by emotions or circumstances *is* extraordinary," Caroline pointed out.

"Your words move me, lovely lady," I said.

"You should know that you have broken one of the old myths of the Amazon jungle," Caroline replied.

"Which one?"

"That some men could never get out and others never managed to get in."

"Then let's have a toast," Jack proposed.

I rang the bell to call for a nurse and ask for some glasses, but nobody came. I got up and went to the doctor's station. It was deserted, and it took me a while to find clean glasses. For a second I thought that that would be a good opportunity for all the patients to escape. When I returned to the ward, Jack opened the bottle and filled a glass for me and one for himself. He poured a little for Caroline, and then we toasted. I took a drink. I was in good spirits. Caroline took a sip and put the glass down. She was sitting up straight in her chair, thinking about something else. I rested my glass on the floor and reached for the box of candy. I opened it and offered it to Caroline. They were fruit candies from Pará. She took one, turning it around in her hand slowly before eating it.

"Thank you," she said.

She looked down at her fingers. I offered her a napkin.

"It's not necessary, thank you," Caroline said.

"When are you going back into battle?" Jack asked me.

"In a few days."

"You should know that there was a guy from Detroit here to see how things were going in the village," Jack said.

"Harry?"

"Yes, that's the one. Do you know him?"

"He came to see me with Rowwe. I got the feeling that Rowwe had a problem with him. That he was afraid of him."

"I think Rowwe's fear is less dangerous than your madness," Jack said.

"How are things in the village?" I asked.

"Well, now we are a truly cosmopolitan city. In addition to Brazilians, Americans, the caucheros that came thanks to you, an Italian dancer, and Argentine, and a Canadian, we have West Indians, lots of West Indians working. Soon, muchacho, we will be like New York."

"Any problems?"

"No problems, don't worry. You'll have it worse than in here but better than in the jungle," Jack said. We all looked at each other and laughed.

They left at dusk. I walked them to the doctor's station, stepped ahead of them, and opened the door for them to leave. When we were saying good-bye I felt like hugging Caroline, but Jack's look discouraged me, and we shook hands. We agreed to see each other soon, when I got out of the hospital. When I returned to the ward I offered the candies to the other patients, took two swigs of whiskey, and put the bottle away under my bed. I was tired and went to bed. I fell asleep quickly but awoke in the middle of the night, with a burning deep in my stomach. The room wasn't dark. There was a full moon, from what I could tell when I got up, and I went over to the window. The vegetation glistened softly, with a luster like that of silver. The night was still filled with the sound of cicadas flapping their wings, and glowworms clustered together spontaneously in random places. Then, unusual for me, I had to throw up. I went back to bed but was able to sleep only until dawn, when the birds began to sing and I smelled the coffee being made in the doctor's station.

In the following days I recovered completely, and I was discharged. I left around nine, and when I went outside I got a surprise: it was cold. I found myself faced with a curious phenomenon in the jungle, almost unbearable for the natives of the Tapajós valley, called *friagem*. The sky remains clear and calm but the temperature falls due to gusts of wind from the Andes. For a couple of days the natives in the Amazon, frozen stiff, interrupt their activities and stop working. They take shelter in their houses and curl up next to the fire. Birds emigrate and fish appear, frozen, on the surface of the rivers. I was afraid that the cold would cause a relapse, but I was wrong. My fever did not return and I felt fine. Enéas, wrapped up in a cotton blanket in which he had made a hole for his head, like a poncho, was waiting for me outside the hospital and he came over to meet me. I greeted him warmly. I felt like walking, and together we went toward the dock, then back along the street where the stores were, passed through the square, by the school, and up toward the neighborhood where the officials lived. I looked through a window in the school and saw one of the U.S. officials, Rowwe's assistant, sitting at a desk in front of the class. The classroom was full of men, and there were also a few women. At the school, named after Henry Ford, reading and writing were taught in the afternoons and evenings, and two mornings a week English and first aid classes were given. Because the administration did not deduct from workers' salaries for attending morning classes, those classes were heavily attended. Rowwe's assistant was teaching an English class and did not see me.

Enéas and I continued our walk along the tree-lined road toward my house. In front of us, at the end of the road, a couple of tractors went by and the smell of gasoline drifted through the air. When we reached the officials' neighborhood I turned around and looked back at the village. Things had changed while I was away. New houses and sheds had been built, and new streets were being cleared. In the meantime, the jungle to the left, to the right, and straight ahead watched, expectantly. I noticed that its green color, like the cold, was more intense. In the final stretch we ran into a group of workers who were warming their hands over a bonfire of firewood and branches, which burned on the ground. I stopped and moved closer to the fire. The workers immediately made room for me, and I felt as if they were looking at me with excessive respect. I stretched out my hands and stayed for a moment, contemplating the fire, and then we resumed our walk. When we were near my house, Enéas gave me a message from Rowwe.

"Mr. Rowwe told me to tell you to read the note on your bed and then go see him at once," he said.

"Alright. How are the new workers?"

"Those that came because of you, mi blanco?"

"No, the other ones, the West Indians, the ones from Barbados."

"Ah! They are Negroes who don't know how to do anything but work. A bunch of slaves."

"I see. And why do you think that they look at me that way?"

"Who? Those back there, where we stopped?"

"Yes, them."

"Your courage is respected, mi blanco."

"For going into the jungle?"

"No, they know the jungle well. You are respected for your courage with the post owners in the area."

"I see."

"Mi blanco, do you feel like you are returning home?" he asked me.

"No, I don't," I responded.

XIV

I went into the house and went directly to my bedroom. It did not smell musty, as though it had been closed up for a while. The window was open and sunlight flooded the room. There was a note and an envelope on one of the beds. Everything seemed to be in order. I opened the closet and inspected my belongings. My clothes were hung up, and my geography book and straw hat were on the shelf. My backpack was on the floor, and next to it, the almost empty bottle of whiskey that I'd bought just before I had left. I leaned down and opened the backpack. Inside I found the revolver that I had taken on the trip and my notebook, which was dirty and damp. I picked up a towel, went into the bathroom, took off my shirt, and got into the shower. The water was cold, and the first spurts were mixed with dirt. As I was drying off with the towel I watched the ants hauling a piece of soap across the floor. I reached down, picked up the soap, and put it in the sink. One ant clung to the palm of my hand, and with some difficulty I shook it off. I went back into the bedroom, picked up the note and the envelope, and went over to the window.

The note was from Rowwe; he was welcoming me back and asked that I go see him at once. The envelope contained a letter from my father. I read the first few lines and put it down. He was writing about himself and his new wife. I crumpled the note and the letter into a ball and threw it on the ground. I looked out the window and saw Frank walking toward the plantation with a tall dark-skinned man dressed in black, European style. I changed clothes and took a swig, which did not taste very good, from the bottle of whiskey. The whiskey just sat in my stomach. I left the house and headed for Rowwe's office. The cold, which a short time earlier had invigorated me, now stung my face and legs. As I walked along I observed the village again: the noise of the sawmill and the smoke from the factory in the calm, morning air, the groan of the tractors climbing the hills, the streets of red earth, the asphalt, the open spaces between the main buildings, the large dock on the river, the Tapajós River that followed its course toward the distant ocean, and on the opposite shore, the wall of trees that closed in on the banks as far as the eye could see. For a moment I thought about Buenos Aires and about the smokey cafés and the nights when too much wine had made my head spin.

Rowwe did not keep me waiting. The door to his office was open, and he was talking on the telephone. As soon as he saw me he hung up and signaled for me to come in and close the door. He stood up and shook my hand. Then we sat down at the conference table, which was covered with papers. Rowwe collected the papers and then set a folder down on the table. He looked straight at me.

"How do you feel?" he asked.

"Fine. I've recovered completely."

"Ninety-two," he said.

"Ninety-two what?" I asked.

"Ninety-two workers have come as a result of your trip. Half are married—some came over with their wives—and half are single. It was a success. Not bad."

"No?"

"No, except for a priest's messenger who showed up demanding the support of Mr. Ford for his mission in exchange for forty workers. He said that he had worked this out with you. Is that right?"

"Yes. The priest's name is Theo, and it seemed like a suitable agreement. I wrote that down in the report."

"I know Theo, and we have already helped him enough."

"I was not aware of that."

"That's okay. We'll just give him a little money. A merchant also came complaining that you had entered his territory. What's that about?" Rowwe asked, with a faint smile.

"It was part of the plan. You knew that."

"Okay. The expense report indicates that there are a few pesos missing, but let's move on to something else; I want to update you on a few things and let you get to work."

"Go ahead."

"Alright. At first glance, with your ninety-two planting trees and forty more that were recruited by the office in Belem who will do general work and two hundred twenty . . . Did you hear? Two hundred twenty that I managed to bring from Barbados to clear the land, we could say that *now* the plan will begin to work better, right?"

I tried to recall the figures in the General Plan, but I could not. I improvised a response.

"I think we still need more."

Rowwe stood up and sat back down again.

"Exactly. We need more and more in order to conquer that damn jungle. Many more. Read this. It's been approved by Detroit," Rowwe said.

His eyes were sparkling, but his voice was cold, inflexible. He leaned forward and handed me the folder. I recognized the title page (Rowwe had shown it to me a few days before my departure), but the title still surprised me. I read out loud.

"Proposal to extend the property, initially, to six million acres, solve the problem of manpower, and move forward and conquer the Amazon." (Rowwe had added "initially" and "conquer" to the title that I had seen previously.) "What is this?" I asked.

"It's simple: if, by catching them by surprise, we manage to evict the merchants, the natives and the caucheros from their lands, from thousands and thousands of acres, and we keep that vast territory, what will happen?"

"We will have more land."

"Right, but that's not the most important thing. The most important thing will be that those people will have no alternative but to work for us. Dozens and dozens of men will have to accept a job at Fordlandia just to avoid starving to death. And so, we will reach our goals much sooner, produce thousands and thousands of tons of rubber for Detroit, conquer the Amazon, and Henry Ford will be at the top, happy and grateful. And the Amazon will be prosperous. Do you understand?"

"Yes, I do. But how will we achieve this?"

"It's a question of ingenuity, yours, Frank's, and, of course, mine. If we need money, there will be money, if we need politics, there will be politics, if we need force, there will be force. Force and courage. Everyone will have his role."

"How much money will we need?"

"A few more million, but that's not your problem."

"What will my role be?"

"Frank and I, with help from Belem, will handle the money and the politics."

"I see. And Detroit has approved this plan?" I asked.

"Well, not exactly, but Harry, who is very close to Henry Ford and to Sorensen, gave me his word. He agreed, backs us, and is going to introduce it."

"What do you want from me?" I asked.

"To help us prepare the entire operation down to the last detail and then to move forward with your part: the infantry, the eviction. We will support you with whatever you need. If you agree, I'll triple your salary right now, and in one year, two years maximum, I'll promote you to an executive position in a branch in Europe. How about London, for instance?"

"Do you drink?" I asked him.

"What kind of question is that? No, not a drop. I don't drink or smoke."

I looked at him, pensive. I had the feeling that Rowwe was going mad and that he did not have the slightest idea of how serious and difficult his plan was. I was convinced that Harry, by giving him his verbal approval, had laid an ambush for him. I looked inside the folder. There were only three written pages and the rest were maps of the Tapajós, with arrows, circles, and numbers drawn on them. There was a quotation on the bottom of one of the written pages. It cited one of Caroline's reports. I looked up and placed it before Rowwe. I thought that the preparations needed to carry out that plan would require a large investment of time, maybe three or four months, enough for me to retire if I thought about it that way.

"Alright, I will start to gather information and we'll see," I said.

Rowwe got up and shook my hand.

"That's what I like," he said. "Whatever you need will be at your disposal. But secretly. As you know—only Frank, you, and me."

We were saying good-bye when there were three sharp knocks on the door. I looked at Rowwe, who indicated that I should open it. It was Frank and the black man whom I'd seen walking with him earlier.

"Ah, what a surprise! Are you better?" Frank asked me.

"Yes, much," I responded.

"Forgive me for not having visited you in the hospital, but I had to accompany an executive from Detroit on his return trip to Belem. You know how it is. Let me introduce you to George; he's from Barbados and acts as a kind of leader for his people," Frank said, referring to the black man.

"Hi," George said, lowering his head slightly.

"Hi."

George had a smile frozen on his mouth. His lips were the color of copper and his teeth were ivory. The whites of his eyes were yellow, and his eyes seemed to suggest that all the evil on Earth was concentrated in him.

"How are your people doing?" Rowwe asked George.

The West Indians had been assigned to felling trees and clearing the jungle, and they were helped, when the terrain permitted, by tractors and other special vehicles that had been designed in Detroit. Some of the Brazilians, more than a hundred, who had been doing that job before the West Indians arrived, moved on to planting rubber seeds under Jack's direction; the others continued with the same task but in an area farther south. The felling of the trees and subsequent clearing were the most dangerous jobs and, therefore, the highest paying. The salary for going up against the jungle was double that received by those who were extracting rubber from trees that were still standing or from those that were already mature, and almost triple that of the men who were plowing, planting, sawing, driving stakes, painting, building, laying cables, storing, hauling wood, or supervising, and of those workers—and many of their wives—who were taking care of the gardens, cooking, sewing, packing, or who were involved in some other general work. Rowwe had managed to get the Brazilian government to permit the import of West Indian manpower with the condition that they not leave Fordlandia. The West Indians had their own huts and their own dining hall, and only through George did they deal with the administration and the authorities. Their workday was longer—thirteen hours—and George, who had recruited them and brought them from Barbados, would physically punish anyone who did not carry out his instructions or who did not follow the rules that he himself had set. Inside Fordlandia, it was rumored that George kept a portion of the men's salary. George looked at Frank, then at me, and finally at Rowwe.

"Everything is under control," he said, smiling.

"Are we finished?" I asked Rowwe.

"Yes, yes, get to work and we'll be in touch."

Frank looked at Rowwe, who nodded his head.

"Wait," Frank said to me, "I want you to look over some other papers."

Frank went over to the desk, opened a briefcase, and came back with an unmarked folder. He handed it to me.

"How about a game of pool tonight?" he asked me.

"Sure, I'll see you there," I said.

I left and walked down the hallway to my office. The window was open and it was cold. I looked around the room. Everything was just as I had left it. I sat down at the desk and opened the folder that Frank had given me. There were maps and approximate dates relating to the extension of the six hundred kilometers surrounding Fordlandia. It also contained a draft of a letter to the governor of Pará asking for the conditions and permission to annex those lands and for guidelines regarding the legal aspects and the cost of the proposed plan.

I closed the folder and put it in a drawer with the one Rowwe had given me. I got up, went over to the window, and lit a cigarette. I stood there for a long time, smoking and thinking. Then I went out for a walk. I walked aimlessly through the streets and then went to have a look at the plantation. I saw ten West Indians following George down one of the paths. They walked stiffly and slowly. They wore shorts and boots, their bare torsos exposing their ribs. A couple of caucheros who were working there stopped to watch them as they passed by. George and the black men kept walking, indifferent, toward the jungle. That day seemed like an eternity. I had given Enéas the day off and was hoping to find Caroline or Jack in the dining hall or along one of the roads, but I was out of luck. At night I went to play pool with Frank, who was in a good mood and asked me about my trip. He displayed a familiarity with me, as if I had crossed the threshold connecting me to a select brotherhood. I spoke very little with him. When we said good-bye at the door of the hall he slapped me on the shoulder and told me that glory and fortune were within our reach. The night was cool, and I hurried home. I got into bed fully dressed, put my hands behind my head, and thought about Fordlandia. I thought that I could probably sketch it from having looked at it so carefully that day, that strange day, that day in which nothing seemed to have substance. With that image in my mind I closed my eyes and fell asleep. I must have been very tired, because I woke up the next morning in the exact same position.

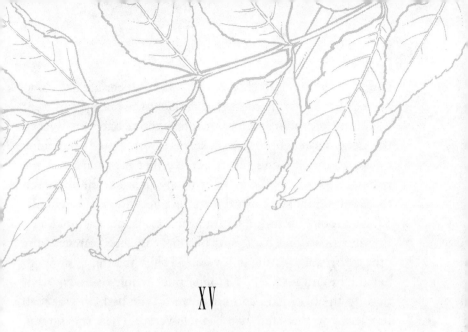

XV

After an early breakfast I decided to go by Caroline's house. Her house was somewhat removed from the other Americans' homes but it was pretty, spacious, and had a well-tended garden out front. To the right of the porch steps was a small table that was painted green. A few meters behind the house was a hedge of thin grayish bushes, above which I could see a few palm trees and some leafy trees. As I approached the house I noticed two men in the bushes looking furtively toward the house. One of the men saw me coming down the street, said something to the other one, and the two took off running, into the vegetation. I walked over to where they had been, and from there I looked toward Caroline's house. A window, the one facing south, was open, and the curtain was pulled back, revealing the interior. Inside, a desk was covered with papers and another one was covered with brushes, mirrors, and small perfume bottles. Native drawings hung on the walls. Sunlight streamed through the window, coming to rest on the papers and on the floor, forming a wide border. The house was quiet. The door to the other room was open, and there, on the unmade bed, with her legs stretched out together and her hands behind her head, was Caroline. At that moment she got up and went out of the bedroom and into the other room. She went over to the desk, picked up a pencil, leaned over, jotted something down, and then stood there, pensive, her eyes staring at the papers. I took a couple of steps to my right and hid between the bushes. I looked toward the street but didn't see anybody. When I looked into the house again, Caroline was holding a tiny mirror in one hand and playing with her hair with the other. She was wearing an oversized shirt that hung down to her thighs and no pants. Caroline put the mirror down, went back to the bedroom, and sat down on the bed. She sat with her legs together and her head lowered. Then she sat up, stretched out her arms, as if trying to touch the ceiling, lowered them, and went back to the desk in the other room. When she stretched her arms I could see her sex, downy and chestnut colored, between her legs. She picked up the pencil, wrote something, and then paused again. For a few seconds she stood there next to the window, straight and motionless. Then she looked at her watch and went back into the bedroom. The bedroom had a bed, a folding screen, and a closet. She opened the closet, took out a pair of pants, brushed them off with her hand, and lay them on the bed. She began to unbutton her shirt and then stretched her arm out toward the door and slammed it shut. I left my hiding place and went back to the street. I approached the house from the front, went up the porch steps, and knocked on the door. A moment later Caroline opened the door halfway.

"Good morning. How are those conclusions coming along? Are they ready yet?" I asked.

"No, not yet."

"I wanted to check out the dance hall and I thought that we could go together. Would you like to go with me this evening?"

Caroline hesitated for a second.

"Alright," she responded.

"I'll meet you there at seven o'clock, okay?"

"I'll be there. See you then," she said with a smile, and she closed the door. I knocked again.

"Yes?"

I thought about suggesting that she close the windows and draw the curtains, but I stopped myself in time.

"I'll be on time," I said.

Caroline frowned. "I assumed so," she said.

I headed toward my office. As I was turning the corner I bumped into Enéas, who was with four workers. He introduced them to me and asked me if I would listen to what they had to say. They took off their straw hats and waited for my response. They were dirty and sweaty. Two were natives of Jocotá (there because of me), and the other two had come from Belem two years earlier. I invited them to come with me to my office, but they refused. We spoke for a while in the shade on the side of the road. I asked what the problem was. The four looked at each other and then at Enéas. Finally one of them, the shortest and most awkward, began to talk. He had a cigarette in his hand.

"We can't take this anymore," he said.

"What?"

"Everything, everything is all wrong," he said.

Once in Buenos Aires I witnessed a workers' strike. The men in the first row carried banners and incited the others. I had been heading to a friend's house when I ran into the demonstration. I stopped, and my eyes met those of one of the leaders. He was jumping up and down and shaking his fists, but his eyes were filled with fear and despair. I kept walking, and a few blocks later I saw the police go by: then gunshots rang out, lots of them. It was a massacre. I had thought about that incident often, and about that man who looked so afraid but behaved so valiantly. The worker talking to me had that same look of fear on his face.

"What is your name?" I asked him.

"Mauro," he said.

"What's all wrong, Mauro?"

"Everything. But more than anything the thing with the foreign blacks," he said.

"And what do you want?"

Mauro turned around to look at the others. He took a deep breath and spoke. His lips were trembling beneath a nose covered with blackheads.

"We want them to leave," he said.

"That's all?" I asked.

Mauro and the others looked at each other and laughed.

"And we want to eat and drink other things, things we like. This is no life, mi blanco," he said smiling.

"What do you want to eat and drink?"

"You know, mi blanco."

"Does everyone feel the same way?"

"Yes, everyone."

"Why are you telling me and not someone else, like the foremen or Frank, for example?"

"Enéas says that you listen to people."

I looked over at Enéas. He was holding himself up against a tree with his hand, as if he were about to faint. When he noticed me looking at him he stood up straight and smiled. I turned back to Mauro.

"If you aren't happy, why don't you go back to your native lands?" I asked him.

"This is our land too," he responded.

"Go back to work and I'll see what I can do."

"We can't take this anymore," Mauro repeated, shaking his head.

He turned around and walked off, disappearing around the corner. The other three followed him timidly. I asked Enéas to accompany me to my office. I opened the window, sat down at the desk, and looked for a blank piece of paper in the drawer where I'd put the folders that Rowwe and Frank had given me. I wrote a message for Rowwe and gave it to Enéas to take to him. "We have to talk," I wrote, "the people are unhappy about the West Indians and the food." Enéas left and returned quickly. Rowwe, in his well-formed and flowing handwriting had responded to me on the same paper: "Worry about our plan and not those slackers. Find out their names, and we'll screw them over." I crumpled the paper up into a ball as Enéas watched and then threw it into the wastebasket. I told Enéas to wait outside for my orders, and I lit a cigarette. Then I took out the folders and spread them out on the desk. I looked over the maps and the figures. I had to begin working, but I sat there staring out the window and thinking about my date with Caroline. I couldn't concentrate the remainder of the day. The heat and humidity had returned. In the midafternoon the clouds hid the sky and a storm broke.

I got to the dance hall at seven sharp, and Caroline was already there. She was wearing a white blouse and the brown pants that I had seen her take from her closet that morning. Her hair hung down over her shoulders. She was truly charming, and she seemed happy to see me. Just before, I had gone by the store to buy something for Caroline. I bought a silver ring adorned with precious stones. After greeting her I gave it to her. She put it on her left ring finger and stared at it for a moment. Then she looked up and smiled. I felt assured. I took her by the arm and we went inside the dance hall. It was a large shed with big windows and a cement floor, a wooden platform in the back, and tables and chairs scattered around the yellow circle that marked the boundaries of the dance floor. There was a white tablecloth and a small floral arrangement on each table. The curtains on the windows were drawn closed, but the reddish sunlight filtered through in spots. There was a phonograph on the platform. A waiter wandered through the tables, talking to those who had arrived before they sat down. Only fruit juice was being served. A sign hung on the door restricting entrance to couples and recommending proper shoes and clothing. The music was just beginning. A dozen couples stiffly followed the movements of the instructor, a thin Italian man with a childlike face and small, round blue eyes who had his arms raised, as if holding an invisible woman. Enthusiastic and lively, he moved from here to there in a square, to the sound of the music. The couples watched him and then, facing each other, took their partners by one hand and put the other on their shoulders (the man must not lower his hand to the woman's waist) to follow the movements being demonstrated by the instructor.

Later, the instructor moved off to the side, watching and correcting the steps and movements of the dancers. The women were dressed in bright colors and the men wore white. The women were checking each other out with quick glances. It reminded me more of a rehearsal for a theater production about to open in which nobody, not even the director, had confidence, than it did of a dance hall.

When the instructor saw us, he interrupted his class and came over to say hello and to invite us to join in. He looked disappointed, and his expression revealed a bit of disgust and contained anger. "These people control their bodies but they can't dance, they are uncivilized," he said to us in English. We stood on the side of the dance floor, watching the couples and the instructor. The air was stifling. I asked Caroline to dance. I took her right hand in my left and placed my right hand on her waist.

She moved a little rigidly, sluggishly, and her hands were cold and soft. As we danced she looked over my shoulder, her gaze drifting from couple to couple. We danced to the boring, out-dated music until we heard the instructor begin to play the same song that had been playing when we had arrived. We decided to go for a walk down by the river.

"You are so beautiful," I said to Caroline as we were walking.

She smiled and looked up at the sky. It had stopped raining, but behind the riverbanks to the west, above the wooded hills, another storm was threatening. It quickly turned dark.

"I hope the weather is nice for traveling tomorrow," she said.

"Are you going somewhere?"

"Yes, I finished my report and I have to go to Belem first, then to Rio de Janeiro, and finally back to Canada."

"Can you postpone your trip?"

"No, my contract with Ford is up."

"Will you come back?"

"I don't know," she responded.

"But would you like to come back?"

"I don't know; professionally, yes, but my feelings are telling me otherwise.

"Are you disappointed?"

"No, afraid."

"What does Jack have to say about that?" I asked.

Caroline stopped and looked at me. Then she burst out laughing.

"What does Jack have to do with it?"

"I don't know, he just came to mind."

"That figures. You can also ask me what some native has to say about it."

"I can't imagine that the good savages might influence your decisions."

"Good savages? What do you know about the good savages?

If you must know, I am afraid of the plans, your projects. This is not colonization; it's just plain conquest based on the opponent's weakness. It's common large-scale murder, justified, apparently justified, by the ideas and ambition of one man—a man who may know a lot about fitting together mechanical parts, about assembling cars, but little or nothing about anything else."

"Do you mean nature?"

"Yes, of course."

"Nature is also brutal."

"Yes. But the difference is that its conflicts are not constant, they don't cause pain, fear or pain, and if someone has to die it's so that someone else may live. They are not isolated parts that can be joined and combined as we see fit. Things in nature happen, they just happen and that's that. Without morals. Without morals that you, for example, should have. Fordlandia is a cruel experiment. What do you think?"

"It's progress, the future."

"Progress? Are you kidding? Is that a joke?"

"Yes, it's a joke. In some way you're right," I said.

"Finally someone around here recognizes that."

We walked around the square, down to the riverbank, and then headed down a side street toward the dock. A few men were gardening in the square. I noticed the smell of freshly cut grass. The street was full of puddles and reddish mud. A tractor passed by slowly and then parked farther ahead under an overhang next to a shed. A few couples were coming up from the river and heading for the village. On the dock, the kitchen employees were gathering the lines and nets. Their baskets were full of fish. Before we reached the dock, we stopped to sit down on a bench. We watched the river in silence. The Tapajós flowed in the shadows, without a single murmur.

"I wish I had more time to get to know you," I said.

"It seems that time is not on our side."

"What time does your boat arrive?" I asked.

"Early, at dawn."

"I'll be there to see you off, if you want."

"Yes, alright." We were quiet for a while. I looked at her and noticed the suspense in her eyes, as if she were waiting for me to impose my will. The situation called for me to make a move, everything seemed to invite it, and, nevertheless, I didn't dare.

"I think it's best we say good night. I have to pack and correct some papers," she said.

She got up and held out her hand.

"Good night, see you tomorrow," she said.

I took her hand and drew her to me.

"Why?" she asked.

"Because I want you, a lot," I said.

I kissed her and wanted to hug her, but she pulled back abruptly.

"No, please, don't," she said.

She looked at me, turned around, and headed toward the village. I watched her as she hurried off. As she walked up the road she turned and waved. I smiled back. Then it began to rain. The drops fell little by little. The lights were on in the village. At dusk, the lights, overwhelmed by fluttering insects, caused a slight low confined glow that made the first stars to appear in the sky look dim. But as night set in, the lights slipped through the village, intense and resplendent, like bolts of lightning, rising and falling, chasing each other through the trees and bushes, toward the rich and sinister darkness of the jungle. I felt like smoking, but I was out of cigarettes. I took a shortcut home along a dirt road, picked up a pack of cigarettes, and went over to the entertainment hall. I crossed the street just as it began to pour. In the light of the doorway the rain looked clear, transparent. I took shelter in the doorway, lit a cigarette, and smoked without pausing. The lightning was incessant and the rain gushed through the gutters. I thought about Fordlandia and about what Caroline had said. Then I looked at my watch. It was almost nine.

Frank was playing pool with Nicky, the dance instructor. I joined them in a game. The dance instructor tried to strike up a conversation with me. He mentioned, in Italian, the names of people, restaurants, and places to go dancing in Buenos Aires and in Montevideo, which he assumed I had to know. His words reflected boredom, fatigue, disgust for everything. Fordlandia was unbearable for him, and I had the feeling that when he spoke of the avenues and promenades of Buenos Aires, the subways or the Montevidean boulevard, that he was really complaining that in the Amazon similar wonders had not been built. He was one of those people who annoy everyone they come across. I answered with a few kind words and some vague remarks, so as not to get too involved. I heard the rain on the roof and thought about Caroline. That night I lost every game.

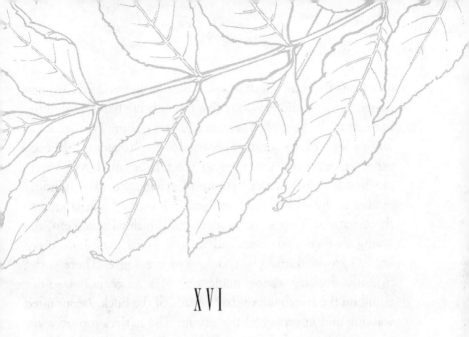

XVI

The Manaus—the English boat on which Caroline would leave—arrived before dawn. I was in bed when I heard its horn. I lay there for almost an hour, watching the light softly enter my bedroom. Then I hurried down to the dock. The river was high, and it was flowing rapidly. The water looked dull, but the green of the jungle glistened in the sunlight. The *Manaus* was one of the best ships that sailed the Amazon, and there was a large crew on board. They had laid two gangplanks down onto the dock. The one closest to the shore was being used to load and unload packages and luggage. The other, in the middle of the pier, was for the passengers to get on and off. There were many more passengers leaving than arriving. Almost all were workers, and after passing through the guard's checkpoint they waited off to the side of the gangplank, festive and ready to board. On the way to the dock I ran into Rowwe and Frank, who were returning from saying good-bye to Caroline. They were accompanied by João, the journalist with whom I had shared a table in the cabaret in Belem. João looked thinner and wore a wide-brimmed hat to protect himself from the sun. He had on a blue jacket and white linen pants, which made him look like a sailor. He had boarded the *Manaus* in the port of Santarem and was visiting Fordlandia to write a few articles for the *Fohla do Norte*. We recognized each other at once and arranged to meet later on. I had barely reached the dock when I spotted Caroline. She was standing almost at the end of the pier, her back to the boat, talking to three natives. Two were women and the third was Teró, the young daubed and conceited warrior from the Munduruku tribe. I stopped and glanced toward the shore. There was a primitive-looking canoe made out of a huge hollowed-out trunk on the riverbank off to one side of the dock. I continued walking and approached the group. The natives moved away from Caroline and she turned to me. She smiled and held out her hand. She did not look happy. I took her by the hand, hugged her, and kissed her on the cheek. She offered no resistance. I noticed she was wearing my ring on her left hand.

"How are you?" I asked.

"A little nervous, but touched that they too came to say good-bye," she said, pointing to the natives.

My eyes met Teró's for a few seconds. I felt in Teró's stare that same sensation of foreboding, hate, and defiance that had been there that night in the Munduruku village.

"Do you know each other?" Caroline asked.

"We met in the village," I replied.

"Are you sad that I'm leaving too?" Caroline asked me.

"Very. I hope you come back," I said.

"I will try to, really."

"When?"

"Maybe after the rainy season."

All of a sudden Jack appeared. He slapped me on the shoulder and remained next to us. He looked serious, upset. He was with a short, fat black woman who had been Caroline's assistant.

The woman began to cry, and she hugged Caroline. Jack tried to console her by rubbing her shoulder, but the woman cried even more. The native women came over to Caroline timidly and also hugged her. Jack and I looked at each other with resignation. When the women had calmed down, I took Caroline by the hand and led her to the edge of the dock, away from the others.

"I don't like good-byes, Caroline, so it's better I leave. Good luck, and I hope to see you soon, as soon as possible."

"I'll be back after the rainy season," she said.

"Promise?"

"Yes, I'll write to let you know when I'm coming."

I hugged her and then left. As I was hugging Caroline I heard some whistles and I looked up at the boat. A group of workers were crowded together at the bow, applauding my move. I walked a bit, then turned around and looked back at Caroline. I felt like destiny was once again separating me from her. Caroline was hugging the women again, Jack still looked upset, and Teró, a few steps behind, was quiet and rigid, like an emperor. My eyes crossed with Teró's. I turned and kept on going.

As I was going up the street toward the village I bumped into Enéas. He was accompanying a friend who was returning to Santarem. Enéas was carrying his friend's suitcase. I told him that I needed him to do something for me right away. Enéas looked at me, surprised, handed the suitcase to the other man, and said good-bye to him with a long handshake.

"What's going on, mi blanco?" he asked.

"Do you see that native's canoe on the shore over there?" I said, pointing to the riverbank.

"What's the problem?" he asked.

"No problem, but I want you to push it into the river, right now. Then, if you want, you can go back to your friend who is leaving," I said.

Enéas hesitated.

"What's wrong?" I asked.

"Nothing, nothing, mi blanco," Enéas said, but he made no move and looked away.

I left Enéas in the middle of the road and retraced my steps. When I was near the canoe I looked over toward the dock. The group surrounding Caroline (two other women had joined in) was still saying good-bye, but Teró was standing there in the sun, watching me with his arms crossed and his head tilted to the left. As soon as he saw me approach the canoe he dropped his arms and took a step forward. I was quite far away from him, about a hundred meters. I noticed his worried look and I smiled. I heard the faint murmur of the waves beating against the side of the canoe. I leaned my chest up against the bow, opened my arms, grabbed on to the edge, and forced it into the water. The canoe rocked and then began to move away from the shore, carried by the current. Teró ran along the dock and dove into the water toward the canoe that was slowly drifting downriver. I watched as he desperately, stroke after stroke, tried to catch up to it. That Indian had a debt to pay me. I felt satisfied then, imagining his dismal return to the village, but later I thought about my behavior and his back in the village, when he had interrupted my night of pleasure with the native woman out of jealousy. Jealousy is odious, and when practiced without any basis it is simply intolerable. It makes me feel pitiful and ill. Nothing good comes from it. That morning I think I was jealous of Teró, just as I had been some time before of Jack. In Buenos Aires, when those fears would begin to take over my feelings, I would resort to other women, and that would reassure me. But in Fordlandia there was little I could do. That run-in with Teró had sealed our enmity, and he would never forgive me.

I met João at noon and we went to have lunch in the restaurant. Rowwe and Frank were waiting for us. On the way, João took photographs of the village (he also took one of me in front of my house). I asked about his colleague, the old Spanish adventurer who was with him in the Belem cabaret. At that time I had read up on the caucheros' revolt in Acre and about the extraordinary events that the Spaniard had recounted, disjointedly, that afternoon as we watched the prostitutes come and go. I was especially interested in the figure who had succeeded the Spaniard as leader of the movement. It was said that that leader, Plácido de Castro, was desperate due to the inferiority of his forces and had traveled through the southern Amazon inciting the seringueiros to rebel against the arrogance of the Bolivians with a simple command: "Get me men or die." When I met Joâo I recalled those stories and thought that I might be able to see the Spaniard again to satiate my curiosity for that unique epic of the early century. "The Spaniard passed on to the other world two months ago," Joâo told me, without a trace of emotion in his voice. In fact, the only reaction I noticed from Joâo was when, after we had eaten and he was jotting down notes and smoking, I told him that some ashes from his cigarette had fallen on his pants.

Rowwe had had the table in the restaurant set as if for a formal meal, with napkins in napkin rings and a set of silverware and special glasses for each course. He had arranged for them to serve corned beef, a luxury, various salads, and a tray of almonds and raisins for dessert. Joâo ate a lot, as if he had just returned from war, and he did not notice my surprise or Frank's when, after dessert, Rowwe offered a toast with a glass of French cognac to the success of Fordlandia. The waiter brought the bottle, served us, and left it on the table. The four of us leaned forward ceremoniously, raised our glasses, and toasted. Then Joâo pushed his dessert plate aside, took a notebook and a small pencil out of an inside jacket pocket, and began his questioning. With scarcely a pause, he asked about the plans, the relationship with the governor, the school, the behavior of the people, and about Henry Ford's personality. Rowwe took charge of answering the questions, but his sentences were often left unfinished. He invited us to another cognac and we toasted again, this time, he proposed, for Brazil and the colonization of the Amazon. Rowwe moved his arm across his eyes, and his head rolled back and forth with an idiotic expression. A lock of hair was covering his white forehead. Shortly after, he excused himself and got up slowly. He walked off toward the bathroom. The three of us watched him zigzag his way to the bathroom and close the door behind him. Then we poured another drink and continued the conversation.

"What do you think? How will this all end, this struggle between tractors and the primitive world, between the ideas of the great American colossus and the customs of some ragged little black people?" João asked, sounding me out, his eyes bulging.

"Reason will prevail, without a doubt," I said.

"And who will ensure that?"

I looked at Frank.

"I don't know, my friend. That is the question of the century," I responded.

"Fine. Everything's fine. Is Mr. Ford happy with how things are progressing?"

"From what I understand, he is," I answered.

"And the West Indians? Have they integrated well with the others?"

"Yes, no problems, they work well and they're paid well. What more could they want?" Frank responded.

"The people are satisfied working under Ford's conditions?"

"Of course they are, just look at them," Frank argued, pointing toward one of the windows. We could see the almost vacant street with a few people coming and going from their jobs. On one corner, leaning against a chestnut tree, I saw Mauro, the worker whom Enéas had introduced to me and with whom I had spoken the other afternoon. He was with another man and was watching us, expectantly. I got the feeling he was waiting for us to finish. I looked at the time. It was after two, and they should have been working. I looked at Mauro. He had now moved away from the tree and was signaling to me with his arm. Neither Frank nor João saw him. I got up and told them I would be right back, that I had forgotten to tell my assistant something. They made fun of me, alluding to the effects of the cognac. I went out to the street and walked straight toward Mauro. He took a few steps forward, took off his hat, and held out his hand. Instead of offering him mine, I grabbed him by the arm and dragged him roughly to the side, out of sight of the restaurant. I pushed him and scolded him, telling him to get back to work at once. Mauro brought one hand up to his chest and told me they were waiting to talk to the journalist to tell him about their problems. I told them again to leave and that I didn't want them to involve me in their matters, and I went back to the restaurant. Mauro's eyes were filled with despair. I entered the restaurant and went back to the table. Rowwe had returned. His face was pale, but he was leading the conversation. He was praising the Ford Company with grandiloquent gestures. Through the window I saw Mauro and his friend walking off down the road. They were walking slowly, and Mauro was limping slightly. We filled our glasses with cognac, Rowwe indicated that he did not want any more by covering his with his hand, and we toasted again. This time to Henry Ford. João told a joke and then asked me to tell one. I told the one about the engineer who goes to build a dam in the middle of the mountains and a few weeks later asks the foremen where he can find women.

João was the only one who enjoyed it, even though he told me that he knew a joke just like it about the jungle. João stayed in the village for a couple of days. He spent much of his time, to Rowwe's disgust, in meetings with Jack and in interviews with other officials. When we said good-bye that afternoon, he told me that Plácido de Castro, the cauchero leader I had been interested in, had been murdered from behind in an ambush. "Do you want to know his last words?" he asked. I nodded, interested. In a rich voice he said, "The man who knows how to live, knows how to die."

XVII

First I heard someone outside the window running, then voices and shouting in the distance. Then an explosion that seemed to come from the sawmill shook the earth. A moment later I heard gunfire, more voices and shouting, and the sound of hurried footsteps up and down the hallway. I stopped reading, closed the folder, got up, and went to the window. I saw Rowwe, Frank, and three guards armed with rifles run by. I heard a voice on the other side of the door say in English: "Savages, they're savages, we have to kill them." I ran out of the office and headed for the street. The rest of the U.S. officials and a few Brazilian accountants passed by, shaken and making gestures. They were carrying three or four small safes and they ducked into Rowwe's office. Outside, about twenty guards had taken up positions around the building. They were expressionless, waiting for orders, and they were aiming their rifles at the mob, a moving mass that filled the street a hundred meters away. Several men, among them office workers, foremen, and doctors, came running toward the building, breaking through the cordon formed by the guards and going inside to hide. Other groups of workers and caucheros drew near the crowd but did not join in. They seemed to come out of nowhere, appearing suddenly. It was as if they had gathered to watch the outcome of a tragedy. Five bodies lay, stretched out, on the ground in front of the crowd. Three were black West Indians. In the distance, sheds were in flames and a column of black smoke swirled toward the sky. The noise of the fire, of posts and pillars being destroyed, of glass shattering against the ground, mixed with shouts of jubilation reached the wing of the building where I was. It was eleven in the morning, and the revolt was two hours old.

In Fordlandia workers were paid weekly. Every Saturday morning, across from the administration building near the sawmill, a long and raucous line of workers in search of their pay would form. The first to be paid were the caucheros and those whose work was directly tied to the plantation. Then the rest followed, according to the job performed. The caucheros formed a line according to age, so that the oldest were the first to receive their money. That morning, the West Indians, a few younger men in particular, had chosen not to respect that practice. At first the caucheros tried to make the blacks conform to the rules with words and later by pushing, and they let an old planter move ahead of them. One of the West Indians, a surly young man with quick reflexes, pulled out a short knife from under his clothing, brandishing it in the sunlight. The old man pounced on the young man and felt the cold steel go in and out of his stomach twice. The old man leaned forward, fell back a couple of steps, staggered, and fell, faceup. A cauchero knocked the young man down with a blow from his right, and he continued to beat him on the ground. From that point on, the morning's tranquillity was drowned out by the noise of shouting and blood. The rest of the caucheros charged the young West Indians. They cornered them up against the payment office and, after a while of uneven hand-to-hand fighting, the conflict swung in their favor. They pounded them with stones, sticks, picks, and hoes and finally stabbed them to death. They unleashed their fury on the other West Indians, who ran desperately toward the jungle and took refuge in a shed that was under construction. A couple of guards tried to stop the caucheros by firing a rifle, which wounded four of them and killed one. Then the guards took off running too. A group of caucheros stopped their pursuit of the West Indians and went after the guards. They caught up to one as he was climbing a tree. They threw him to the ground, dragged him by his hair to another, taller, tree, wound a rope around his neck, and hanged him from a branch. The crowd reached the shed under construction. They doused the door and windows of the shed with gasoline and set fire to it. The tremendous roar of the fuel resounded around the village, announcing what was happening. The mob watched the flames for a while and then headed for the main offices. On the way they unleashed their ire on other buildings, and as they closed in on the upper part of the village, more rebels joined in, arousing the attention of curious onlookers and provoking panic and the hurried flight of the authorities and officials. They stopped a hundred meters away from the offices, just as the guards, grouped together and kneeling down, threatened to open fire. They were carrying five bodies, and they left them there on the rough pavement in the street.

I stayed there, astonished, outside the offices but behind the guards. Frank came over to me. A few beads of sweat had formed on his forehead, but he did not wipe them off. He was scared. A simple mathematical calculation tilted the odds in favor of the mob. I asked him what was going on. "Downright criminals," he said. Suddenly, two men came out of the crowd and came toward us. They walked slowly, cautiously, like old men. Frank called to the leader of the local guard. He was a tall Brazilian, born in Manaus, with yellowish skin, no eyebrows, a bald head, and very fat (although he gave the impression that he had been even fatter at one time because his skin was flabby with wrinkles and folds). He had removed his gun from its case and now held it in his right hand. "Go see what those two want and tell your men to open fire as soon as I say so," Frank ordered. The fat man bowed, said something to one of his assistants, and then went straight over to the two caucheros. He moved forward confidently. The guard remained tense, aiming at the mob. They met halfway. I looked at Frank, pushed my way through the guard, and hurried over to the three men. I understood what was happening, but I felt no sense of responsibility. I did not, however, want to be passive or remain in the dark. As I was walking over to them someone called out my name, but I kept going. Mauro saw me approaching, elbowed his friend, and smiled faintly. He had a lit cigarette hanging from his mouth. When he was face-to-face with the fat man he began to speak. Then the fat man slapped him right across the face. The cigarette fell a few meters from Mauro.

"I don't want you smoking while you talk to me," he said to him.

Mauro turned pale but said nothing at first. Then he asked if he could pick up his cigarette. The fat man said no. Mauro stepped to the side anyway and began to reach for the cigarette butt. The fat man cocked his gun and aimed it at Mauro's head. "One more move and I'll blow your brains out, caboclo," he said. I felt beads of sweat forming on my forehead. I stepped between the leader of the guard and Mauro, bent down, picked up the cigarette and took a drag. Then I handed it to Mauro.

Mauro stood up straight, took the cigarette with one hand, and wiped off the trickle of blood that was coming from his mouth with the other. Mauro's friend spoke to the fat man. I could not understand what he said to him, but the fat man, with his gun still raised, made a gesture as if he were going to smack him across the head. Then he turned around and glared at me, resentful and threatening. Sweat ran down over my eyelids. For a few seconds we were frozen, staring at each other. I realized that I had put him in an uncomfortable position. I looked back to where the guard was and spotted Frank. Jack was next to him. I raised my hand, indicating that he should wait, and I addressed the fat man. "Lower your gun and step back, I want to find out what these people want," I ordered. The fat man hesitated, looked at Frank, and then took a few steps back. Mauro's friend stammered that the only thing they wanted was for the blacks to leave. I told him that I would speak to Rowwe, provided some of the people leave at once with a patrol to put out the fire and to ensure that there were no more deaths. He agreed. Mauro came over to try to tell me something, but I cut him off, ordering him to take charge with his friend of carrying out the agreement. On the way to Rowwe's office I ordered the leader of the guard to send a patrol with the caucheros to put out the fire at once. The fat man, still resentful, obeyed. A short while later, in the hallway outside of Rowwe's office and with all the officials watching and George urging him on, he came up to me aggressively and challenged me to a fight. George stood by his side, showing me his ivory teeth. I told him that if he took off his watch and put the gun aside, I would gladly accept his challenge. While the fat man was distracted removing his holster, I pitted myself against him and kicked him with all my might between the legs. The fat man opened his mouth like a fish out of water, clasped his hands below his waist, and leaned over. I took one step to the side, leaving the perfect distance for me to land a blow on the back of his neck. I clasped my hands together, raised my arms and then lowered them, quickly and sharply, on the greasy area that connected his neck to his back. The fat man moaned in pain and collapsed to his knees.

Negotiations with Rowwe were not as difficult as expected. When I entered his office, Rowwe's eyes were filled with fear. He was surrounded by the Americans (Frank and Jack arrived after me) and four Brazilian officials. He was pacing nervously, hurling insults and uttering aggressive but powerless stupidities against the people, the jungle, and his destiny. His words seemed filled with hatred, but they revealed weakness and confusion. For the first time I felt able to impose my will on him. I told him to calm down and that we had to resolve the situation. Still hysterical and still pacing, he told me to start talking. I stood in front of him, blocking his way, and told him that I would do so provided that only Frank, Jack, he, and I were present. Rowwe abruptly moved aside to continue pacing, raised his voice, and insulted me and everyone else there. Then he asked the others to leave us alone for a moment. Frank and Jack, who had followed me to Rowwe's office through a kind of ceremonial corridor that the officials and guards had cleared for me after the scene in the middle of the street with the workers, came in and observed our conversation in silence.

"We have to get rid of the troublemakers and execute the criminals," Rowwe said.

I stared at him and saw the fear in his face, which emboldened me.

"They want to kick out your West Indians and the dance instructor, and they want to eat and drink other things. They gave me one hour to think it over. If we don't give them what they want, they are threatening to burn down the village and leave on the first boat out," I said.

"What do they want, champagne and caviar?" he asked me.

"No, beans and liquor," I replied.

"We have to get rid of those idiots," he muttered.

Then he walked over behind his desk and let himself fall slowly into his chair. There was a two-week-old edition of the *Folha do Norte* open on the desk. The main article included a photograph of Rowwe. He was feigning a smile and pointing to some tractors working in the jungle. He was so proud of that article that he was having it copied and translated for his family and for the offices in Detroit. Joao's opening lines read, "In Fordlandia, where the civilization of the Amazon begins, a million dollars are spent each month. Work is Yankee style, and alcohol is not permitted." Rowwe lowered his head and pounded on the desk.

"No," he said.

"No what?" I asked.

Rowwe was slow to respond. He sat with his head down and his forearms on his knees, staring at his hands. Frank and Jack came forward and stood next to me. I asked Jack for a cigarette, as did Frank. Jack quickly took two cigarettes out of his shirt pocket, one for me and the other for Frank. The three of us smoked while Rowwe sat there in total despair, his head still down. Frank and Jack smoked nonstop, exhaling slowly. I looked out the window. Several Brazilian officials were crowded together, watching our meeting. I got up and closed the window.

"Why do we only have an hour to decide?" Frank asked.

"An hour is enough time to make a decision," I said.

"As far as I'm concerned, I have no problem with what those bastards are asking for. We could organize the work better and do just as well without the West Indians," Jack suggested.

Frank looked up and glared at him.

"You're to blame for what is happening," he said.

Jack made a fist and put it in his face.

"One more like that and you'll have no teeth left," he said.

"And you'll be left with no job, no salary, no support from us, and on your way back to prison in Detroit with your little engine," Frank told him. Frank lowered his fist and walked over to the window. Then he drove his fist through the glass, which shattered in pieces. The Brazilians on the other side of the window ran off, alarmed. Rowwe raised his head.

"No," he said.

I took a step forward and rested my hands on the desk. I looked him in the eye.

"No what?"

"Detroit mustn't find out about this, mustn't . . . ever . . ."

"What will we tell people?"

Rowwe sighed, then got up abruptly, took some long strides over to one side of the office, and opened a drawer in the filing cabinet. He took out a folder (that must have contained his plan) and waved it in my direction.

"And what do we do with this? Huh? What do we do?" he shouted.

"Rowwe, listen to me. If we don't give them an answer, those people are capable of burning all of us alive," I said.

Rowwe wiped a hand across his forehead, and in an entirely different tone of voice, almost trembling, he said, "Alright, you and Frank take charge of getting rid of the West Indians and the dance instructor."

"And the food and drink?"

"Only on Sundays."

"And the movies?"

"Who said anything about movies?"

I pointed to Frank. He looked at me, surprised.

"We did," I said.

"I'll ask Belem for a projector and some movies," Rowwe said. "Now leave me alone."

Frank asked me to convey our decision to the caucheros. He would handle the dance instructor and George and his West Indians. I left the office. Most of the officials were outside, expectant. The leader of the guard was also waiting for me along with George, who was ready to defy me. When I reached the street the guard was still aiming at the crowd, which seemed to be under control. Enéas came out to meet me, and he walked next to me proudly, without a single extraneous gesture. Sunshine filled the sky, and the air smelled of smoke and ash. Mauro came forward and asked if the answer was positive. I nodded my head and kept walking. Mauro remained where he was, laughing. I stopped in front of the crowd. The bodies were still there. The eyes of one of the West Indians were open and blood was dripping from his throat, forming a small puddle next to his head. Insects were buzzing around the bodies. I climbed an oil tank and let the people gather around me. I looked out over the mob. The street had a slight grade, and I could see almost the entire village. I saw the fire in the sheds subsiding and the patrol and the other men putting out the final flames. A small cargo ship was pulling up to the dock. The deck sparkled in the sunlight. Then I looked down and saw the worried expressions on a dozen faces. Women had joined the crowd. I realized that people were pushing up against each other to see me. I felt I held all the power and that just a few words from me would be enough to end it all. I spotted Mauro in the crowd and looked at the dirty, sweaty faces that surrounded him. Then I spoke to them.

"Caboclos," I said, "we have decided to send the West Indians home, and on Sundays you will be able to drink and eat whatever you want. Now work together to repair what you broke and bury the dead, all of them. It's over."

The people exploded in an irrepressible cry of joy, and those in front tried to lift me up on their shoulders. I resisted, but they were insistent, and with Enéas's help I shoved them aside. The mob slowly began to break up, and I looked for a tree to give me some shade. I stayed under the tree branches alone, watching as some headed back to the plantation, others began to repair the damage, and a small group, made up of doctors and policemen, saw to the bodies. Then Frank and Jack came over to me. The street was soon empty and calm.

At night the caucheros organized a party in an alleyway next to one of their huts. Jack and I were the only foreigners to attend. Liquor, music, and dancing filled the street. The vigil for the caucheros was set up inside the hut, and there was a continuous flow of people entering the hut and then leaving to return to the party. Some were crying as they came out. I saw women dressed in black and a few men wearing bracelets of the same color. Two women next to us were crying, and they told us that the bodies of the West Indians had been thrown in the river. A quartet was standing on some chairs next to the hut, playing and singing various songs. The people offered us liquor, but Jack and I opted for the whiskey we had brought. We sat in a circle on the side of the road with Antonio and the two other Brazilian doctors. The moon was high and the sounds of the night—insects or whatever they were—did not bother us. We drank two bottles in all. At one point I saw Enéas go by. I called to him and offered him a drink and we toasted. Around midnight, Jack went back to his house to get his guitar, and then he tried, unsuccessfully, to join the quartet. Later he left the guitar with us and went off to dance with several of the workers' wives. He looked happy. The dances were frenzied, and the dancers moved skillfully and confidently. I felt like going to look for the dance instructor and dragging him there by the nose so he could demonstrate how to move to the sound of the music. A woman who was alone came over to our group and we made small talk. She looked upset. She began to cry and she hugged me. She was wearing a red-and-white-striped dress. Her straight black hair and her large rounded breasts were her greatest assets. When she stopped crying, I took her hand, said good-bye to the group, and took her back to my house.

After a few days, everything had returned to normal in Fordlandia. Life went on as always for those who worked on the plantation. While it is true that many workers returned to their villages, they didn't do so out of fear of retaliation by the foremen or the guards but rather because they simply could no longer put up with any kind of discipline. They had found the orders and rules very strange, incomprehensible and intimidating. Those who stayed complied with the new system of work. Since there had always been strict orders in place, they had no difficulty adapting to the innovations and the division or repetition of jobs that Rowwe, inspired by a few manuals Jack had written, imposed. The felling, clearing, and planting remained as active as when the West Indians and additional workers had been there, thanks to the model conceived by Jack (an adaptation of the one in place in Detroit). The rubber trees grew throughout thousands of acres. Relations between the authorities and the workers became less rigid, and Rowwe only had to worry about maintaining order on Sundays, when each person was able to buy and drink a half bottle of alcohol. The West Indians, with George as their leader, left for the Colombian Amazon (George had obtained a residency permit there), and the dance instructor, after pleading in vain for a contract in

Detroit, left for Montevideo. Mauro disappeared. One day, the caucheros said, they saw him walk off alone toward the jungle. He did not return to his hut that night, or the next, or any other day. Rumor had it that the leader of the guard, while drunk, had bragged about having killed him with his own hands and hidden his body in the jungle. The leader must have also said that I knew about that death too. I was never able to confirm it, since I found out about it after the fat man had already left to join George and his West Indians.

A month after those events, a movie projector and five movies arrived from the Belem office. For a few days the movies were shown in the entertainment hall in private showings for directors, but after a while, bored to tears with the small misfortunes of Buster Keaton, Charlie Chaplin, Douglas Fairbanks, and Greta Garbo, the projector was handed over to Antonio and his doctors so they could organize mass showings on Saturday nights and Sunday afternoons, in the hall that had previously been used for the dance classes. As far as I was concerned, I was completely happy watching movies and had always said that I could wait for the end of the world sitting in a movie hall, under the flood of light from the projector. But I agreed with the decision, and I only got excited about going to see movies in the dance hall when Antonio told me, jokingly, that the natives of the Amazon applauded tragic scenes and were frightened by the normal escapades of the heroes. Rowwe's plan was postponed, the Americans occupied themselves with scheming and gossiping, one against the other, and I was left to work with Jack in his pursuit to tame the jungle. We contented ourselves with laying down numerous paths through the dense growth and sowing thousands of seedlings in the clearings. But every day seemed the same, and it was hard to get used to my new activities. What's more, at night the jungle destroyed, without fail, almost all the progress achieved during the day. Time turned back as night fell. I felt as if we were living a tragedy that had only reached the end of the first act. And so the summer passed. Then the rains began. After the rainy season Caroline returned, just as she had promised.

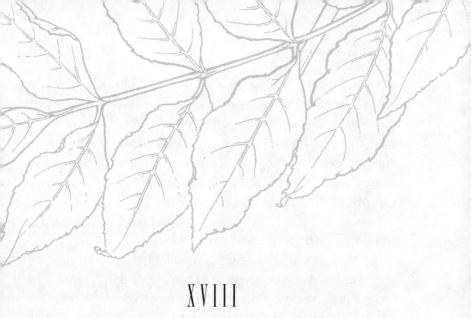

XVIII

John was standing in the long corridor of the crankshaft section when a small, thin older man with a youthful appearance stopped by his side. John immediately sensed the man's presence, but he did not take his eyes off the conveyor belt, and with the aid of a tool about the size of his forearm he continued to adjust the parts of welded metal that passed by, waist high, one after the other. John was in training (at that time there were thousands more like him in the Rouge plant), but he knew the rules that had been set at the complex in response to union pressure.

The union was fighting to affiliate automotive machine workers. It had replaced the old plant representatives with more aggressive organizers and was using the same methods of propaganda and unrest that it had successfully used in the steel industry. The policy of high company salaries had collapsed with the depression of 1930, and in order to intimidate the union (even though, in fact, no hint of internal protest had ever been tolerated), the authorities had introduced new rules of conduct. Sitting, crouching down, singing, talking, and smiling were prohibited. Explanations were required to walk from one place to another, bathrooms were monitored to insure that no meetings or smoking took place inside; and outside the complex, company agents patrolled the bars and nearby stores in an effort to detect possible conspirators. Product loyalty was also controlled. Employees and members of their family could drive cars manufactured only by the company. And, most important, the assembly line was accelerated, tardiness was not tolerated, and the lunch break was reduced to fifteen minutes.

John was not smiling, singing, or talking to his coworkers on the line. He was just nervous, sweaty, and the presence of a strange man observing his movements with such interest made him even more uncomfortable. Instead of stretching out his arm without bending at the waist, finding the piece and adjusting it with a backward motion, firmly and precisely, in fours seconds, as the operations manual stipulated, he was leaning forward too much and was a few centimeters too far away, so he was taking more than twice as long. His inexperience, exacerbated by nerves, was holding up production in the section, which was not acceptable. John thought they had come to fire him (there had to be some reason that guy was standing there by his side, watching all his mistakes), and he thought about his future. For a few seconds he was overcome by doubt. Should he turn around, apologize for his clumsiness, confess that he had wasted time in the bathroom two days earlier, and given the difficulties of finding a job in Detroit, ask for another chance? Or should he resign without a word in the face of his misfortune and just ask for a certificate of good behavior that might be of use to him in joining the navy, or head west, to California, to paradise, as his fiancée so wanted. Once on the street nothing is sure, he thought. Nothing, nothing in life is worse than being without a job, without money. You're a nobody, you don't even exist, he thought, and the more his mind wandered, the faster and more unmanageable, almost spectral, the movement of the belt and the crankshafts became. He had to rid himself of those thoughts. He recalled how in the training course for new hires it had been driven into them that a blank mind was a guaranty for keeping up with the rhythm of the machines, and if that, for some strange reason, was impossible, the expert recommended fixing one's attention on the pieces passing in front of him and associating them with anything that might provoke a special disgust or a special fondness: a mouse, a spider, a pig, a cockroach, an ass, a tit. He drew closer to the machine and stubbornly tried to concentrate on the movement of the pieces. But that morning it was no use. Despite trying as hard as he could, it was impossible for him to focus on his work. He stood there, in front of the belt, talking to himself, asking himself, "And now what?" and then answering himself, "Nothing, nothing at all. It's over."

After a while the man watching him tapped him on the shoulder, asked him for his tool, and took his position on the line to perform his job. John turned around and obeyed, timid and resigned, his eyes on the floor. The man told him to watch how he did the job and then try to imitate him. John watched the man's unique skill and saw how he adjusted a dozen crankshafts effortlessly and without the slightest hesitation. Then the man leaned forward, looked down, read the name on his overalls, and gave the tool back to him. "Now, John, you try it, calmly, let the machine do the work, you just go with it. That way you won't be so tired when you get home," he said to him. A touch of color spread across John's pale cheeks. He clenched and opened his hands, which were also sweaty, picked up the tool, shook his head, and went back to work. Then he looked quickly over his shoulder and saw the peculiar man, who was wearing a jacket with leather elbow patches and some old shoes, walk off down the corridor with a lively and uneven step. To avoid sanctions, the workers had learned to communicate with each other without moving their lips, and when it was important, they would communicate by writing messages on the pieces that advanced along the conveyor belt. The first thing John felt when he read the message was pure astonishment. Then he looked back down the corridor and the corridors beyond that and smiled at his coworkers in the section who had identified, piece by piece, the strange man. "Do you know who that man was, John? Henry Ford."

Ford arrived at the plant in Rouge early that January morning. On the way from the Fairlane mansion to the complex he had been quiet, speaking only when he had asked the driver to stop the car on the side of the road as they passed the house next to his mansion. The young Dahlinger was driving an old Model T through the gardens. Ford sat back in his seat, looked for a moment through the little window as that boy, suspected of being the fruit of his relationship with Evangeline, drove the car from here to there, between the trees and the plants, and then he ordered the driver to keep going.

The executives who saw him arrive at Rouge a while later noticed his somber, gruff expression, as if he had been struck by lightning, and they knew, right off, that that day there would be trouble. A few executives, accustomed as of late to the boss showing up annoyed, attributed his malaise to the depression that was threatening the country's economy. Others, the older ones, attributed his suddenly irritability, his whims and unexpected comings and goings, to the influence of old age on a unique personality. The depression had hit the industry hard, especially Detroit. Nevertheless, the Ford Motor Company, due to its bold reactions—first it ordered the prices of its cars to be lowered and then salaries—and to its extensive fortune, showed signs in those days of solid survival amid the merciless competition that was rocking the industry.

True, union struggles were increasing, and President Roosevelt, whom Ford detested, was courting him in order to have him join their conciliatory measures, but Ford did not lose sleep over that, and he managed, with brutal responses and rebuffs, not to show weakness: a defect that, in his opinion, corrodes man's spirit like no other. No. It was not just the depression, the union presence, or Roosevelt that had given him a hard time. Nor were those fits of anger and superiority due merely, as his former subordinates maintained, to the displays of senility of a brilliant and conflicted mind. Those who presumed to have known him forever were sure that those outbursts could be ignored without major consequences, and they were convinced that age—Ford had turned seventy— played a part in the boss's new obsessions. In some way, in the last few months, his experiments—practical science, as he called them—had bordered more than ever before on that thin line that separates eccentric, peculiar ideas from those that simply have no pretext. A few weeks earlier, his granddaughter, Edsel's daughter, had surprised him in flagrante at the washbasin in his bedroom. Fascinated by his beliefs about how to restore hair follicles, he was washing his hair with water oxidized from razor blades. The foremen and workers in the motors' section had also been left speechless when one winter afternoon, with no shame, he had gathered them together to inform them of and recommend one of his latest findings: they should breathe carbon monoxide if they wanted to rid their bodies of heart trouble and tuberculosis.

Around the same time, the press reported the strange meeting he had had with a scientist named Carver, who had visited

Ford in Greenfield Village upon his request. Ford, in the middle of a long speech in which he was advocating the consumption of vegetables, told the scientist that cows would soon be on the verge of extinction because humans would produce synthetic milk. Carver agreed and referred to his own experiments, which purported to convert weeds into food for humans. Ford lost no time. He invited his guest to accompany him on a walk through the park to gather weeds, and then, with the utmost normality, under the stupefied gaze of the scientist, he sat down on the grass and began to chew them, with the delight of a cow chewing its cud. Perhaps those idiosyncrasies and others like them were a consequence of old age. Maybe the death of his friend Edison, the only person in front of whom he felt embarrassed about his eccentricities, had left him without inhibitions. But a streak of madness lives in all extraordinarily intelligent men. Ford had always had moments of imagination and madness, and it was excessively arbitrary to associate those moments, the changes in his mood and his insistence on always getting his way, with a decrepit state. No. Old age, like the economic crisis, was only part of the problem. Ford, in fact, was angry at the era. Terribly angry. He believed that the crisis was a necessary and healthy purge after the excesses of the jazz era, and he acted consequently. He was openly opposed to the charity and philanthropy that the government and some of his colleagues were advocating, and he continued to espouse the merits of individualism, self-sufficiency, personal effort, the decentralization of industry, and the return to the countryside as unique and infallible remedies. In his newspaper, the *Dearborn Independent*, and in his six-minute speeches on his nationwide radio program, *The Ford Hour*, he promoted his points of view emphatically. But reality had changed for millions of people. Signs of social decay were easily noticeable on the streets, and his words now sounded hollow, ridiculous, meaningless to those who had lost their jobs and were rummaging through garbage in search of food. Ford, who had always been a hero to the man in the street, felt alone, that his reputation was vanishing, that his cause was passing into the land of shadows, and that there was nothing worse, nothing comparable—not the unions, not old age, not other makes of cars, not the most sworn enemies, not the death of a friend—than to see his glory fade, inevitably, like the slow fading light of a late summer afternoon.

When he arrived at Rouge that cold January morning, Ford got out of the car, and without saying a word to the driver he headed, determined, to the engineering and development laboratory, where his men were designing the Model V-8. Just as with the Model T and Model A, he was personally involved in the project. He spent almost three hours discussing even the smallest details with the engineers and designers, and he left the laboratory threatening them, for no reason whatsoever, saying that he was aware they were selling industrial secrets to Walter Chrysler.

He went from the laboratory to the accounting department. Ford despised paperwork. When he had arrived at the complex he'd seen a line of shivering suppliers waiting to get paid. Ford entered the department and asked the person in charge why those people, representatives of companies that he'd known for a long time, were being made to wait. "It's bureaucratic routine," the employee responded with a smile frozen on his face. Ford asked him to open a window as he picked up a few ledgers and other items from the employee's desk. Then he went over to the window and threw them out onto the street. "Sir, I don't see any reason for following your routine or for keeping these books. Put the money in a barrel, and if you have to pay someone, stick your hand in the barrel and take out what you need!" he shouted at him.

As he left the accounting department he bumped into
Sorensen and his assistant, Harry. Sorensen informed him that
Harry's report on his trip to the Amazon was ready and that he
was at his disposal. Ford was fond of Harry. He liked his swag-
gering air, the nonchalance with which he carried out his whims,
and his rough and confident personality. He considered him the
prototype of masculinity. Harry was uncouth and devoid of
imagination, but he had gradually won Ford's trust, and later,
Liebold and Sorensen himself would pay for it. Ford spoke with
the two for a moment and told Sorensen to bring the report with
him to the conference room at lunchtime and to inform Edsel
and Liebold of the meeting. He said good-bye to Sorensen and
to Harry with a quick, firm handshake and then left to tour one
of the sections of the Rouge complex.

Years ago, Ford used to walk along the assembly lines of the old
Highland Park plant. There he'd felt like the benign monarch of
a peaceful kingdom. But Highland Park, with its five floors, fifteen thousand production and assembly machines, and its complex furnaces for cylinders was a miniature compared to Rouge.
Rouge was simply unwieldy. Ford thought about the old plant
when he reached the crankshaft section and had a look at the
long corridor and the enormous assembly line. By that time his
mood had improved. Minutes before, Harry had told him that
his reputation and his ideas about the social order reached as far
as the South American jungle. He had also asked him why he
was wearing that jacket and the old shoes. He explained that it
was his contribution to creating a spirit of sacrifice among workers to confront the difficult times, and after his response, he had
noticed admiration in the eyes of Harry and Sorensen too. Ford
walked slowly down the crankshaft corridor and took the time
to correct the actions of a nervous new employee who was dis-

turbing the rhythm of production. Then he climbed the stairs to the first floor, turned right, and at the end of the hallway, before entering the dining room, he looked out a large window. The sky was cloudy and the wind was blowing columns of smoke from the chimneys toward the west. For a moment he recalled the Arrow and the world record for speed set by that automobile, which had been prepared entirely by him in the middle of the winter of 1904, on the frozen surface of St. Clair Lake. Every time the car went over a crack, it jumped up into the air, and when it didn't jump it skated, but he had managed to keep it steady, straight on the surface, and its 150 kilometers per hour made news around the world, for him and for his automobiles. It was a terrible experience, but the successful outcome proved to be infinitely superior. Clara, his wife, was there that day, along with the small and obedient Edsel. The image of Edsel, jumping up and down on the ice to get his blood circulating and waving his hands to say hello to him before he stepped on the accelerator and let the Arrow loose, overcame him for a few seconds. "That boy, so unlike me," he said to himself. Then he entered the dining room.

Inside, just as he had ordered, Edsel, Sorensen, and Liebold were sitting around the table, waiting. Ford greeted them, sat down, and asked Edsel to begin with the day's business. Edsel did not feel well. His health, affected by a rebellious ulcer that would soon develop into cancer, had worsened, and he had spent the morning until just minutes before the meeting lying down on the couch in his office. He had three matters to discuss. He made an effort to conceal his pain from his father and began with the structure of the company. He advised the preparation of a flowchart that would describe the executive duties. To reinforce his arguments he cited the successful experience of General Motors. General Motors had developed a form of decentralized management to facilitate cooperation between the different departments and to open the game to the initiative of the employees, a game in which the company would be regarded as a machine whose movable parts were human and the lubricant was merit. In fact, Edsel was introducing new organizational ideas not just to emulate the good performance of its most dangerous competitors but also to establish once and for all the precise limits of his own authority as president and that of his closest associates. Ford did not seem to be listening. But he shifted in his chair, looked at him, and did not hesitate to respond.

"No organization, no specific duty associated with any position, no line of succession or authority. I don't want any of that. What else do you have?"

Edsel stared at his agenda.

"According to the financial plans that Liebold prepared, I think we have to start thinking about increasing capital with a public offering of stock," he said.

Ford became livid. He put one hand on the table and leaned forward, drawing his face close to Edsel's. He looked at him seriously and intensely. He assumed that Edsel was insisting on liquidating his power in the company. He was right.

"I would rather tear down Rouge and all the plants, one by one, before some Jewish investor acquires our stock," he said.

Edsel buried his face in his hands. He was silent for a moment, and then, without looking at his father, he asked if he wanted him to bring up the third item that he had planned for the meeting or if they should request lunch directly.

"What is it?" Ford retorted.

"Buying the rights to manufacture the Zephyr. I think that model would suit the tastes of our middle-class customers, and we could place it between the Ford and the Lincoln in terms of price and quality."

"How much is the investment?"

Edsel wrote down a figure with several zeros on a piece of paper, which he passed to his father. Ford picked up the paper and read it. He looked at him and nodded.

"Okay, buy them. Anything else?" he asked.

Edsel remembered his father's mood when he arrived that morning, and he was content with having obtained one positive response out of three. He left the ideas of a test track and of separating the design section from the engineering section for another occasion.

"I have nothing else," he said.

Liebold interrupted.

"I have a problem," he said.

"Oh, yes? What kind of problem?" Ford asked.

"With Harry. I think the guy is out for himself, a tough guy who's leading the confrontation with the union to unsustainable limits, and he is going to create problems for us, all of us," he remarked angrily.

"Oh Ernest, you seem nervous, you need a break. The three of you should know that Harry was behind a decision that I want to tell you about," Ford said.

Sorensen listened, leaned back, and smiled. He was smiling less with his mouth than with his eyes.

"What decision?" he asked Ford.

"I'm taking a trip."

"Where to?" Sorensen persisted.

"Do you have Harry's report?" Ford answered.

"About the jungle?"

"Yes, about what they call Fordlandia?"

Sorensen picked up a folder on the desk and showed it to him.

"Here it is," he said.

"What does the report say?" Ford asked.

"Well, it says that the idiot in charge there has to be replaced, that he has delusions of grandeur, with our money, of course, but that the project, even if difficulties continue, will be a success," Sorensen said.

"I think the only thing that that project is good for is spending money," Edsel intervened.

Ford looked at Edsel and then turned to Sorensen.

"What else does it say?"

"Not much. That the natural surroundings are impressive, exotic. That life there is primitive, but that the people are happy with you, that they see things your way, Henry."

"Well, that's where I'm going," Ford said.

The three men exchanged glances. Edsel sat up straight in his chair.

"It's an inhospitable, difficult place," he said.

"As inhospitable and difficult as this country. Or perhaps you think that I am only good for staying at Fairlane and tending the roses?" Ford replied.

"No."

Ford, without looking at anyone, gave his order.

"Well then, I want an itinerary prepared for me in complete secrecy, and choose the most suitable dates. Agreed?"

Sorensen and Liebold nodded in agreement. Edsel looked at his father astonished, his mouth agape. He thought that while his father was digressing, the company was going adrift. The waiter came in to set the table and serve lunch.

XIX

In the middle of May the skies turned blue. The leaves began to change color and the swarms of mosquitoes and gnats disappeared. I realized winter was over. Once again you could walk along the roads, through the village, and look out onto the Tapajós. In winter, because of the rains, the Tapajós rises almost three meters, overflowing its banks and covering the shores and beaches. During those months the water becomes dark brown, and it flows, dirty, sluggishly, and tumultuously toward the Amazon. No sooner does the rain stop and summer begin than its level drops rapidly and its color turns a beautiful clear green with bluish patches. I took advantage of those first days of summer to take long walks through the village and along the banks of the Tapajós. Days became longer again, and the hordes of birds returned. That year the *guarajubas* arrived first. They flew over the village for hours and then dotted the treetops with their yellow and purple plumage. In just a short time the sun dried up the muddy spots; myriads of butterflies appeared, and at dusk the shrill song of the cicadas was heard once again. In the air and in the countryside there was a sense of renewed life.

On the plantation, however, things were not going well. An unidentified disease had attacked the rubber trees and was making them wither at lightning speed. Jack was the first to find out about the disease from the workers, and after inspecting the seringales with the health patrol he immediately reported the damage to Rowwe, who requested help from the Belem office. The epidemic was spreading at a rate of a hundred acres per day, and although it had started in the fields in the south, it had already spread north and west. The Belem office sent a Japanese expert on the first boat bound for the Lower Amazon. The boat brought supplies, a group of new workers, and mail. There was a letter for me from Caroline.

She had had a pleasant trip, and in Montreal she'd met another Argentine (an engineer from Rosario who was finishing his studies at the local university). Her colleagues were fascinated by her research and frequently invited her to speak at gatherings and lectures. But she was awaiting news from the Ford Company—she had requested tickets and money—so she could visit the village at the end of June. She said she was anxious (she used the Spanish word *ansiosa*, a gesture I interpreted as a sign of affection for me) to return to the Amazon. As soon as I finished the letter, I put it in my pocket and went to meet Jack.

We had both gone down to the dock to greet the expert, and we had both received a letter from Caroline. But whereas I chose to read my letter in the privacy of my office, Jack had left at once to tour the plantation with Frank and the Japanese expert. I was not indifferent to the epidemic. Not at all. I simply was not at all acquainted with the practices and problems of silviculture and thought that I was facing one of those cases in which one is in danger of believing, falsely, that he is an active part of the solution. What's more, I had had some run-ins with

Jack over that very issue. Jack had assumed responsibility for the seringal epidemic as if it were a grave family problem, and his character changed, becoming too surly and excessively responsible for my taste. The changes in an individual's personality when he either transforms or blurs the basic features (whether they be charisma, generosity, or audacity) that distinguish him from mediocrity, terrify me and evoke feelings of rejection. In all the time that had elapsed since we had first learned of the problem to the time the expert arrived, Jack had done practically nothing other than walk the southern paths, alone or with his assistant, verifying and measuring the damage, asking questions, and talking with people about the possible origins of the plague. In those days, Jack carried a small ax with him, and on each path he chose one of the most affected trees and cut it down. Then he gathered several branches and some dead leaves and studied them in silence. He exchanged opinions with the caucheros and kept walking, speaking only to give instructions about some job or other in a defiant tone of voice. I seldom accompanied him on those walks. Jack considered the problem very serious, almost hopeless, and as a result he went against Rowwe's orders to continue the work of clearing and sowing at all costs, as if nothing were going on. My opinion at the time was that the plague, if we relied on the help of an expert, could be controlled. But neither Jack nor I, or even Rowwe or Frank or the caucheros had any reasons or knowledge on which to base our opinions. It was merely conjecture based on a greater or lesser hope. Nevertheless, Jack was bitter, and he firmly defended his pessimism. This, along with the changes in his behavior, was the origin of our heated arguments. In some way, those disputes damaged the good relationship that we'd had during the winter, when activity in the village was almost entirely limited to the sawmill and to repairing machinery, and the men and women who did not return home spent most of their time locked up in their homes.

In the Amazon, a winter day seems like an eternity. Day breaks with a thick mist, then it begins to rain, and it's rain and nothing but rain until dusk. Everything smells like water, everything sounds like water. The roads are covered with thick foliage and the earth dissolves, sinking, soft and heavy, due to the overgrowth of moss, weeds, and brush. It is the desolation of the end of the world. During the rainy season the trees seem left to themselves: they draw near and embrace each other, as if for protection. The nights cloud up and the moon, which appears now and then, mysterious, in the middle of the misty sky, leads to false expectations that the next day will be better. One wakes up and goes to bed with damp clothing, surrounded by mud, harassed by insects. Even tobacco must be kept in small jars so it doesn't decay.

The first weeks of winter were the hardest. I was tormented by the desire for a woman. I did not think only about Caroline. I thought about all the women I had known, all those I had loved, and my bedroom and my office were filled with all of their faces. Jack arranged for a woman to visit me. My activities at that time were limited to reading, either in the office or at home, and playing pool and poker with Frank and the Americans. When I got bored with the games, I went by Jack's house. He opened the door, wiped his hands off on his shirt, greeted me, and offered me a cup of coffee and a whiskey. Then I followed him to his workshop, where he continued to work on the still unfinished engine. Parts were scattered all over the workbench. Antonio was also there, helping Jack. They were working in the midst of an infernal confusion of nuts, cylinders, bolts, files, wrenches, hammers, and other things I detest because I don't know what to do with them. On some occasions they would stop their work and open a bottle, and we would spend long hours talking and drinking. Jack, between the occasional joke, would tune his guitar and sing a song that I would, without fail, relate to Caroline.

When the angel of sadness
comes near my bed
dragging a ribbon of darkness
across my eyes
I ask for a last breath
to say goodby to my girl
to say goodby to my love.

One night Jack told us (though by Antonio's calm manner I assumed that he already knew the story) why he had been sent to prison. In his hometown, he had left a dance drunk, and in front of the saxophonist and the drummer of his band he beat to death a man who had been flirting with his fiancée. He had openly admitted his guilt before the jury, alleging self-defense, and the jury, moved by his admission, sentenced him to five and a half years in jail. No sooner was he out on parole than the Ford Company, on the recommendation of an ex-convict, added him to their staff.

That morning I left them to their work and departed. As we were saying good-bye, Jack asked me if I would mind if he got me a woman. I smiled. "Of course not," I said. "I'll see what I can do for you, my friend," he said. Some time later, in the middle of a foggy night, a mulatta knocked on my door. She had been sent by Jack, and she stayed until dawn. I would never see her again, and I never found out her name. Those things happened in the winter. But then the blue skies returned and the weather changed. I had received a letter from Caroline and was on my way to meet Jack, Frank, and the Japanese expert to find out what we should do, if there was anything we could do, about the plague that was destroying the seringales.

I walked a while along the paths in the southern zone. I spotted the group through the trees, about two hundred meters to my right, and I headed over to them. The Japanese expert was using a magnifying glass to examine a leaf in his hands. Jack and the others surrounded him, expectantly. The caucheros working in the area had also crowded around. Jack looked troubled. I joined them and silently awaited the scientific opinion. The flapping wings of some white herons flying in pairs could be heard above. The expert looked up, put the magnifying glass away in his jacket pocket, and spoke quietly.

"*Microcyclus ulei*, it's hopeless," he said.

"What's that?" Jack asked.

The Japanese expert used his index finger to point at one tree and then the next.

"It's a terrible, devastating fungus that is transmitted by the leaves, from seringal to seringal. A leaf disease."

"How can it be controlled?" Frank asked.

The expert shook his head.

"Are all the trees planted in the same way, the same distance from each other?" he asked.

"Yes, all of them, there are almost seventy million plants," Jack said.

"It's hopeless then; sooner or later they will all die."

Frank grimaced and puffed on his pipe, making a small cloud of smoke. Nervously, he went over to the Japanese expert.

"Do you know who is behind us?" he asked him.

"Yes," the expert replied.

"So then, you are fully aware of who we are? Where we come from?"

"Yes, I suppose so," the expert responded.

"Then, you big idiot, explain why, why you believe that everything we have worked for all these years will come tumbling down just like that," Frank shouted at him.

The expert was impassive.

"Because the trees were planted very close together, and the disease has no obstacles to prevent it from spreading."

Frank bit his lip. Then he turned around toward me.

"Look, Argentino, look at this sorry little man defying Henry Ford's plans, and here we are listening to him as if he were a god. Bullshit! What he is saying is pure bullshit! We plucked you out of your hole and are paying you to help us," he went on, staring into the Japanese man's eyes, "not so you can spit in our face. So think of a solution fast!"

Jack intervened. He grabbed him by the arm and pushed him back violently.

"Shut up, leave him alone," he said.

"You're telling me to shut up, you who planted the trees this way so that one day they'd all die," Frank protested.

Jack held up his small axe and brandished it at him.

"One more word and I'll cut your throat," he threatened.

Frank stepped aside and was quiet.

"Why doesn't that fungus attack the trees in the jungle or the rubber plantations that were already there, the ones we left standing?" I asked.

"You too with your nonsense," Jack said.

"I'm not Frank, calm down," I said to him.

The expert looked toward the jungle.

"If you look carefully, between each rubber tree in the jungle you will see that there are almost fifty meters, a distance far enough to stop or neutralize the plague if it appears," he said.

"Is there any solution?" I insisted.

"None, except uprooting all of them and starting over," he said, as naturally as if he had said good morning.

Jack punched the palm of his left hand with his fist.

"I knew it, I knew it, from the very first day I knew it," he complained.

"So why didn't you warn us, you bastard!" Frank shouted.

Jack turned around and looked at Frank. I stepped between the two of them and restrained Jack by putting my hands on his chest.

"Calm down, let's see what we can do now," I said.

Jack pushed my hands off and stepped back.

"Shit! That's what we can do," he said, brandishing the ax in my direction.

We were silent. I looked around and realized that more workers had gathered to listen to our argument. Some of them were squatting down.

"How long will it take for the plague to spread throughout the plantation?" I asked the expert.

"I don't know. It could be a matter of days or months. But that's not the entire problem."

"There's more?" I asked.

"The fungus attracts insects. They will probably attack en masse," the Japanese man said.

"Mosquitoes?" I asked.

"Mosquitoes, mosquitoes, you don't understand anything, anything about anything," Jack interrupted.

"No, mosquitoes no," the expert said, "hymenopterons and orthopteons."

"What are they?" I asked.

The Japanese expert had a smug expression.

"Locusts, ants, beetles, it's hard to say," he said.

Frank came over to me and took my arm. He looked at the expert.

"Of course, yes, of course, there will also be another world war and they will bomb Fordlandia, Detroit, London, Paris, and then the planets will collide and everyone, absolutely everyone, will die. You are going to explain this to Rowwe. I refuse. Now let's go, Argentino, let's stop wasting time with these two witch doctors," Frank said.

The expert looked at him and shrugged his shoulders. Frank shot him a threatening look and headed for the village. I caught up to him and we walked away quickly, side by side. Along the way Frank complained about and insulted Jack and the Japanese expert. He was enraged. Every so often he looked to me for confirmation of his blasphemies. "Don't you think they're nothing more than a couple of imbeciles?" he asked me. "Maybe, who knows," I responded. "I do, I know, of course I know," Frank insisted. We climbed the hill along the shortest, narrowest path, which was partially overgrown, and then went down to the road leading to the main building. We arrived in no time. Rowwe was waiting for us at the entrance. His hands were on his hips and he looked very worried. After greeting us he asked us to follow him to his office. We went into his office, but none of us sat down. Frank went to the window and opened it. He took a deep breath. He was upset and had to cough. Rowwe looked at him and then at me.

"So? What's going on?" he asked, standing in the middle of the office.

"He says we're going to lose everything," Frank said.

"Who says?"

Frank remained by the window.

"Who else? That damn Japanese guy that Belem sent."

"Why are we going to lose everything?" Rowwe inquired.

Frank stretched out his arm and pointed to me.

Rowwe looked at me, intrigued. Beads of sweat had formed on his forehead. I took a cigarette out of my shirt pocket, lit it, and took a long drag.

"Are you going to speak or not?" Rowwe asked.

I looked him in the eye.

"The Japanese expert says that the plague is caused by a fungus that spreads from leaf to leaf and that there is no way to stop it," I said.

"A fungus is going to destroy us?"

"Yes, that's what he says."

"A fungus is going to stop us, we who invented the most colossal, most fabulous machine ever invented?"

Frank turned around.

"He's a bastard," he said.

"Give me your take," Rowwe asked.

Frank stretched out his arm with the palm of his hand facing down.

"He's like any other Japanese guy, short and puny," he said.

Rowwe turned red.

"The fungus, you idiot! What does the fungus look like!" he shouted.

Frank frowned and looked down.

"It's almost invisible," he said.

For an instant Rowwe was pensive, motionless. He put his index finger and thumb together and yelled, "A minuscule thing, this minuscule, a thing like this, is going to destroy us? Huh? Answer me! Huh?"

"Yes," I answered.

"That's impossible, and if you say it's so, you will have to be the one who explains it to Henry Ford. I won't do it!"

Rowwe turned around, picked up a chair, and smashed it against the wall. Then he went to his desk, gathered some folders that were scattered about, and threw them violently on the floor. He dropped into his chair and buried his face in his hands.

"Shit, shit, it's all shit," he repeated.

I took one last drag of my cigarette and threw it on the

ground, making sure to put it out so it didn't burn Rowwe's papers. Frank and I looked at each other. He shrugged and gestured with his hands, indicating that there was nothing left to say. After a while, I went over to Rowwe's desk.

"Rowwe, are you listening to me?" I asked him.

Rowwe opened his hands, revealing his face.

"If what you are going to say provides a solution, yes, if not, no," he said.

"I have an idea. While we call on another expert," I said in order to gain Frank's support, "why don't we try to isolate the plague, contain it to where it has already developed by burning the trees, creating a barrier to protect the remaining ones? Sacrifice a part to save the whole?"

There was a long silence. Then Rowwe dropped his hands and got up. He walked around the desk and came over to me. His eyes were clouded over.

"How will you know where the plague has spread to and which trees to set fire to? On whom will you rely?"

It was a fair objection. I hesitated and replied,

"On Jack."

Frank stepped away from the window.

"Jack is a traitor. He thinks everything is lost."

Rowwe looked over his shoulder at Frank.

"That's right, don't count on Jack, he's through," he said to me.

"I'll go with Enéas then. First with Enéas and then with the health patrol," I said.

"How many acres will you burn, approximately?"

"I'm not sure, maybe twenty thousand, thirty thousand."

"How long will it take?"

"Maybe a week or two."

Rowwe just looked at me for a moment, weighing my suggestion, and although his expression was unchanged, the muscles in his face tightened. Frank came over to us.

"Sacrifice a part to save the whole. Good idea, boy, a good idea, go ahead, do it, set fire," Rowwe said.

Frank agreed and slapped my arm.

"I'll go with Enéas tomorrow and mark off the affected area," I said.

Then I said good-bye and left the office. When I opened the door, several office workers, who had crowded together in the hallway trying to hear our conversation, looked at me, waiting for some revealing comment. I went to my office and locked myself in. Through the windows I could see the village and the square. It was a bright day and the colors were vivid. I saw the Japanese expert arriving with Jack. His diagnosis had impressed me, but I wanted to make a final attempt, perhaps foolish, to try and remedy what appeared to be irremediable. In addition, if things turned out as the expert predicted, my life would soon change. I read Caroline's letter again carefully. I wondered if, in the event that the plague put an end to the plantation, I would be able to continue with the Ford Company in the United States or in Europe and continue to see Caroline. Probably not. During the winter I had thought about the possibility the plantation would fail, but, clearly it's one thing to think about failure and another for it to happen. I heard the Japanese expert and Jack arguing with Rowwe in the hallway, and then I saw them pass by on their way back to the village. The expert was walking calmly, but Jack looked deeply depressed. I put Caroline's letter in my pocket and left. One of Rowwe's assistants delivered a message from me to Enéas, notifying him to come find me early the next morning. I walked, slowly, and for a long time. I went over in my head what I had said to Rowwe. I corrected myself; my proposal did not consist of sacrificing a part to save the whole; it meant, simply and directly, going down with the ship. It was a moment of triumph for the jungle. Its attack had been unexpected and vengeful. I suddenly felt as if I had already lived through these circumstances. I went to the store to buy the newspaper from Belem and headed to the restaurant. As I was eating, two Brazilian officials came over to me to inquire as to the origins of the plague and the future of the plantation. I would have preferred to be alone, but I had coffee with them and told them what I knew. Then I paid and went home. I closed the bedroom window and drew the curtains. I filled a glass with whiskey and, sitting on the bed, passed the time reading the newspaper. In Brazil there were peasant uprisings, and a revolutionary process was under way. A box in the sports section reported on Argentine soccer, and it mentioned that the leading scorer of the championship was the center-forward from Boca Juniors. I picked up the bottle that I had set on the floor and poured myself another drink. I drank until I was completely drunk. Then I lay down on the bed and fell asleep. That night the temperature fell, and the sounds of the jungle could not be heard.

XX

For the second day in a row Enéas walked slowly through the plantation, without any indication that there was a serious problem. He wore a straw hat, and his hair hung down below the crumpled brim. He told me that he had left his hut before dawn, and it was obvious from his face. He looked as if he were sleepwalking. I, on the other hand, had slept well, but I was nervous. I had never entered so deeply into the plantation before, and it felt strange to walk up and down the uneven terrain in the middle of all those trees, surrounded by the silence and stillness of the jungle. The landscape was magnificent, and the atmosphere was shrouded in mystery. The mild air, still filled with humidity, released whisps of fog toward the sky, which was now completely clear. We walked along together, and two foremen and a team of workers followed a few feet behind, ready to mark off the boundaries as I indicated.

Some areas had been hit hard by the plague, and the trees were devastated. Every so often I would stop to examine, as best I could, the dying leaves and trunks and then resume my course toward the southern boundary. Everything I had seen until that point was contaminated and in accordance with my plan had to be set on fire. During a break I informed the foremen. They agreed; Enéas showed neither opposition nor enthusiasm. The previous day we had performed a test on the well-marked paths in the western zone. We hauled a few cans of fuel to the area and sprinkled it over more than a kilometer of trees and foliage. No sooner had we thrown the lit torch than the wooded area became a flaming mass, and we had to retreat in a hurry to prevent the suffocating smoke from overtaking us.

It must have been nine or ten in the morning when we stopped at a tallymen's cabin for coffee and a smoke. The tallymen were disheartened by the situation. We then continued south. My plan was to arrive at the last cabin in the southern zone after midday. We took a path that bordered the uncultivated jungle, making our way through slowly, brushing back the growth that was covering the path. On our right, there were rows of young rubber trees. On our left was an abundant and thick wall of vegetation that looked like it was about to fall on top of us. The ground was soft and moist, and it was muddy in spots. Above the jungle the heat began to rise, the cicadas sang in their shrill tone, and in the interior of the forest, birds chirped softly. All around it smelled of fermented sap and humidity.

At one point I had the feeling we were being watched from the dense growth. It was completely quiet, but my intuition made me uneasy. It was then that the first of that morning's many disgraces occurred. I told Enéas how I was feeling. Enéas stopped, looked toward the jungle, and shrugged. I went over to him and offered him a cigarette. "The older you are, the more afraid you get," I said. Enéas smiled and took a cigarette wrapped in gold paper from his pants pocket. But I insisted, and Enéas put his cigarette away, took one of mine, and carefully placed it between his lips. "A good cigarette scares away the fears," he said to me. He just stood there, his legs apart, his hands in his pockets, and the cigarette dangling from one corner of his mouth. He looked calm. I lit a match and cupped my hands so he could light the cigarette. Enéas took a step forward and leaned over my hands. His back was to the jungle, and for a second his head was even with my chest. Suddenly I heard a buzzing in the air and a sharp blow, like a punch to the chin. Enéas reeled and lost his balance, as if his heart had stopped. As he collapsed I caught him by the arms, and I saw the arrow sticking out of the middle of his back. I looked deep into the bushes, and through the leaves and branches I thought I saw the fierce face of Teró. I heard more buzzing in the air, and, driven by the miserable and obscene instinct to survive, I lifted Enéas's body up and pressed it against me, shielding myself from the furtive attack. The second arrow sunk into Enéas's neck. I took a few steps back, his body still pressed against mine, and then I let myself fall to the ground, between the rubber trees. I propped Enéas up next to me and used my hand to support his back. A trickle of blood ran down his chest toward his waist. When I took hold of the arrow in his neck, with the intention of yanking it out, he looked at me in an extraordinary, profound, and familiar way, and he asked me not to.

"Let me die," he murmured.

"It's not right, amigo, don't go," I said.

Enéas closed his eyes for an instant and then opened them again. His eyes were filled with a strange glow.

"All men die, but some, like you, truly live. I couldn't," he stammered.

"That's not true, Enéas. You are a great person, forgive me."

His eyes, sparkling and inquisitive, captivated me. I gently ran my hand through his hair. Shortly after, he let out a short breath, and the sparkle in his eyes vanished. He died in my arms with a peaceful expression on his face. I removed the arrows from his body, dried the blood on his mouth with a handkerchief, laid him on the ground, and placed his straw hat atop his bare chest.

A long time passed before I could forget Enéas's death and the circumstances surrounding it. It was clear that the intended victim of the attack had been me and that destiny had favored me once again. I stayed there next to the body, frightened and dazed. After a while my hatred won out over my fear. I don't know if it was my past, my friendship with Enéas, the problems at the plantation, or a combination of everything. But I set out in search of revenge. I stood up, ordered the foremen to take charge of the body, and then, stumbling, falling, and getting back up again, I ran toward the village. I was in a hurry to get home, get my gun, and set off for the Munduruku village in search of Teró. On the last hill I bumped into Jack. He tried to detain me, taking hold of my arm and asking me what had happened, but I kept going. The hatred and confusion did not let me speak. I entered my house and went into the bedroom. I looked for my backpack and put the gun inside along with two cartridges, the straw hat, some cigarettes, maps, and a bottle of liquor. Then I took some money from a drawer and left for the dock. There were three boats belonging to the company moored there. I argued with the guard, saying I had to leave on an urgent mission for a few days, and I told them to give me four cans full of gasoline. Rowwe, I said, would deliver the departure and boarding permits later. They listened to me suspiciously, but while the boss was talking on the phone with the main office requesting authorization, two of his subordinates were already bringing the gas cans. I quickly loaded them, untied the lines, and jumped aboard the boat.

I started the motor and took off. I had to go with the current, and I estimated that it would take me a day and a half to reach the village. It was very possible, however, that I might make contact with Teró much sooner. That depended on whether, after committing the crime, he chose to come out of the jungle and head home immediately in his canoe. That was the scenario that best suited my plans. As I sped along, I yearned with all my heart for the moment I would find myself face-to-face with Teró. I wanted revenge, death and revenge, and I wanted to be rid of him, like a bad dream. Luck was on my side. A few kilometers upriver, on a deserted sandy beach on the right bank—which was also property of Fordlandia—I spotted Teró with another native. He was sitting down, relaxing in the sun. There were two canoes on the beach. Since the Munduruku traveled in groups of two or more, I assumed there were other natives in the area. In one of the canoes, in addition to oars, there were arrows, nets, and spears. I slowed the motor and pointed it to the beach. When the boat was almost scraping bottom, I dropped anchor and jumped out. Teró and his friend had stood up as soon as they noticed the boat heading their way. They looked surprised. They were daubed and hid their nudity with frayed cloths. I wasted no time. I seized the gun, removed the safety catch, and went to meet Teró, who was also walking toward me. He moved proudly, confidently, as if he were expecting me to get out of his way. He seemed to be smiling, which may have been the effect of the paint on his face. We stopped a few feet from each other. I raised my gun and aimed it at his chest. He looked calm, cold, unfathomable. We looked at each other without lowering our eyes.

"Your end has come, evil Indian," I shouted. Teró raised his hands, his palms up, indicating that he was unarmed. I thought about whether or not that Indian deserved to die heroically, defenseless, with a bullet to his chest. I hesitated for a few seconds. Then I dropped the gun on the sand and unleashed all the rage and contempt I felt for myself on that wretched Indian. Yelling, I rushed at him and attacked. A relentless silent brawl broke out between the two of us. That Indian was strong, and even though I was taller than he was, he knocked me down twice. I managed to hit him squarely a few times with my fists and my legs. Then we grabbed hold of each other desperately, by our arms and heads, and we fell to the sand in a tight hold as we continued fighting, sweating, and hitting each other.

When I was young I was intrigued by the slums, and at times had come up against troublemakers. But that was the first time I had kept up a fight from beginning to end, with real warlike rage and every kind of blow and attack. Blood gushed from my mouth, and there was blood on my hands. But the fight was wonderful; it made sense—living, landing blows, bleeding, drawing blood. We rolled toward the shore. We turned over and over, and in a second my feet were in the water and I found myself on top of him, squeezing his neck with all my might. I had his life between my hands and I longed to put an end to him once and for all. But Teró endured the pressure, and with a decisive effort he managed to shift my body by moving his arms and his legs and reverse our position. I was now on bottom, my feet on the sand and my head in the water. Teró butted me on the forehead with his head. Then he put his knee on my chest and made a kind of crowbar by putting his forehead and fist across my neck and chin, pushing downward to submerge me, to drown me in the water, as if I were a pup. Remorseless horror shone in his eyes. He was on the verge of achieving his goal. The water flooded my lungs, and I felt myself about to pass out when his muscles relaxed and he collapsed on top of me. I sat up on my elbows and shoved him off me. I leaned over a little farther and saw him, floating next to me, facedown, and I pushed him out into the river.

Bubbles broke on the water's surface around his head. I did not understand the sudden outcome of the fight until I looked up, and against the sunlight I saw the silhouette of Theo, the German priest. He was standing there, with a small log in one hand, offering me the other so I could get up. I accepted, sat up in the water, rinsed off my face, and coughed. Exhausted, I sat there, coughing, surprised by that ending, even though such a tragedy, the second time around, ceases to be terrifying. Theo seemed happy to have been there at the right time and for having landed a good blow to the back of the Indian's neck. Somewhat joyously he said, "The Lord protects his flock."

I stood up, coughed again, and looked toward the river. Teró's body was slowly sinking in a tide pool. On the beach, Theo's young native assistant was aiming my gun at Teró's young friend. Theo swung the log and threw it in the water. Then he squatted down and washed his hands, sticking them in the small waves that washed up onshore.

"Now it's your turn," he said gravely as he stood up.

"What do you mean?" I asked.

Theo pointed to the Munduruku native.

"Him," he said.

I looked over at the two natives. Theo's assistant had now climbed a sand dune and continued to aim at the Munduruku, who remained still, waiting. He looked over his shoulder at us. He was small and fragile. In his right hand he was holding a wooden spear.

"What's wrong with him?" I asked Theo.

"Nothing really, but you have to kill him," Theo said.

I looked at him, in disbelief.

"I have no reason to do that," I responded.

Theo ran his hand behind his neck and slowly began to walk toward his canoe. He took a few steps and then turned around. He looked at me, shook his head with an air of annoyance, and kept walking. When he got to his canoe he reached in and pulled out a black book, opened it, read, and raised his eyes. There was not a single cloud in the sky. The sun was setting, forming no shadows on the beach. A pair of herons were flying high, very high in the sky, toward the west. Theo left the book in the canoe and went over to the sand dune. He was twice as tall as his assistant. He took the gun away from him and ushered the Munduruku over to the shore, where I was. The native walked alongside, frightened. He couldn't have been more than fifteen. He stopped in front of me, looked at me, and then looked down, resigned to his fate. His face began to cringe. He was crying. Theo stood next to me, continuing to aim at him.

"Do you want a war with them?" he asked me.

"No."

"I just saved your life, right?"

"Yes."

Theo handed me the gun with the butt facing me.

"Then kill him!"

"I can't do that, there's no reason," I answered firmly.

Theo took hold of the gun again, annoyed.

"It's simple. If you don't kill him, he will run off to his tribe and tell them what happened, and then you will have serious problems. Or perhaps you want to die here in the jungle, here at the end of the world? Is that what you want?"

I felt ashamed. His attempt to convince me was useless. I stood in front of Theo and looked straight at him.

Theo took a handkerchief from his pocket and dried the sweat from his forehead. He lowered the gun for a moment.

"I came for Teró because he tried to kill me this morning, but he killed my assistant, Enéas, instead. That was all, and the matter is closed."

"How do you know it was Teró if I saw him here fishing just two hours ago?" Theo asked me.

I did not want to argue and so I said nothing. Theo changed his tone and continued.

"One way or another you have to kill that Indian. If you don't, your boss's visit will be tarnished by bloodshed and turmoil."

"What do you know about Henry Ford's visit?"

The Munduruku stepped back. Theo cocked the gun, aimed it at him, and shouted something in his language. The Munduruku was trembling.

"Here everyone knows everything. Perhaps you are unaware that Mr. Ford will visit the village in the next few days? Remember our deal," he said.

I thought about the comments that Frank and Rowwe had made about the plague. They, too, had mentioned Ford as if they would soon have to give him an explanation. I looked at the Munduruku and then at Theo.

"Let him go, Theo, please. No innocent man deserves to die."

"That reasoning does not work, son, least of all here," he said. "Or perhaps you believe that conquering this kingdom is a farce? That the world is a farce? Or he, or they, or we . . . don't you get it? There is never just one culprit. Kill him! Kill him once and for all!" he ordered.

I had only one choice. Take the gun and force Theo to back off and to leave that Indian in peace. I controlled my anger and reached my hand out toward him. But the instant Theo offered me the gun, the Indian took off for his canoe running, and in a second, with a single dry, bloodcurdling noise, it was all over. In one single, simple movement, Theo, with his quick reflexes, had seized the gun again and hit the fugitive in the back. The native fell to the ground, flat on his face, mortally wounded. I ran after him and tried in vain to lift him in my arms. Theo walked right by me, without stopping, on his way to his canoe. He dropped the gun on the sand. I looked at him.

"You're a murderer," I said.

"Only a twisted man can talk that way to the one who saved his life. You poor thing. You don't love your own nor do you hate your enemies," he replied.

Theo called to his assistant and got in the canoe. The assistant pushed it into the water and they left. They had barely set off when Theo leaned forward a bit, his hands on the edge of the canoe.

"We'll see each other soon, son. We'll see each other when Ford arrives. And don't forget our pact," he yelled.

I remained on the beach. I don't know how much time went by. It made no difference whether I stayed there. My mouth was swollen and my tongue was dry, and it was difficult to spit. My body ached. I rested on my back on the sand, watching the birds soaring. Way up in the sky some clouds offered a sensation of absolute calm, but my spirit was in turmoil. Enéas's death, even though he had never really been my friend, made me extremely sad. I sat up and smoked as I thought. The silence of the jungle was magnified by the silence of the water, creating an extraordinary effect. I recalled my childhood and the long conversations with my mother. "The years don't change our essence, and one always ends up getting used to the course of our destiny," she would say. Around dusk, when the first shadows appeared, I put the body of the Indian in the Munduruku canoe and dragged it toward the current. Before letting go I picked up an arrow from among the many on the ground. It was just like the ones that had ended Enéas's life. I let the canoe go and watched it for a moment as it slipped down the river. Then I swam after it, grabbed on to the stern and turned it around. It had no keel. The Indian's body disappeared down the Tapajós. I swam over to my boat, climbed over the side, started the motor, took a long swig of liquor, and headed for Fordlandia.

———

The return trip seemed shorter than the outbound journey. By the time I reached the village it had begun to grow dark. As soon as I spotted the lights and the dock in Fordlandia I decided to throw the gun into the river. There was my house. My only thought at that moment was that that house offered refuge, peace, light, protection. But I was not a hero who returns from battle wounded. I didn't sleep that night. The sun had not yet risen when I went to see Rowwe. I told him that I wanted nothing to do with the problems of the plantation and I expressed my desire to leave the village as soon as possible. It was then that Rowwe told me of Henry Ford's imminent visit.

XXI

Suddenly the thundering of a plane filled the sky. It swooped over the village twice before gliding gently and landing on the Tapajós. The people who had been waiting in the square since early that morning applauded and watched, in amazement, as the plane came to a stop. As soon as the skids of the plane began to glide across the water, the crowd, which Rowwe had organized in a military-like formation, broke, and ran toward the edge of the high riverbank. Rowwe, the Americans, and I were all on the dock. Rowwe elbowed me and pointed at the plane. "We are also responsible for that technology," he said proudly. I nodded and remained silent. "Come on, boy, smile, you are about to see God in person. What's wrong with you?" Rowwe kept on. I looked at him and backed away. I was thinking about Enéas. His death continued to wrench my heart. Rowwe looked at me disapprovingly, straightened his tie, and went over to Frank. He whispered something in his ear. Frank turned toward the people who were crammed together on the edge of the riverbank and shrugged.

The Americans were euphoric over Henry Ford's visit; their

eyes were filled with an inflated pride. Ford would only be in the village until the late afternoon, and Rowwe, as had been agreed upon with the office in Belem, was put in charge of planning the agenda and the welcoming festivities. The schedule included a ceremony that had been planned for the square and for which a platform had been set up facing away from the river, a ride through the village in a convertible Model A Ford, the christening of the school with the name of the illustrious visitor, a stop at the hospital and the factory, a private banquet, replete with a variety of local dishes, and, finally, meetings with the authorities. At some point in the afternoon, Ford would meet with Jack, Antonio, and me. Theo, who would be officiating at the christening ceremony, had arrived at dawn with several other residents of Jocotá, including the mathematics teacher, who was also lobbying for a meeting. A financier who had come from Rio de Janeiro was also soliciting a meeting; when he had been denied permission by Rowwe to moor at the dock the previous day, he had anchored his luxury boat in the middle of the river. Nobody knew for sure how he had found out about Ford's visit, but he intended to see him in hopes of convincing him to invest in a fantastic project that dealt with the exploitation of iron mines in the jungle. The Americans said that that guy, who had been born and raised in New York, had lost most of his fortune and dozens of men because of an obsession with the construction of a railway in the extreme southwest Amazon.

Rowwe had arranged for a band to accompany the scheduled activities. Ford would speak to the single residents from the platform, and then he would walk through the streets and greet the married couples. Rowwe had instructed the couples to wait outside their homes for Ford to pass by. The banquet was for Ford's entourage only, and the only officials from the village who were invited to join in were Rowwe and Frank. There was another menu for the officials, which was served in the movie hall, and a feast and dance were organized for the workers in three sheds that had been air conditioned especially for the occasion. Rowwe had taken precautions; the night before, a patrol had searched all the houses and sheds and confiscated all cigarettes and alcohol. The report that would be given to Ford, however, contained all the makings of a catastrophe (the plague already covered seventy percent of the plantation), and as I saw it, it was very unlikely that the music, the food, or the displays of affection and admiration would soften the heart and ears of the supreme leader.

When the propellers stopped spinning and the plane had come to a stop about a hundred meters from the dock, Rowwe boarded a motorboat and went to meet Ford. One of the doors on the plane opened, revealing the figure of a man. The band thought it was Ford, and it launched into a popular march by Sousa. Rowwe raised his hands, exasperated, and ordered the band to stop. The music stopped as quickly as it had begun. The man, the director of the Belem office, waved to Rowwe and went back inside the plane. Ford had flown to Belem, where he had had a top-secret meeting with the governor of Pará and then had transferred to the jungle by hydroplane. At the suggestion of the director of the Belem office, an agrarian scientist had been included in the entourage. A moment later I saw Harry appear, and finally, after him, came Ford, who looked up at the sky and then waved toward the shore. Rowwe signaled to his assistants, who blew their whistles, and the people, who were crowded together along the riverbank, responded with an ovation. The band began to play again. Ford smiled and nimbly climbed down onto the deck of the motorboat. The financier was at the bow of his boat, watching what was going on through binoculars. As soon as Ford sat down in the boat, the financier's boat sounded its horn. Ford turned toward the boat without losing his smile. The financier raised his arms, but Ford watched him indifferently. As the boat moved toward the dock, the guard made sure that the workers returned to the square. Ford climbed the stairs, still smiling, escorted by Harry and by Rowwe, and he greeted us one by one. The line began with Frank, who was followed by Rowwe's assistants, Jack, and, finally, me. Ford walked with exaggerated steps. His hands were like a pianist's, long and thin, and they were in constant motion. He wore a cream-colored English-style linen suit, a white shirt, a felt hat, and no tie. The ring of wrinkles around his eyes emphasized his ingenuous smile. As I stretched out my hand and introduced myself, Ford stopped for a second and looked at me carefully.

"Argentine, right?"

"Yes, sir."

"The Argentine, well, well. I'll talk to you later," he said.

Rowwe, who was next to me, patted me on the shoulder, satisfied. Then he went with Ford to the end of the dock, where they greeted the maestro, and then into the car and slowly climbed the hill, amid the collective roar, toward the platform. Ford's speech was brief, too brief perhaps, but the people, who didn't understand a word anyway, applauded his words enthusiastically. Making no gestures, Ford spoke: "I am happy to meet a new civilization, the civilization of tomorrow. I am happy to have laid the foundations for a place unlike any other, removed from the filth and depravation of the cities. I ask you to continue in this way, in peace and harmony, and with respect, as, slowly but surely, our values will triumph throughout the jungle, throughout all the jungles and all the world, and what will happen here will be an example for all of mankind. Thank you. Thank you very much," he said, and then he glanced around him, sighing excitedly.

After his speech, the band struck up again. A flock of magpies, tired of all the racket, flew off in search of the opposite shore. Ford pointed to the flock and remarked to his colleagues how they seemed to be in such a hurry. A locust with grayish wings came to rest on Rowwe's shoulder. Ford picked it up with his fingers and forced it to fly off. The locust flew around in circles but came back to rest on Rowwe's shoulder. "One of you must be feeding it; if not, it wouldn't come back so quickly," Ford said, alluding to Rowwe in a joking manner. Rowwe took the remark seriously, but Harry, Frank, and the rest of the group burst out laughing.

I saw Ford again that afternoon. I had to wait almost an hour at the school, in a classroom next to the room where the officials were meeting. The school had been painted white, and the interior walls were decorated with photographs that depicted the history of the automobile and of the company. Two armed guards, who were standing next to the door to the meeting room, ensured the privacy of Ford's meetings. I sat on a wooden bench and waited. Jack and Antonio were also there waiting. They were both pondering the outcome of the brief meeting they would soon have with Ford. Success or failure? Light or darkness? Promotion or downfall? The atmosphere in the classroom was filled with such conjecture.

I recalled those nights when a friend, an accomplished poet, had asked for my advice on scheming a way to meet President Alvear in a café in downtown Buenos Aires. It was not vanity on his part but rather desperation. A recommendation from Alvear, even if scribbled on a napkin from that old café, would have enabled him to support himself. Since then I had thought that the elusive compassion of a powerful person can set the life of a man with simple ambitions on the right track. In the past, I had been energized by those moments of tension that precede an important event, and I would have waited for Henry Ford with the same excitement as Jack and Antonio, but that afternoon my expectations were reduced to the chance to meet a genuine legend. Nothing more. Antonio desperately wanted funding to invent a machine that would make it possible to study the workings of the human brain, and Jack had brought the plans of the prototype of his engine and was anxious to tell Ford about his innovations, with the hope that it would change his life.

Jack was quiet, pensive, but Antonio talked to me almost nonstop. I felt as if he were rehearsing the arguments that he would put forward to Ford. "If it is agreed that the body of wild animals starts with the throat, where do you think the human body starts?" He asked me right off. "In the eyes," I responded. "You're mistaken. The starting point is the brain, and we know nothing, absolutely nothing, about it. We don't know what it does when we are awake and even less when we are asleep," he assured me. Just then the door to the room opened and Harry came out. He walked over to the three of us, holding a piece of paper. He spoke to Antonio abruptly, asking him to jot down quickly and briefly the reasons he wanted to see Ford. Antonio held the sheet of paper up against my back and wrote down a few words. He handed the paper to Harry and remained standing, undaunted, waiting for a response. Harry returned quickly. Ford would grant him a position in the hospital in Detroit with the only condition being that instead of studying the human brain, he research the possibility of extracting medicines from tropical plants and fruit. Antonio received the news as if he had just won the lottery. He got up with a triumphant shout and gave Jack and me a long hug. Harry interrupted the celebration, reminding us that Ford was waiting. Jack picked up his plans, straightened himself, and headed toward the room. I followed two steps behind.

The atmosphere in the room was not the warmest. Rowwe and Frank looked as if they were at a funeral. Their faces were serious, and there was an intensity in their eyes. Ford was seated at the head of a rectangular table. He was frowning, and he looked tired, as if he had seen more than he could take in. I saw that he was clutching a book in his hands. As soon as he saw us he smiled, put the book down, and directed us where to sit, one at the other end of the table and the other two on opposite sides. Harry walked around the table, whispered something in Ford's ear, and then sat down next to him, on his left. There was a long silence. Ford looked at Jack.

"Let's let Jack say what he wants to say, and then we'll listen to Horacio. I can call you Horacio, right?" he asked me.

I responded with a confidence that I did not feel.

"Yes, of course."

Ford nodded without saying anything. Jack opened his plans and put them on the table. His hands were trembling. He hesitated and then said, "Mr. Ford, in my free time I have developed a six-cylinder engine that starts automatically and is cooled by a water pump. I would like you to see the plans that I brought, and if you wish, I can also show you how it works. I think that with these innovations, our cars will be very successful, incredibly successful."

Ford raised his eyebrows. Edsel, after a trip through Europe some weeks back, had suggested similar innovations, assuring him that they would soon be the order of the day in the automobile industry.

"Let me see those plans," he ordered, not looking at anybody.

Harry got up, took the plans out of Jack's hands, and handed them to Ford. Ford looked them over for a second. Then he shook his head disdainfully and gave them back to Harry. He spoke without addressing anyone in particular, and his tone had changed.

"I am not the slightest bit interested. Six-cylinder engines are only viable for the luxury market. I travel thousands of kilometers to find out about a failure, and those responsible for that failure not only do not want to assume responsibility, although they will, in fact, assume it, but some of them even pretend to work and think like mechanical engineers."

Ford let his eyes fall on Rowwe, and he continued, "One question, Jack, just one. Did anyone warn you in all this time that a plague could destroy the plantation if the trees were planted as they are? Tell me, yes or no?"

"No, sir."

"Do you think, as biologists do, including the one we brought with us today, that the fungus will wipe out everything we have done here?"

"Yes sir, I do."

"Do you know anything about the natural sciences?"

"I've learned a few things here, sir."

"Did you bother to study any more?"

"No, sir."

"Do you think your knowledge is sufficient to give well-founded opinions?"

"No, I don't, sir."

"I could say, then, that you don't know anything?"

"It's possible."

"Well, my boy, you don't know anything. Thank you for your efforts. You can go now."

Jack got up, walked slowly to the head of the table, shook Ford's hand, picked up his plans, and left.

Ford was silent for a moment, then stood up. Harry also got up and indicated that we should all do the same. We obeyed. Addressing Harry, Ford said, "Does anybody else wish to see me?"

"Yes, Harry, the priest who was at the ceremony this morning. His name is Theo, and he wants help for his work in the jungle."

"Oh, the fat guy. What kind of fellow is he?" Ford asked.

"You know him well, right?" Harry inquired of Rowwe.

Before Rowwe could answer I raised my hand.

"May I tell you what I think, sir?" I asked, addressing Ford.

Harry looked at me, disgusted. Ford nodded his head.

"That priest is an opportunistic adventurer. He does things only for his own advantage. So I suggest that you not give him a meeting and that you not give him money either," I said.

Ford walked over to me. He stopped by my side and from there addressed the rest of the group. He appeared thinner and shorter than he had that morning.

"Well, gentlemen, that's enough for today. What I have to discuss with this young man can be done while we walk. Get me my straw hat and make sure no one bothers us on our walk."

Harry and Rowwe looked at each other, surprised by their boss's behavior. Then Rowwe walked over to a cabinet, opened it, took out the hat, and handed it to Ford respectfully. Ford took off his jacket and put on his hat, folding the brim downward. He looked like a peasant on a holiday.

"Which way should we go?" he asked Rowwe.

"This way," Rowwe said, and he hurried to the school's side door, which opened onto the back of the square.

Rowwe opened the door and stepped aside, like a hotel porter. In the meantime, Harry went to look for a guard. Ford gestured for me to follow, and we left together. We skirted the school and began to walk along a gray stone path that led down to the riverbank. Harry, Rowwe, Frank, and a guard followed a few feet behind. In the distance we could hear the lively music from the workers' celebration. The sunlight was beginning to fade. Ford walked along for a while, saying nothing.

All of a sudden he took me by the arm. He pointed to a tree on the path.

"It's a mango, right?" he asked me.

"Yes, it is."

"Have you had the chance to see the Amazon and our territory from above, in a plane?"

"No, no sir."

"Ah, it's a dream, a simply marvelous dream."

Ford looked over his shoulder.

"Tell me, Horacio, tell me the truth. Rowwe and that guy Frank are a couple of idiots, aren't they?"

"I think so, sir."

"I thought so. It's impossible to fail here. So much wealth within reach, just waiting to be seized!"

Ford looked up at the sky and continued. I was glad he did not ask me anything about my life or about why I was there.

"Do you know whose idea it was to name this place after me?"

"I don't, sir."

"Sir, sir, can't you leave out the 'sir,' Horacio?"

I shrugged.

"I had an assistant who always referred to me as 'mi blanco,' " I said to him.

"Yes, but you and I have the same color skin. Are there many blacks in Argentina?"

"No."

"And Jews?"

"Yes, they're an important group."

"That's not good."

I looked at him. Ford sensed my bewilderment and turned toward me.

"Yes, that's not good," he said.

I did not respond, and we kept walking. Ford stopped several times to watch the birds flying overhead. At one point a paca crossed the path.

"Do you believe in reincarnation," he asked me.

"I don't know much about it."

"I am interested in the influence the past has in determining who we really are. For example, I believe that when a person dies, his spirit goes into a newborn. If the man who dies is a creator, his spirit will make the baby a genius like Leonardo da Vinci or Edison. On the other hand," he said pointing to the spot where the paca raced by, "he surely got screwed in his previous life."

Ford laughed at his own remark. Then I reached into my pocket and took out an old newspaper clipping that talked about (and caricatured) Ford's presence in the Amazon. I showed it to him. Ford took it in his hands and, with a magnifying glass that he removed from his pocket, looked it over carefully. He repeated the title of the article with a hint of pride.

" 'Civilization and Work.' May I keep it?"

"Yes, of course. It's for you."

Satisfied, Ford smiled, turned around, and called to Harry. Harry ran to catch up to us.

Ford told him to save the article. Then we kept going until we reached the river. I saw a small boat setting off from the financier's larger one and heading toward shore. There were three people aboard. On the edge of the riverbank, the village police were standing guard.

"Do you know what life was like for Leonardo da Vinci, the inventor of the bicycle?"

"I've read a bit about him," I said.

"Perhaps you know how I started out?" Ford asked.

"Not really."

"I was working as chief mechanic at Edison Illuminating, and at night, every night, in a small workshop that I had set up on the back patio of the house I was renting on Bagley Avenue in Detroit, I spent all my free time, going without rest, assembling a machine, my automobile. It was my obsession, my boy, my great obsession. I defied everybody. I made my way, defying even my father. I had an assistant, the good Mr. Bishop. Late one rainy summer night, after many months, we finished our work. I felt, son, felt, yes, that's the word, that that machine was going to change everything. Nothing would be the same, nothing on Earth would remain the same after seeing my machine. I told Bishop that I wanted to test it right there, in the streets of Detroit, that very night, but he objected. 'Henry, it's late,' he said, 'and we might get in trouble with the police or with the horse-drawn carriages. Let's go tomorrow, early,' he said. 'No, Bishop, no, it will be tested now or never. Don't you understand what is happening? Don't you realize that we are initiating a new era, a new era for mankind, that we will be immortal?' I asked him, determined. Bishop was convinced, and we agreed that he would go in front on his bicycle in order to avoid problems. Bishop left his house on his bicycle, and I, my boy, pulled the throttle, turned the crank, and when my car had come to life, when that little engine began to roar like a little lion in the middle of the jungle warning his kingdom, I got in and took off. It had chain traction, like a bicycle, and the seat was also like a bicycle's. But it was much more than that, it was an automobile, a vehicle with a combustion engine. In the blink of an eye I left Bishop behind. Ha! I went down Grand Avenue to Washington Boulevard. Eight miles an hour. There goes crazy Henry, with his diabolical toy, changing the world, in the rain, at eight miles an hour," Ford spoke nostalgically.

I thought about Jack. I went over to him and said, "Jack also worked very hard to show you his machine."

I noticed that he was barely paying attention to me. His answer was not what I was expecting.

"My father," he said, "didn't even want to get in. A week later, we went with Clara and little Edsel to his farm. My entire family was amazed by my automobile, the neighbors clamored around me, the press wanted to photograph me. But he, stubborn and indifferent, did not move one step beyond the door to the house."

We reached the riverbank. Ford stared at the flowing current. The small boat was now approaching the shore. The guards grouped together and ordered him to go back. A stout bald man stood up in the boat and, with a loudspeaker in his hands, began to shout "Henry, Henry." The guards took out their weapons and threatened him. Ford noticed what was going on and asked me to order them to let him speak.

"Henry, I want to team up with you on a great project—iron mines in the southern Amazon. It's a fantastic project. Please, let's talk about it. Forget about rubber. Listen to me, please."

Ford brought his open hands up to his mouth.

"What do you know about rubber? The entire world needs rubber; automobiles, industry, everyone is desperate for rubber. What do you know?"

"The rubber here is cursed. I failed. I wanted to build a railway to carry the rubber. I had a fleet of boats for transportation and I lost a fortune, millions of dollars. That's why I am proposing iron, believe me, I know what I am talking about."

Ford shook his head from side to side. Then he shouted, "Who are you?"

"Don't you remember me? Percival, the Titan, we met in New York."

"Tell me, Percival, why should I trust a man who has failed? Eh? Why? What's more, you should know that the time for dreaming, for creativity, has ended in this world. If you're living in a dreamworld, then so be it," Ford replied.

The man was quiet. Ford made a gesture of disapproval and turned his back on him. The little boat slowly headed back toward the larger boat. Ford began to retrace his steps, and Harry, Frank, and Rowwe surrounded him. Ford stepped off to one side of the path and called to me. I went over to him. He looked at me intensely, and I noticed the preoccupation in the depths of his hollowed eyes. He spoke very softly.

"I know that you want to leave. I've heard that you are a courageous man. If you choose to continue with the company, there's a spot for you as Harry's assistant. In Detroit there are also disturbances like those you had here, and you can lend Harry a hand. Or, if you want to stay in the jungle, you can join us in the search for revenge. But if you do not continue with us, I'd like to know what your price is."

It was then that I understood the reason for our walk. But I wanted to hear him say it.

"I don't understand, sir."

"Nobody can ever know that things turned out badly here, that I couldn't succeed with these deformed and impassive giants. Least of all Edsel, my son. I will keep going, I will do battle in another era, maybe downriver. My mind is made up. We'll leave this territory and occupy another. But I don't want to hear a word about this unsuccessful experience that unfortunately bears my name, not a word, ever. Let the devil himself cover it up! Trees don't talk about the tragedies they cause, but men do. I have to look out for myself. What is the price for your silence, Horacio? What is it?"

The others were watching us, waiting.

"Tickets and money for me and Caroline."

"Who is she? A sweetheart?"

"Something like that."

"Women are harmless. Well, my boy, it's a deal. I'll have Harry arrange the tickets."

Ford smiled. We shook hands, and then he went over and joined the gringos. He took a few steps and turned around.

"Horacio, you know what?"

"What?"

"Your Firpo knocked out our great Dempsey. No doubt about it. I was there, ringside in Madison Square Garden. It was robbery, my boy, highway robbery."

I smiled at him. I watched as he walked off pretentiously, leading the others. He was not a thinker. Nor was he a man of science. But there was something about him that revealed a man of extraordinary qualities. In his eyes, passionate and nostalgic, one sensed a strange and precise mixture of pride, conviction, and rebelliousness—qualities of a man who does not leave things as he finds them.

When he reached the school, the band began to play again and there were fireworks. An hour later his plane left. Ford left explicit instructions with the directors to destroy the files, photographs, films and all other material dealing with the village that they could get their hands on. He also ordered a campaign to get journalists and politicians to join in the cover up, and if that were not possible, to at least minimize the size of the project and the size of the failure. The plane took flight, and I watched it until it was just a dot in the sky, just beginning to fill with stars. Shortly after, the financier's boat raised anchor and disappeared down the river.

The celebration continued into the night, but none of the Americans took part. I could not find Jack or Antonio. I hung out in one of the sheds with the workers for a while. The music had ended, but the air was full of voices, shouting, and laughter. Around midnight, a swarm of pesky locusts, like the one I had seen that morning, began to smother the lights and the tablecloths. Theo, Roque, and Flavio, the mathematics teacher, entered the shed. It had been months since I had seen Roque. The three walked toward me, and they were drunk. Theo came up to me with an expression of disgust on his face that looked grotesque given his drunken state.

"That wretch didn't want to see me, so to hell with him and

this filthy village. To hell with it all," he said, threatening with his index finger.

Roque and the teacher came over to us. I shook both their hands.

"What have you been up to Roque?" I asked.

"I'm heading south, in search of gold. Do you want to come?"

"Who is 'we'?" I asked.

"There are three of us; the priest, the mulatto, and this teacher, who is tired of pondering life as it goes by," the teacher intervened, his breath reeking of alcohol.

"Join us, Horacio. We need men like you, men with scruples," Theo said.

"We're going a hundred kilometers south, where they say you can find gold wherever you look," Roque added.

Roque had a pack of cigarettes in his hand. He shook it until two appeared and he offered them to the teacher and to me. The teacher took one, put it between his lips, and stood there staring at Roque's hand, waiting for him to hold out a match. The teacher let the cigarette fall to the ground, pulled out a small bottle from inside his jacket and handed it to me. I took a drink. It was good liquor. We stayed there, drinking and smoking, but I was quiet and reserved, and after a silence that seemed unbearably long, they realized that their presence was bothering me. They left in a hurry without saying good-bye, and they headed down toward the river. I never saw them again. The grayish locusts were everywhere by that time—buzzing around the lights, jumping along the walls, and flying into the women's hair.

XXII

Caroline was lying underneath a clean, faded sheet. Her eyes
were closed and her hair disheveled. She looked fresh, fragile,
calm, like honey melted by the sun. I stood in front of her for a
moment, looking at her gentle face. Then I leaned over and
kissed her on the cheek. She smiled slightly. I moved away
from the bed and walked across the room. A dense light was
slowly beginning to fill the air, and the obscure and remote
sounds of the port drifted through the open window. The
room had a bed, a black folding screen, three chairs, a table, a
mirror, and a shelf. The table was buried beneath a camera and
some of Caroline's books, folders, and perfumes. Several pic-
tures depicting apocryphal love scenes hung on the walls. I
went over to the folding screen, got dressed, took some money
off the shelf, emptied the ashtray into the wastebasket, and
left. Before closing the door I turned back to look at Caroline.
She had covered her shoulders with the sheet and brought her
hands up next to her head. I closed the door without a sound
and went down the wooden staircase to the main floor of the
hotel, the hotel where we had stayed since our reunion in

Santarem two weeks ago. The lobby was empty, except for the porter who was sleeping on a bench. I felt like taking a walk, and I went outside.

I walked along slowly for a long while. I felt free. At first I avoided walking by the port, and I walked down the adjacent back streets, which were narrow and dirty and crammed with stores and houses made of mud and straw. But the hustle and bustle of the people, crowds of people, shouting as they bought and sold their goods, disrupted my thoughts, and I decided to go down to the walk that ran alongside the river. The hum of the city bothered me, and I detested those people who did nothing, or did not know how to do anything, other than compete for the money of others and dream—if what they did could be raised to that category—of vulgar and ridiculous things.

As I walked along I thought about Caroline. She was the most beautiful woman I had ever loved. The first few days, our love had been like a game, continually reinventing itself. After the fall of Fordlandia, brought down first by the leaf disease and then devastated by a brief but terrible invasion of locusts, we had arranged to meet in Santarem. There, halfway between the deepest depth of the jungle and the civilized world, we would decide our future. We spent our first night in the hotel (the only decent one in the area) awake, talking and laughing. The following days were filled with caresses and kisses, and we spent most of the time lying in bed, exchanging secrets, compliments, and laughter. We left the room only at dusk, to watch the sky turn a beautiful saffron color and to have dinner in the hotel dining room. Nevertheless, as the days went by, I realized that we would not be able to get along forever. We were too different and too much alike. The previous night Caroline had wanted to be alone with her thoughts. She didn't speak at all, and I let her lose herself in her meditations. She was quiet during our walk around the port, in the hotel dining room, and in the room too.

At one point, after we had finished eating, she asked me for a cigarette. I handed her one already lit, and she inhaled deeply, as I have only seen men do. Then she twirled the cigarette around in her fingers, leaned back in her chair, and just stared at me. I realized that it was difficult for her to say what she wanted to say. I wanted to help her, but I couldn't find the words. I shrugged. Caroline rubbed her forehead with her left hand, and maintaining that revealing silence, she let me see the tears in her eyes. A moment later, confused, she put out her cigarette, and with a great effort, got up and left without finishing her cognac. Those tears had a lasting effect on me.

Around that time I had the opportunity to meet an Englishman to whom a shipping magnate had entrusted a project in a remote region of the Amazon. The meeting could not have been more untimely. The enormous project consisted of clearing the land in order to make way for a sawmill, a plantation for rubber, rice, jute, and pepper, and a ranch for imported cattle. They were prepared to invest a fortune, had the benefit of good relations both inside and outside of Brazil, and were hoping not to commit the same mistakes that had been made in Fordlandia.

Shortly after the locust invasion, everyone (the American directors and myself) had left Fordlandia in a hurry on a modern ferry barge. The barge took us down the Tapajós at twice the speed with which I had gone up it for the first time on the *Moacyr*. We sailed along in virtual silence. I got off in Santarem to join Caroline, and the gringos kept going; some were headed to Belem, others to San Pablo, and the two bosses, Rowwe and Frank, were returning to their country reluctantly, hoping to find new jobs.

The Plantation never recovered. The locusts finished off in a couple of days what the fungus had started. The natural beauty in the village quickly withered, and the buildings, which were soon swallowed up by the jungle, with time looked like mere shadows of old failures. The curtain fell on this pitiful drama without spectators, amid a sickly atmosphere and with the stigma of defeat attached to it.

A torrential rain was falling as we boarded to leave. I sat in the stern on the starboard side and watched the village until it disappeared from sight. It was a flower from yesterday. All that remained were a few caucheros who were left to themselves, and Henry Ford II, after the death of his grandfather (the life of Edsel, his father, had ended much earlier), turned it over to the government of Brazil for a small amount of money.

The Englishman, who was an expressionless fellow with cold eyes, told me that he had met two Americans in Belem and that they had recommended me as someone who might want to join him on his venture. They told him to ask for "El Argentino." He wanted to know what my conditions would be for accepting the job. Also at that time, some merchants from Manaus who were staying at the hotel for the weekend proposed I team up with them in the exploitation of a bauxite mine in the heart of the jungle that surrounded that city. Caroline was furious when I told her about those projects, even though I knew just by looking at her what she would say. In fact, I could read her mind, even though I never reached her inner core. Caroline wanted us to follow in Jack's footsteps and set out for Spain. She wanted to work as an anthropologist and was very excited about the political future of Spain. Jack knew people in Barcelona, and in defiance of the American justice system, he had headed there. Before leaving Fordlandia and just after Henry Ford's visit, he had sought out Frank and broke his nose with his fist. Jack had left me his revolver, a sheet of paper with the words to two of his songs (my favorites), a cylinder cap for his engine, which could be used as an ashtray, and a letter for me to deliver to Caroline.

After walking around the port a while I stopped in front of a small bar and entered through its blue door. I ordered a coffee and a drink while, out of the corner of my eye, I examined the rows of bottles on the counter, the mirror, the worn rug, the little yellow tables, and a couple talking softly. I sat at the bar for a while and then moved to a table next to the window. Outside it was almost completely dark. The sky had clouded over, but the storm had not yet broken, and the thunder could be heard in the distance. Through the window I watched as the fragile boats in the port, with the caboclos seated in the bow, sought refuge on the shores of the wide and turbulent Amazon. I thought about how things would have been had I stayed in Buenos Aires, if I had chosen a different life, if I had, by accident, taken another train, if what at the time seemed unbearable to me would have become hell. I also wondered if I was still the same man who one and a half years ago had come to that place intending to bear my anguish and mull over my secrets. I had the feeling I had lived intensely in the jungle, but in a way that was not true to myself. I couldn't leave, but I couldn't stay either. I was at a crossroads; and that September morning, any route, any opportunity, seemed the same to me. Through the glass I saw that it was beginning to rain. The lightning cut through the sky in brilliant and bold streaks as the rain got heavier. I looked at my watch. I had not even been gone three hours. I finished off my drink, paid, and left the bar. I had made up my mind and was anxious to get back to the hotel. After all, the world was the sphere of whim, chance, and error, and up until then, I had had nothing to regret.